MW00882607

IN CASE YOU DIDN'T KNOW

IN CASE YOU DIDN'T KNOW

STEPHENS BROTHERS BOOK ONE

SHEA BRIGHTON

Welcome to
Stephens Construction!
Enjoy!
xoxo

This is a work of fiction. Names, characters, places, and incidents are products of the author's imagination or are used fictitiously and are not to be construed as real. Any resemblance to actual locales, organizations, or persons, living or dead, is entirely coincidental.

In Case You Didn't Know Copyright © 2020 by Shea Brighton

All rights reserved.

Cover Art and edits by Victoria Miller

No part of this book may be reproduced in any form or by any electronic or mechanical means, including information storage and retrieval systems, without written permission from the author, except for the use of brief quotations in a book review.

https://www.sheabrighton.com/

To my Book/Wine Club crew - thank you for being with me from when I first decided to do this, to encouraging me, heck, even harassing me to finally finish it. It's been five years, but I don't know if I would have ever gotten the first draft completed without you. Thank you for being an amazing group of friends who mean the world to me.

CHAPTER ONE

"Good morning. Stephens Construction, this is Valerie."

"Val? Is that you?"

Rolling her eyes, Valerie Milner stared at the phone in her hand. *Who the hell else would be answering the phone at my desk?* Placing it back against her ear, she replied, "No, it's not. Can I take a message?"

"Ha ha. Very funny." The deep voice came crackling through the phone. "You know I sometimes lose reception on this stupid Bluetooth."

Then by all means keep using it. She stowed her purse in the bottom drawer. Val was smart enough to not say anything though. Drew may be one of her best friends, but he was also one of her bosses. Working for the three Stephens brothers was nothing if not *interesting*. At least, that's the kindest word she could use. Most of the time they simply drove her crazy. Yet it was crazy in a good way. She couldn't even imagine working anywhere else. And truthfully, wouldn't even want to. They were pretty much the closest thing to family she had around here. Hell, they were her family, period. She never thought, when she moved out to the East Coast and got this job, she

1

would find a family. She just wanted to escape the sadness and mess her life had become back in Arizona.

"Are Matt or Jon in the office yet?" Drew's voice snapped her back to the present.

Figuring she could get some work done at the same time, she pulled up her e-mail and started checking the messages that had come in overnight. Technically, she was the executive/personal assistant to the president of the company, the oldest brother, Matthew, which meant she was never at a loss for work. However, that didn't mean a good portion of her time wasn't spent doing work for all three men. *Sigh.* By the number of e-mails already, it seemed like today would be non-stop. Not that that was unusual. The company had been busy enough when the sole focus was construction. They recently expanded into designing their own buildings when Jonathan finished his degree in architecture and business had taken off. Val wasn't sure how any of them knew which way was up anymore.

Pushing a strand of hair behind her ear, she scrolled through her inbox. "Drew, it's eight o'clock in the morning. Do you really think Matthew's not already here?" Matthew always was the first person in the office, and true to form he was sitting at his desk. No matter how much of a workaholic he was, Val believed it was for more reasons than just the business that pushed him here early. "As for Jon, I haven't seen him yet, and since I sit by his door, I'll go with no." Her centrally located desk, in the middle of the three main offices, made it easy for her to keep track of the brothers' comings and goings.

"You're being a little extra sarcastic today. Guess that means you had a date with Mr. Stick-in-the-Mud last night. You know, Val, you always let your inner brattiness shine through after you've spent

time with him. Shouldn't you find someone who doesn't crush half of your personality? Think of the better days at work the rest of us would have if you did." Laughter pealed through the phone line. She was fairly sure Drew could keep this up all day. She was also sure he could definitely act like an ass.

"Because it's my mission in life to annoy you, Drew. I'm sure that's the only reason I go out with Evan. There could be no other reason at all." Val didn't know why she kept doing this. Talking about her relationship, or really any guy she dated, was the one sore point in her friendship with Drew. Or *past* relationship? For some reason, she'd never mentioned to Drew that she had been planning to break up with Evan last night. Normally she told him everything, but lately she had been a little more hesitant to talk about her love life. For some reason, every time she went out with Evan, it felt more and more wrong. Conflicting feelings and thoughts were running around her brain, and she wasn't sure she liked it. And all those feelings always seemed to center around one person: Drew.

She could almost see his smirk as he chuckled. "Well, I've already decided it's not great sex."

"Andrew!" Valerie was sure she resembled a fish with her mouth gaping open. Heat started to flood her body and not merely because of embarrassment. They had an unspoken agreement that there would be no talk about each other's sex lives, even if they talked about who they were dating all the time. For reasons she didn't want to fully accept, the thought of Drew being intimate with another woman didn't sit right with her. Nor did she want him thinking about what she was doing. He cackled like a fool on the other end of the line, and all she could do was sputter. "I…I don't ev… Drew!"

Val shouldn't have been surprised that her shout of indignation brought Matthew out of his office. Though she wasn't related by blood to the Stephenses, Matthew had treated her like a younger sister from the moment she started with them. He was the protector, Drew the instigator, and Jon the peacemaker. Although, at times, they could take on each other's roles. All together they made for a wonderful family to be around, most of the time— if that family came with overbearing brothers. And right now, Matthew's protective instincts were at the forefront, and he didn't even know what Drew had said.

Snatching the phone out of her hand, Matthew spoke, "Andrew, why are you harassing Valerie? And why the hell aren't you at the office yet?" He stopped talking for a few seconds, presumably to listen to whatever Drew had to say.

"You know what? I don't care. Valerie's sex life is her business, not mine and not yours."

Thinking she should defuse the situation, Val wrote a note on a piece of paper. While Drew was adept at trying the patience of most people, his big brother was special in that regard. It seemed no matter what the topic, Drew could find the right, or maybe the wrong, thing to say. She slid it in front of Matthew and hoped he took her, "Just leave it alone," to heart, but it appeared as if her note came a fraction of a second too late.

Face turning bright red, Matthew seethed his response into the phone. "Mine isn't your business either, Andrew. Now get in here!" Slamming the phone down, he stormed away from Val's desk and into his office, the door banging in his wake.

"Well, I can see this is going to be a fun-filled day." Luckily, most people who spent any time around her got used to the fact that she talked aloud to herself all the time. On the plus side, she hadn't started responding to herself yet, but there was always tomorrow. Putting her head in her hands, she tried to figure out how long it would take Matthew to calm down.

"Talking to yourself this early in the day is not a good sign."

Lifting her head, Valerie couldn't help but smile at Jonathan standing in the doorway. All of the Stephens brothers were tall like their father, but Jon was the only one who'd inherited the light blond hair and unique navy-blue eyes from their mother. An image of Drew's dirty blond hair and sky-blue eyes filled her mind. Sometimes, she felt pierced by his stare, in a way she never did by Matthew or Jon. She was never sure what to make of the feelings when they arose. Giving her thoughts an internal shake, she re-focused on the brother in front of her. The one who also inherited his mother's propensity to try to smooth things over, so Val would have some help bringing everything back to a normal work environment.

"You look exasperated, which can only mean Drew must have done something. You know you have completely different expressions depending on which of us pissed you off, don't you? Not that I have ever done that." A quiet *aren't I so innocent?* whistling followed that last statement.

Val could tell Jon was enjoying himself from that start of a grin that tugged at the corner of his mouth. If he thought he could pass himself off as the angel of the group, he didn't realize she could see right through him. He seemed to take great pleasure in both adding to the crazy and keeping the peace. Sometimes she thought he egged everyone on merely so he could smooth things over and provide a little entertainment in the process. Jon, however, was always the one trying to defuse the most stressful moments.

"Yup, right now you're sporting the 'I can't believe he went there, and I want to hit him, but I also kind of want to kiss him' look that is synonymous with Drew."

Apparently, it was her day to resemble a fish because her mouth was hanging open yet again. She had heard a lot of crazy things from the brothers over the years, but this, this was insane. How could Jon think she would ever want to kiss Drew? They were best friends, nothing more. Would never, could never, be anything more. *Suuuuuuuuure, go with that. Like there's never been a thought of having more before.* Telling her inner self to stuff it, she tried to form words to respond.

"It's a little early in the day to be drinking, isn't it, Jon?" Hoping that she could deflect whatever conversation he thought would be good to have.

5

Cocking his head, Jon stared back at her. He didn't have the piercing gaze that Drew did, though he could intimidate when necessary. He came off as easy going, until there was something he set his mind to, and then he became singularly focused. Somehow, he could also make a person feel as if he were delving into their soul and innermost thoughts. Slamming the door to those thoughts, Val crossed her fingers that she was able to shut out him and his suggestions.

"Guess you're still not ready to go there yet, so let's move on." Strolling over to her desk, he casually leaned on the corner. "What did the older brothers do this morning to get your day off to a downhill start?"

Val was absolutely going to take this opportunity to change the subject and ignore whatever Jon had been hinting at. It was best not to even entertain that topic, at least not in the harsh light of day. No thoughts of kissing Drew, none at all. That needed to be her mantra. Unfortunately, now that it was mentioned, the scene kept replaying itself in her mind. Not exactly what she needed at the beginning of her day. Putting it out of her mind for now, she figured that maybe later she would ponder why Jon even thought to bring that up.

No one knew where her thoughts sometimes drifted when she was alone. She'd never even told her best friend how Drew invaded her dreams, more and more lately. She needed to keep those to herself and never let them get the best of her. She had been down that road once before, and it was not one she wanted to travel again. But would it be the same road? Drew was nothing like her long ago ex, Timothy. She was so much different than the girl she'd been at that time, but still the worries lingered.

"How about we just forget about that? *You* deal with Drew when he finally shows up. I'll let Matthew cool down a bit before I go talk to him about the day ahead." She jerked her head toward the computer screen. "There's an e-mail about the Lewis site that I need to talk to him about." Jon cringed as he realized why she needed to let Matthew simmer down.

The Lewis site had been problems from the word go, mainly because Mr. Lewis had shown himself to be a pain in the ass. She was pretty sure that Matthew regretted ever bidding on that job, especially since it should have been the least complicated of all the jobs they currently had going on. A simple, no-frills building. Get it designed and get it built. And it would have been, if Lewis and his son didn't decide to change their minds about every single thing they were doing. Not to mention, the site seemed to be possessed, 'cause if something could go wrong at a construction site, it had gone wrong at this one.

Of course, Matthew didn't really have much of an option going for the job or not. Lewis was a long-time friend of his in-laws, and there was no turning them down. About anything. Now, between the constant on-site issues and the fact that father and son seemed to think they could waltz in to discuss anything, at any time, they were all ready for this project to be over.

Jon nodded. "You've got it." Standing, he straightened his jacket, turned to walk into his office, stopped and looked back and gave her a strange look. That soul-searching look again. Why was he so damn good at that look? "Val, don't let Drew make you too crazy. One day he'll figure it out, and so will you." And, with that, he walked into his office and shut the door.

Val stared at the closed door, her gaze narrowed in confusion. What the hell did he mean by that? Figure what out? Did he suspect that sometimes her thoughts turned to Drew? Well, best to not even worry. She went through the rest of her e-mails, handling what she could. Figuring it was as good a time as any to venture into the bear's lair, she picked up her tablet, stood, and strolled over to Matthew's office.

7

~

DREW STEPHENS PULLED into the parking garage next to the building housing Stephens Construction and turned off the engine to his SUV. It would be odd not coming to this building anymore, once the new and bigger office they were working on was completed. Their dad had started the company out of this location, and for so long, it worked well. But now they were simply growing too quickly—not that it was a bad thing—and needed the space the new office would provide. And besides, Drew thought proudly, it would be nice to see their name on the building. No longer would they be tenants, they would have their own place to call home. But that was still a little bit down the road.

Now, well...now, he had to face the mess he caused this morning. Teasing Val was one of his favorite things to do. Even though he couldn't see her that time, he could just imagine her green eyes starting to sparkle and the flush spreading along her cheeks. Her light blonde hair, a bob cut, a perfect accompaniment to her pale skin and frame for her face. Sometimes, when he managed to get her really riled up, the redness creeped down her neck, on to her chest. Wondering how much lower the color went was probably wrong. No, *no*, it was definitely wrong. Friends, that's what they were and what they would remain. No matter what his brain, or his dick, sometimes tried to tell him. Drew was pretty sure they were both crazy.

Grabbing his briefcase and his keys out of the ignition, he opened the door to jump out. Shutting the door behind him, he hit the remote and heard the telltale *beep* as he strolled toward the building. No reason to rush the dressing down he was bound to get in the office.

He paused on the sidewalk as the front door to the building swung open. Lewis Jr. sauntered out and made a sharp right. He exhaled silently as the man strode in the opposite direction.

After the phone call, he was definitely not in the mood to deal with their most annoying client. How Matt put up with them he didn't know. With the coast clear, he made his way into the building.

The elevator ride to the tenth floor seemed to get slower every single time he rode it. Finally, he stepped out, striding down the hall to their office. Checking his watch, Drew realized it was still before nine, which explained why the reception area was still quiet. Pamela had been with Stephens Construction since he and his brothers were practically still in diapers, but she never set foot into that office before nine a.m. sharp. Considering how efficiently she ran that side of the house, Drew was happy with whatever time she wanted to come in.

Walking through the empty reception area, Drew headed toward the back where his and his brothers' offices were. It was also Val's office "home." Even though, technically, she was Matthew's EA, her desk was in a big open space, centrally located to all of them for convenience. Noting her empty desk and Matt's closed door, he surmised that they were already hard at work. And Val was probably trying to keep him out of Matt's line of sight at the moment. He did have a knack for pissing off his older brother, but this time, even he could admit he went too far. He knew better than to make a crack about his brother's marriage, no matter what he thought about it.

"Nice of you to show up today, considering the havoc you've already caused."

Jon was leaning against the doorframe to his office, a smirk making him look even younger than his twenty-eight years. Flipping his younger brother the bird, he waltzed past him and sank down in a chair facing Jon's desk. Following him and taking his own seat behind the big modern desk, Jon just sat back and grinned.

"Can it, wise ass. I know I stepped in it this morning with Matt. I'll apologize later, after he's calmed down." Of course, there was no telling when that could happen—a week or so maybe, but he would eventually.

"What about Val? No apology to her? Not that I know what you said; she wouldn't say. But I do know she was talking to herself before nine."

Well, shit! That doesn't bode well for the rest of us today. If Drew knew anything about Val, it was that if she started talking to herself, she was truly miffed. Drew leaned back in his chair and crossed his left ankle over his opposite leg. Might as well get a little comfortable since he was sure the inquisition was coming about what he said to Val. Running a hand through his dirty blond hair, he pondered how to answer this. Lately, Jon had been hinting at things Drew really didn't want to think about. Little good that did him, because want to or not, he thought about it, or more specifically *her*, more and more lately. *Valerie.* His best friend. And definitely not in a "friend" way. But he did everything in his power to make sure those thoughts didn't stay in his mind too long. And he definitely didn't let them show through. Ruining their friendship was not on his agenda.

"Do you want to hear it all, or just where I really fucked up?" Hoping he didn't have to do a play-by-play of this morning's conversation, Drew stared at him.

Jon crossed his arms behind his head and reclined back in his chair, then propped his feet atop his desk. "How about the highlights? I don't need to know everything."

Clearing his throat, Drew thought about his answer. Maybe he could spin this. "See, it's not really that bad the more I think about it. All I did was mention that I was sure she wasn't seeing Evan for the great sex." He pasted his more innocent, angelic-like smile on his face.

Jon just glared and gave him that *are you that much of a dumb-ass?* look.

"What? You've seen Evan. Does he really look like the kind of guy to make a woman scream? He's probably the missionary only, do it in the dark with all their clothes on type." *I would definitely get Valerie out of all her clothes.*

What the fuck! There was that totally inappropriate voice that had started in his head lately. Though Drew feared it wasn't the big head on his shoulders that was the source of the voice.

"Whether you think that about Evan or not, what were you thinking saying that to Val?" Jon just shook his head. "You can't tell me that you didn't realize saying something like that would piss her off."

To be honest, Drew didn't know why he said it. He had a pretty strict rule about not talking to Val about either of their sex lives. They often teased each other about the people they were dating though. Their personality or hobbies or even the car they drove. But never had either of them crossed that line into talking about sex. The last thing Drew wanted to do was think about Valerie and sex in the same sentence. *I don't know if it's the last thing. More like it* should *be the last thing.*

"What's the frown for brother?" Jon saw way too much. Sometimes Drew just wanted to shut that little voice in his head up. This was a perfect example. There should be no thought in his mind about sex and Val, none at all.

Shaking his head to clear his mind, Drew responded, "I don't know why I said it, Jon, and that's the truth. The words were out of my mouth before I could stop them."

"Look, I'm not necessarily disagreeing with you. He doesn't seem all that wild and crazy to me either." A sly look crossed Jon's face. "And God knows, Val is probably just this side of freaky. You know, with all those books she reads, she's probably a wild one in bed." With a waggle of his brows he added, "Or wherever."

"What the fuck, Jon?" Bounding out of his chair, it took everything Drew had to not jump across the desk and try to throttle his brother. How dare he talk about Valerie like that! Pacing in front of Jon's desk, clenching and unclenching his fist, he finally looked at his brother. His grinning-like-a-fool brother.

"Fuck you. That meant nothing, Jon." *Great.* He hadn't even seen the trap Jon set before falling on his ass right into it. Flopping in the chair he had abandoned, he tried to regain his cool. "I just don't think there is any reason to talk about her like that."

Leaning forward to rest his forearms on his desk, Jon tried to stare him down. He had a feeling he knew what was coming, but he'd be damned if he really wanted to hear it. Picking up his briefcase that he'd put next to the chair when he came in, he turned his back on Jon and started to walk out of the office. This was not a conversation he wanted to have now. Or ever, really. If he could simply learn to ignore those thoughts and feelings, everything would be fine. He had to ignore them.

"Andrew. Take the chance you want to take. You never know where it may lead. Don't let yourself be held back and miserable like someone we know."

Having stopped at the sound of Jon's voice, Drew stood there right by the door. Hanging his head, he quietly responded, "I can't. It will lead to the loss of my best friend."

He was stepping across the office's threshold when he heard Jon say, "Or to gaining your greatest love."

CHAPTER TWO

*V*al was able to avoid Drew all morning, though it was not by actively trying. After dealing with Matthew ranting for twenty minutes about how unbearably rude his younger brother was, she finally managed to get him focused on actual work. Not that that was any better in terms of getting him to calm down. Before she had even gotten to the e-mail, Franklin Lewis Jr. had waltzed into the office like he owned the place and demanded a minute of Matthew's time. That minute turned to ten, which left Matthew seething. Then she had to bring up the Lewis e-mail from overnight, which had him all fired up again as soon as they finally got around to tackling it. She left him on the phone with the site foreman, trying to get the latest information on what was happening.

Snatching her purse from her desk drawer, she slung the strap over her shoulder, looked at the closed doors to all the brothers' offices and headed out to lunch. Passing through the reception area, she noticed Pamela wasn't at her desk. They often went out to lunch together, but this was probably for the best. After the morning she'd had, she really just wanted to decompress. Normally, if she went out to get a bite to eat, she asked the guys if they wanted anything, or to join her, but today she just wanted to lay low from interacting with any of them. At least until she made up her mind about what she wanted to say to Drew.

Leaving the building and heading out into a beautiful spring day, she plucked her phone out of her purse and speed-dialed Chelsea, her best friend since childhood. As luck would have it, Chelsea and her husband, Rick, wound up moving to Virginia just two years after Val had settled here. Rick's military career had them leaving after a time, but they recently returned. And this time it looked permanent. Having Chelsea around was a definite plus, especially at times when her mind was racing with crazy thoughts and her bestie's input was needed.

"Hey, girlfriend!" Chelsea answered. "Guess it's lunch time. You have one of the hotties with you?"

Laughing, the stress of the morning rolled off of Val's back. It never failed, but Chelsea could always get her to smile. Deciding to sit for a little bit before getting a quick bite to bring back to the office, Val found an unoccupied park bench and settled in to talk to her friend. "Not today. Needed some alone time for a bit. How are things by you?"

"I'm in packing hell! That's how things are. How the hell did we manage to have this much stuff crammed in a one-bedroom apartment? Where did it all come from?" An audible sigh came over the line, and Valerie smiled to herself as she pictured her friend pulling herself together. There was a definite plea in Chelsea's now calmer voice. "Don't forget you can't abandon us tonight. I'm counting on you."

Chelsea and Rick had just bought a house now that they decided to stay in the area long term. Unfortunately, that meant packing up again—one of the things Chelsea hated to do. If Chelsea had her way, she'd leave everything in the apartment and buy new stuff. Luckily for her, and their bank account, Rick was having none of that. Hence the hell that her bestie now endured. It also meant Val got roped into the moving festivities that were going on.

"I'll be there. Don't you worry. Already have the address of the house in my GPS." Shifting on the bench, she tipped her head back. "You better have some wine for me though. I'm only helping because you promised wine and food. I'm holding you to the wine at the very least." She sighed this time as she looked into the bright blue sky. A blue that reminded her of Drew and all those confusing thoughts. "It's been that kind of day already."

Bringing her gaze forward again, she watched people wander past. Some in a rush and some strolling along. Businessmen and women in suits merged with all of the DC-bound tourists in shorts and T-shirts. She loved to sit and people watch, sometimes making up stories about the people who intrigued her the most. A harried mother pushed a stroller in front of Val, with a little red-headed girl, about five or six, walking next to her. Making eye contact with the little one, Val waved and got a shy wave and smile in return. *Well, that just brightened my day a bit.*

"Oh, I have wine and beer. And Rick will probably run out and get something for us to eat. We spied a couple of places to grab food in the area around the new house. Might as well start testing them out now. You know how much I enjoy making calls for takeout for dinner."

"Great. I'm leaving work a little early today and brought clothes to change into. I'll head right to the new place from here. See you later, sweetie."

"Later."

As Val disconnected, she thought again how happy she was that Chelsea was staying in the area. The move even put them a little closer to each other. Though Val could admit Chelsea would get all up in her business over the Evan breakup, and God forbid she should tell her whatever stray thoughts about

Drew she may have running through her mind. Damn Jon for putting them there.

Yeah, 'cause I sure didn't have any on my own. Only friends. Riiii-iiiiiiiiiight.

Focusing on the people wandering the street, Val was in her own little world. Today would have been a perfect day to take out her Kindle and read some more of her latest erotic romance book, but she was so engrossed in it last night her battery died and she forgot to grab it off the charger this morning. Instead, she occupied her time making up her own story about a couple across the street. So completely in her own mind, she didn't hear someone approaching the bench where she sat.

"This spot taken?" A deep voice emanated from the tall man staring down at her. The voice and man were all too familiar. Both had started occupying her nightly thoughts, no matter how much she tried to shut them down. And no matter how much she told herself they didn't belong there.

Closing her eyes, Val considered her too few options. She could get up and walk away or she could just tackle the situation and put it behind them. Walking away would be childish, and what would it really accomplish? It's not like her friendship with Drew would end because of what he said this morning.

"Only if you sit down." Lifting her lids and raising her head, she looked into light blue eyes filled with an emotion she couldn't quite decipher. One that puzzled her. She could sense that Drew likely regretted what he said, but his gaze told a deeper story. It wasn't only regret or embarrassment reflecting back at her. It was something much stronger and much more foreign to what she had ever seen there before.

SITTING DOWN, Drew leaned forward, putting his elbows on his thighs and clasping his hands between his legs. He turned his head to gaze at Val, then took a breath and looked away again. Drew had spent most of the morning locked in his office thinking and re-thinking about what he said this morning. He hated that Val was upset, and he was reasonably ashamed of himself for the comments he had made. He also believed he had to get these thoughts, these feelings about her, under control. Losing her was not an option. Nor was exploring a relationship. There was no way she had those types of thoughts about him, so why sign up for rejection?

Still not looking at her, he said, "I need to apologize, Val. I know we tease each other, but not like I tried to do this morning. I crossed a line in an entirely inappropriate manner." Flexing his hands, he plowed on before she could say something to stop him. "Not that it's an excuse, but I really don't feel Evan is right for you, but that's neither here nor there. You're my best friend, apart from my brothers, so if you're happy then I'm happy." He exhaled audibly. The pressure that had been weighing him down all morning, lifting slightly from his chest. He still needed her forgiveness though.

Finally looking up, he caught her stunned expression—emerald green eyes open wide and light pink lips slightly parted. He'd shocked her, which, considering things that normally came out of his mouth, was not that unusual. This time though something was different. Was it his apology? Did she not think he would recognize he was wrong and say so?

Moistening her lips with her tongue, Val let out a small sigh. "Drew, I can't say I wasn't slightly taken aback by what you said. But it's okay. I know you were teasing, or trying to tease." She gave him a little grin. "Don't beat yourself up about it. We're good." Placing a gentle hand on his arm, she gave a slight squeeze.

The tension in his shoulders gave way, and Drew let out the breath he was holding. Now he could fully relax. He wasn't surprised, not really, but he would be fooling himself if he didn't admit he'd worried that Val would make him work a little harder for forgiveness. She was looking at him quizzically, head tilted a little. Like she was trying to figure out all the emotions and thoughts going through his mind. *Good luck with that, 'cause I can't even manage to do that right now.*

"I promise that's the last time I make comments about your sex life." A sex life that would never be with him. *Nope, not going there.*

Sighing, Val leaned forward a bit. Positive she was going to say something, he looked over at her face.

"Well, that won't be hard to do. I won't be having a sex life right now." Still not looking at him, Val gave a minute shrug. "You were right. I did see Evan last night, but only to break up with him. So, for the moment, you have to promise to not tease about my non-existent sex life." Leaning in to his shoulder, she gave him a little nudge with a smile playing on her lips.

Well, fuck me. This was absolutely not what he wanted to hear. As conflicted as he was, he felt a whole hell of a lot safer with Val in a relationship. He may not have liked Evan, or any other jackass she had dated recently, but at least if she was involved with a guy, he kept his thoughts at bay. *Except lately, you fool. Lately it wouldn't have mattered how serious her relationship was. You were still thinking about her. You were definitely thinking about her naked.*

"Why the frown?"

Great. Guess he hadn't been able to keep his feelings from showing. Tonight. He'll pull himself together, get through the day and worry about this tonight. Besides, he had the whole weekend ahead of him and had no plans of seeing Val. Plenty of time to shore up his defenses.

"'Cause we usually share things, Val. How come you didn't talk to me about this?" This was as good of an excuse as any to justify his expression, and Drew was honestly a little perplexed as to why she didn't tell him she was breaking up with Evan.

They had definitely gone through breakups together, usually doing the whole *should-I-shouldn't-I* thing with each other before making the decision. That she didn't this time was strange and hopefully not telling. Though he wasn't sure what it may be telling about.

Leaning back on the bench, Val turned and looked at him.

"To be honest, I don't know. I think it's because I could sense you really didn't like him." Bumping his shoulder again, she smiled. "Not that you've liked many of the men I've dated. But you really had something against him, didn't you, Drew?"

Thinking hard about how he wanted to answer this, he considered his options. Bringing up the disaster from this morning probably wasn't the best idea. But what he said on the phone was true. Val was a bit of a brat. Sarcastic, teasing, and confounding. The few times he had seen her and Evan together, her whole personality had changed and he just didn't like it.

"He stifled you, Val." Looking at her for her reaction, he acknowledged her slight nod. So maybe he wasn't going to be the bad guy by saying this. "You weren't you when you were together. Not to mention, you could do so much better."

"You're right. And I do deserve better." Grinning, she said, "Maybe I even deserve the best."

"Good thing I'm still available then."

Val closed her eyes and threw her head back laughing. When she opened them again, he gazed into sparkling green eyes full of pleasure and just a bit of mischief. "Available for what?" Picking up her purse, she started to stand, looked at him and winked. "I said the best."

Chuckling, he rose with her and clutched at his chest jokingly. "You wound me! But you don't know what you're missing." *Warning! Change the topic soon or you're going to be in trouble.* "C'mon. Let's grab a sandwich and head back inside."

Standing next to him, she gazed up into his face. There was something that flashed in her eyes with that look. He just

19

couldn't decipher it, but it intrigued him. Tempted him. Because that was a look that spoke to those thoughts running around his brain. Spoke to the visions that kept him awake at night and his cock hard as a rock.

She curved her arm around his, linking them together. "Yeah. Take me to lunch."

CHAPTER THREE

*T*he rest of the afternoon went by in a flash. With all the Friday afternoon work rush, she didn't have time to contemplate all those feelings winding their way through her mind after her talk with Drew. There would be time for that later this weekend. She was really hoping the manual labor of the next few hours would quiet her mind for a restful, Drew-less night's sleep.

Pulling up to Chelsea and Rick's new house, Val let out a laugh. There was Chelsea, obviously nearing the end of her rope, judging by the hand motions she could see coming from inside the sedan. Before Val even opened the door, she could hear Chelsea cursing. Hoping Rick wasn't on the receiving end of her tirade, Val killed the ignition, pulled the key out and stepped out of the car. Strolling toward the house, Chelsea's rear end was sticking out of the back door of her car. A frustrated scream echoed from the backseat.

"Son of a bitch! Move, you fucker."

"Babe, I don't think that's going to help move it." Rick was striding up the front steps of the townhouse, carrying boxes of his own. They were having the big pieces of furniture moved professionally, but doing the bulk of it themselves over the next few weeks. That meant free labor like Valerie getting sucked in to the "fun."

"Stuff it, mister! That's what you did to this damn box. Stuffed the fucker so far under the seat that it's stuck. With any luck, it's your shit in there and I'll just drive around with it forever." If there was one thing that Val knew it was that Chelsea's vocabulary, which was normally a little on the rough side, went on a downhill slide when she got frustrated.

Her sense of humor also generally took a nosedive, so Val was going to play this one on the safe side. Biting back her grin, she walked up to Chelsea's car and leaned in the opposite side. Her bestie appeared to be having the fight of her life with a box that had managed to get wedged underneath the driver's seat.

"Hey, girlfriend. I'm here and ready to be put to work. What do you want me to do?"

"You can work on freeing this damn box while I go kill my husband?" Giving a final glare at the box, Chels glanced up and smiled. "Welcome to the new abode."

Both of them backed out of the car, just as Rick emerged boxless from the house. Looking up at the three-story townhouse, Val nodded as she took it in. So many townhouse communities in this area, with their cookie-cutter houses. This one was different though, with the facades of all the houses having different styles and elevations, giving some individuality to each one. It fit the couple, newer and, from what Chelsea told her, renovated to a much more modern aesthetic. Still, Val liked her little one-story cottage that she bought a year ago.

"Congrats. This is a housewarming gift. I'm drinking your liquor tonight." Handing over the bottle of sparkling wine she brought with her, she gave her friend a hug. "I see that my evil plan to keep you in the area has succeeded." Turning to Rick, she shared a hug with the man who made her best friend so happy.

Reaching into the trunk of Chelsea's car, Rick grabbed another box and put it on top of a growing pile. Laughing as he threw an arm around her neck, he looked at his wife. "See, Chelsea, I told you she put some sort of hex on us to keep us here."

"Yeah, the control I have over government jobs is amazing. You should see what I can do with Congress."

Rick was able to secure an excellent job with the government after finishing his service in the Army. Apparently, he was really good at whatever he did—some secret mumbo jumbo Val really didn't want to know about—and had agencies tripping over themselves to scoop him up. Really all she cared about in the end was that they were here and happy. So, consequently, she was happy.

"You amaze me, Val." Giving her a thumbs up, he lifted the boxes from the ground and reversed course to make another trip into the house. "Can you work on getting them to lower gas prices again? 'Cause if I get stuck in this damn DC traffic for as long as I did yesterday, my entire salary is going to go solely to gas."

Val laughed and turned toward her best friend. "Jesus, stop drooling! You're married to the man."

"Hey, I can't help it. I like his ass, and it looks damn fine walking up those steps while he's carrying heavy things. He is so getting lucky tonight." Chelsea finally looked at her and gave a wink. "Just don't tell him. I want to make him work for it a little more."

"You are insane. Have I mentioned that before?"

"Maybe once or twice." Walking over to Rick's truck, Val followed her. "But honestly, it's why you love me right? I'm insane but lovable."

Nearing Rick's car and what would undoubtably be more boxes that had to be unloaded, Val couldn't help but think that Chelsea was right. She was a little crazy, and sometimes the things that came out of her mouth just made Val shake her head, but it definitely was one of the reasons she was her bestie. If they've been side by side this long, there was no doubt their friendship was going to last.

"Sailor! Sailor, come back here!"

Val turned toward the direction of the shout. A small, fluffy dog was trying to climb Chelsea's legs. As a woman, probably only a few years older then their own thirty-two years, came hurrying after the little guy.

"Sorry about this." Clasping the leash onto Sailor's collar, the newcomer regained control of her wayward pup. "He heard you talking and escaped when I went to walk outside. I'm dog-sitting for a friend this week. He's normally leashed or inside, so you don't have to worry about that." The woman was a combination of mortified and worried that she had somehow offended her new neighbors.

Judging by the fact that Chelsea had kneeled down and was almost as playful as the pup, it seemed as if her worries weren't justified. Nevertheless, it didn't seem to make the woman any less nervous.

"Don't worry about it." Chelsea replied while giving Sailor one last pet and regaining her feet. "Happy to meet a new neighbor." Before introductions could be completed, a delivery car pulled up in front of Sailor's temporary house, and she hurried off with a "Nice to meet you, too."

"Well, a bit abrupt, but I'll change that." There was no stopping Chelsea's optimism sometimes. "Let's get back to the heavy lifting."

Looking in the flatbed of Rick's black pickup truck, she gazed upon what seemed like an endless sea of boxes and bags. Luckily, Val figured that the truck could only hold but so much, so maybe it wasn't as bad as it seemed. Of course, since Chelsea and Rick had helped her move into her house, turnabout was fair play. Didn't stop her from raising her brows at her friend.

"Hey! You got off light. There's a ridiculous amount of boxes back at the apartment, but we just ran out of room in the cars. I told Rick it has to be mostly his shit because I couldn't have accumulated this much crap." Chelsea opened the door and laid the bottle of wine in what looked like a full laundry basket. Grabbing the basket, she shut the door and walked toward the back of the truck.

"You're kidding right?" Looking at her friend, Val could do nothing but chuckle. "I've been shopping with you. You aren't exactly the dictionary definition of restraint."

"I only buy important stuff." Laughing herself, Chelsea lowered the truck's tailgate and started pulling boxes forward. "Well, important to me."

Hefting two boxes out of the truck bed herself, she turned to find Chelsea positioning the laundry basket on top of another box and picking up her load.

"You're too much." Turning, they both proceeded toward the steps leading up to the front door. "Let's get a move on and get this stuff inside before it gets too late."

TAKING a step back from the kitchen windows, Valerie turned in a circle around the room and looked over her handiwork. If she said so herself, she did a damn fine job putting the blue painter's tape around the windows and along the cabinet edges. Between the kitchen, living room, dining room, and powder room, she was pretty much taped—and tapped—out. After having unloaded both vehicles in quick order, she offered to help Chelsea get some things done in the house. Rick had grabbed the opportunity to run to the local home improvement store and pick up the paint Chelsea had already selected.

"Rick just called. He's waiting on the pizza to be done. Should be back here in about twenty minutes," Chelsea relayed as she came down the stairs. While Valerie had tackled the main floor, she had handled the bedrooms and bathrooms on the second floor.

"Sounds excellent, and I'm starved. So, what do you have to combat this thirst? You promised me wine."

"Yeah, yeah. There's both wine and beer in the fridge." Chelsea wandered over to the stainless steel appliance and opened the door. "What'll it be?"

Felt like a beer and pizza kinda night to her. "I'll take a beer."

Chelsea leaned into the fridge and pulled two longnecks out. Passing one to Val, she walked over to a small box on the counter. Putting her own bottle down, she rummaged around until she finally gave a shout of triumph.

"*HA!* I knew I packed one in here." She yanked the bottle opener from the box with a small grin. "I remembered the priorities." Popping off the cap from her beer, she passed the bottle opener over to Val. "Let's take a load off and wait for Rick to come back."

They moved from the kitchen into what would eventually become the dining room. Looking at the hardwood floors, Val wasn't really all that excited about sitting on them. "Hey, Chelsea, you have anything for us to sit on?"

"Never fear. Let me grab some throw pillows we brought over. I know these floors aren't exactly made for comfort."

Picking out a couple of red cushions, she tossed them on the floor. Val moved over to one, sitting down on it and leaning up against the wall. Taking a long sip of beer, she watched her friend get settled in, knowing what would come next.

"So, did you break it off with Evan? Inquiring minds want to know." Smirking, Chelsea looked her way.

"Yup. Last night." Val thought back to the previous evening and tried to figure out what to say. "I told him we needed to talk, so he came over to my place. At first he seemed to take it okay, agreeing with me that we really were different in a lot of ways that made growing a relationship tough. But then..."

"Then what?" With a quizzical look on her face, Chelsea leaned over into her shoulder. "What did he do?"

Val didn't even really know how to explain it to herself, let alone her best friend. The whole evening had taken a surreal turn, and looking back on it, she was just glad she was able to get Evan to leave as quickly as he did. Taking another sip before setting her bottle down, she tried to put voice to her thoughts. "We talked for a bit and everything was fine, or at least I thought everything was fine. He went in to use my bathroom before he left and literally walked out of it a changed man." Even remembering what had happened the night before sent a little shiver through her. "It was the most bizarre thing. When he came out, he went on about how much he loved me. How good we could be if we kept trying. That he didn't want to let me go."

Chelsea's raised eyebrows signaled her confusion too. "I didn't know things had gotten to the 'love' stage between you two?"

"That's just it, neither did I. Or, at least, he hadn't said he loved me up until that point. I sure didn't say it to him. We'd only been dating about five months. I know that's not too fast for some people to fall in love, but it is for me. And the way he changed. It was just really, really strange."

"I don't know, babe, but considering how odd that encounter was, it's good you're rid of him." Chelsea tilted her bottle toward Val in the universal symbol of *cheers*.

Picking her bottle back up, she clinked it against Chelsea's. Nodding, she said, "I completely agree. I was just really uncomfortable last night." It had been the right move last night, and Evan's behavior just cemented her feelings. She was free again to look forward. Maybe to really look for someone who was the right match for her. "But now on to bigger and better things."

"Speaking of bigger and better." Chelsea's grin was as wide

as she'd ever seen it. "Does that mean you're going to go after middle hottie? Cause I'm pretty sure he's definitely bigger."

For some reason, all roads seemed to lead back to Drew today. Or more specifically, thoughts of Drew. Romantic thoughts. Sexual thoughts. *Oh, so many sexual thoughts.* Maybe she was deluding herself into thinking that she didn't have these feelings for him. She had always thought him attractive. How could she not? All three Stephens men were, but there had always been something more about Drew in her mind. Yet only recently, those thoughts had taken on a sexual edge. More and more she started comparing men she dated to Andrew and the time she spent with him, and they always seemed to come up lacking. Their humor wasn't as funny. They weren't as polite. The list just went on and on. She kept telling herself she was exaggerating Drew's good qualities, but that didn't make a difference to her brain. She still managed to find something wrong with all of the guys she dated.

Evan had been a little different, but now she couldn't really see how. It was almost like he was the exact opposite of Drew, so that made him better. If Evan wasn't really funny at all, then how could she compare him to Drew. If he never held the door open for her, she just told herself that he saw her as an independent woman. Not everything had to come back around to Drew. Looking back on it, she clung to things with Evan because he was so different, which would make sense if Drew was an ass. But he wasn't. Neither was Evan, but he just wasn't for her.

So where did that leave her with these confusing feelings for Drew? She definitely didn't want to lose a friend. That was a road she wasn't traveling down. Again. And it's not like she had any indication that he had these feelings for her. He hadn't ever done anything that hinted he thought about her like that. Yeah, they joked all the time. They even flirted, but that was all in fun. Just teasing. *Was it? What if it wasn't? What if both of us have feelings for each other? What if one of us made a move?*

"Earth to Valerie. Come in, Valerie."

Turning her head, a knowing smile on her best friend's face greeted her. An all too-knowing smile. Which meant she was going to be in for it now. Maybe she could deflect. At least it was worth a try.

"Why are you bringing up middle hottie?" Taking another sip of beer, Val hoped Rick would show up soon. She needed something to distract Chelsea, and nothing did that better then her own man. "And why do you now have me referring to them as the hotties?"

"Because they are hot. I'm married, not blind. All three of those men are just F-I-N-E. Don't you think what's under the clothes is probably just as impressive as what you can see when they're dressed?" Wiggling her eyebrows, Chelsea licked her lips, though not to wipe off any moisture. Unless you counted the drool that would probably start any minute if she kept this up.

Shaking her head, she laughed at her friend.

"You know you can admit they're hot without admitting to any other feelings, right?"

Val looked at Chelsea. There was a wealth of knowledge and understanding in her gaze. If one person knew where she was coming from, it was Chelsea. She had been there for the aftermath with Timothy. Now she was fighting something inevitable, or maybe, if she gave a voice to some of these feelings, she'd realize they weren't real. Weren't tying her up in knots for no reason.

"Fine. You're right. All three of them are hot. Are you happy now?" Laughing, she took another swig of beer, and again hoped really hard Rick got home soon so this conversation could end. She didn't know why it was so hard to admit to an interest in Drew. What if voicing it made them real? Wouldn't it be easier to ignore if they weren't real? *But that's not true, is it? Because it's never out of your mind, so how can it be real?*

"I'll be happy when you're happy, Val." Chelsea gave her that knowing look only best friends could give. Val had seen that look before. The one that meant Chelsea knew her better then she really knew herself. She had been there for the highs with Timothy and then was her support after the crash and burn. Her friend understood her fears and worries, even when Val didn't want to face them. "And I don't think you really are. You won't be until you have exactly what you want, and to get that, you have to admit what it is you want. And to admit that the past is the past and won't be repeated."

With those words of wisdom, she heard the front door open. Her time was up. She just had to figure out what to do with her best friend's advice.

CHAPTER FOUR

"So what's put you in such a miserable mood, Matt?"

As the three of them walked to the driving range, Drew threw the question out to his big brother. Something had been eating at him, noticable by the tension in his shoulders and his more-clipped-than-usual tone of voice.

Matt threw him an *F.U.* glare. "I'm not the only one, Andrew. You've been walking around like you lost your best friend."

The sideways look from Jon told Drew that he thought it too, and he would have to agree with both of them. Ever since that conversation with Val, he'd been worried their friendship was on shaky ground. Not because she didn't forgive him, but because he was afraid his feelings and thoughts about her would eventually come out. What then? He couldn't show them, but he was having a harder and harder time keeping them at bay.

Walking up to his spot on the driving range, he dropped the bucket of balls. The three of them were somewhere on a piss-poor skill level for golf, but as their business grew, more clients wanted to talk during an afternoon on the course. Not to mention, whacking dozens of balls at the range sometimes helped relieve some stress. At least it wasn't the whacking off he'd been doing in the shower lately.

"Got some things on my mind. I'll deal with them." Lining up his first shot, he swung and watched the ball take flight. "Besides, I asked you first." Nothing like reverting back to childish ways to get the focus off himself.

He looked over to see both his brothers taking their first swings of the morning. He also noticed a couple of attractive ladies looking their way. How sad was it that he couldn't even manage a passing interest, mentally or physically. Lately, all thoughts led to Val, and that was something that could only go nowhere. Matt didn't even bother giving the women a glance, and Jon, ever the peacemaker, shot them a devastating smile that had them giggling. At least the mild flirtation made up for being passed over.

"It's that clusterfuck over at the Lewis site. Every damn day brings something missing, or confusion with the order, or any one of a number of other issues. If it was one or two, I'd take it in stride, but this is happening all too damn frequently. If I didn't know better, I'd think this was all deliberate." Moving another ball to the tee, Matt took his next swing. "But who the hell would be doing that to us? There wasn't even damn competition for the bid. Lewis came directly to us."

Drew had worried that doing business with friends of Matt's in-laws would come back to haunt them. Sounds like that may be coming to fruition.

"Val mentioned that there was some weirdness going on over there." Jon replied as he stepped up to the ball. "But I don't think that's the only thing that has you in a snit."

"Fuck off, Jonathan. I'm not in a snit." Whacking the next ball as if it was Jon's head, Matt turned away.

"Yes, you are. You both are. I guess some women will do that to you. I'm planning on finding one that won't give me any trouble." Drew let out a peal of laughter at his brother's declaration. All women gave men trouble, that was a given.

"I'm not talking about Cassandra." The tone of his brother's voice made that final.

Under the best of circumstances, and there were very few of those, Drew would call his brother's marriage strained. Usually he considered it the fucking Titanic, a sinking ship that neither would get off of. Cassandra because she was just a bitch and thoroughly enjoyed making Matt's life miserable. Matt stayed for their son and reasons only truly known to him. Though, Drew surmised, both he and Jon knew what, or rather who, those reasons led back to.

"I feel like I'm making the semi-annual offer to you, but when you need to vent or finally do something about the hell you call a marriage, we're both here for you." Jon gave Matt a pat on the shoulder and turned his eagle eyes to Drew. "Now I know what's causing you to PMS. Just make a move already."

"What the fuck? I'm not PMS-ing! And you know nothing." Drew didn't want to have this conversation, especially with Matt around. Matt focused on two things: his son and his business. If he thought for a minute that Drew was interested in Val, he'd have the coniption to end all coniptions. Workplace romance and drama were things he just wouldn't deal with.

"You're finally going to make a move on Valerie?" Matt chimed in as he hit another ball. With his back to them, Matt couldn't see Drew's mouth drop open. Even Jon paused in the middle of his swing with a mirrored expression. When there was no response, he turned and saw both of them standing there with their mouths agape.

"You do know I'm not a complete idiot, right? My love life may be hell, but even I can see the fucking mooney-eyed stares you give her. And damn, those looks she gives you. I've been ready to go get the fire exstinguisher a couple of times. Some days, I'm stunned that I don't walk into the office and find the two of you going at it on her desk."

Drew didn't think his jaw could drop any farther. Matt was looking at him like he was a fool, and Jon busted out the biggest grin ever.

"Did you really think I didn't know?" Matt's eye-roll told him he thought he was a jackass. "Or did you not know she's checking out your ass everytime you walk away from her desk?"

"Yes."

"Yes what, Romeo?" Well, at least his brother was smiling, even at his expense. A smiling Matt was a rarity, so he'd take it.

"Yes to both. And what the hell do you mean she's checking out my ass?" Drew was pretty damn sure Val had no interest in him. He couldn't be that off the mark, could he?

"I would have thought that was pretty self-explanantory." Grabbing a golf ball, Matt started tossing it in the air. "She stares at your ass like she wants to take a bite out of it. Sort of exactly how you look at hers."

Jon was of no help to him, standing there as his shoulders shook in a silent laugh at his expense. Snatching the ball out of the air, Drew leveled a stare at Matt. "So what? You've just been watching all of this going on and haven't said anything?"

Drew had spent hours beating himself up over his thoughts, even as they inevitably turned him on. He was exhausting himself every day making sure that what he felt for Val wasn't a blaring headline across his face. And now his brother, his least relationship-aware brother, made it seem like Valerie was interested in him. What if there was a possibility for them? Did he really want to take it? It was easy to tell himself no when he believed the attraction wasn't shared. But if it was? *If it is, that means getting to have some down and dirty sex. Go for it.*

"What the hell do you want me to say? 'Um, Andrew, did you know you liked Valerie? You want me to pass her a note in study hall for you?'" Jon's shout of laughter earned them dirty looks from quite a few fellow golfers on the range. "This isn't fucking middle school. You're thirty-two years old. I assumed you knew you were interested in her."

"Yes, jackass, I knew, but I didn't know she was interested back. You could have done your brother a solid and told me."

"I said she stared at your ass, not that she was interested in you. Maybe she has a thing for scrawny asses?" Matt ducked just in time to miss getting beaned by the ball Drew threw at him. Pretty soon they were going to get kicked off the range for acting like children, but Drew couldn't think about that right now.

"Seriously though, Andrew, if I had to put money down on it, I'd say she was just as interested in you as you are in her. Why not do something about it?"

"Because she's my best friend after you two dolts. I don't think I could take it if I did something to ruin that."

Walking the few feet from his tee area, Jon chimed in. "I told you already, brother, take that chance. I don't think you'll be disappointed."

Drew stared out on the driving range. The thoughts and emotions were a jumble in his head after listening to his brothers. Could he really take the risk? A part of him was definitely not willing to go down that road unless he was sure Val thought about him the same way. It would be one thing for them to both risk their friendship together, but him making a fool out of himself by saying something she didn't reciprocate was a whole other matter. That was emotional suicide because she would never feel comfortable with him again. But maybe, just maybe, there was hope for him. If Matt was right, he had hope that he didn't have before.

"Regrets are something that can eat at you. Regrets for what you did or didn't do. I don't want to see you live with those regrets, and I don't want to see you live without happiness. Take that risk, Andrew. We'll be there for you no matter what."

Matt's words conveyed a lot. There was experience behind them, the kind that could torture a person for years. He saw those regrets in Matt's eyes all the time and swore he would never experience them himself. Maybe it was time to risk it all and see where it got him.

CHAPTER FIVE

"*M*orning, beautiful."

Val looked up from her computer as Drew strolled in to work with a grin spread across his handsome face. Dressed to impress in a charcoal gray suit, white shirt, and cobalt tie that made his light blue eyes pop, it was all she could do to stifle a sigh. She had done her best to avoid him over the last week, though that was only so feasible given her work environment. She didn't linger at work, instead going home to run errands, clean, and workout. Doing anything she could to make herself fall into an exhausted, dreamless sleep each night. But that all escaped her over the weekend. Too much time with nothing to do, and a few pleading phone calls from Evan, had placed thoughts of Drew front and center of her mind. Consequently, after the weekend she had, filled with dreams and fantasies about the man standing in front of her, Monday was off to a tricky start. She had to get a grip on these wayward thoughts. Otherwise, she would eventually make a fool out of herself in front of him.

"Good morning, Drew. You've cleaned up well this morning.

I'm impressed." *If I can just get him past me and into his office, I can get on with my morning.*

"Well, you know I can appear professional if needed." Flashing a cheeky smile, he gave her his "professional" pose. Even with the most stern, intimidating look on his face, there was nothing that could distract from his good looks and masculine presence. "Trying to woo Monroe this morning and win the contract from the state."

The state job was a big deal for Stephens Construction. A brand new, state-of-the-art forensic laboratory would mean some serious bolstering for the company's resume. Matthew, Drew, and Jon had tirelessly outlined their proposal. While a completely new beast for them to take on, with specifications they had never dealt with before, this just made the three of them all the more determined to show their best and win. They'd been researching and talking to experts for months now, all leading up to today's final presentation.

"I can't imagine them not being impressed with the proposal that's been put together. All the hardwork you three have put in will pay off."

"I hope so. While we don't 'need' this job, I can't say it wouldn't be a feather in our cap to land it. And I know Matt is banking on this to push us to another level in the field."

Matthew was driven by demons Valerie knew little to nothing about. He worked like a man possessed the majority of the time. He'd agonized over this bid since they first heard about the opportunity and knew he was determined to show that a small, family business could compete against some of the giants in the area. Drew and Jon had been doing everything in their power to make sure that Matt succeeded. Although they fought at times and didn't always get along, they were brothers, after all, and Val had never seen a tighter-knit family than the Stephenses. While they may all share in the successes of the company, they each worked their asses off to make sure their brothers were proud.

"All I know is that I'm going to be able to enjoy the quiet. With all three of you out of the office for most of the day I'll finally be able to get some work done. Do you know how tricky it is, and the lengths I have to go to, to keep all three of you happy?"

Looking down, an e-mail notification popped up on her screen, and she thought she heard Drew say something that sounded like, "Oh, you could definitely keep me happy." *Yeah right. Those crazy thoughts are putting words in his mouth again. No! Stop thinking about his mouth!* Raising her gaze back to Drew, a funny expression had crossed his face. Lately, he had been looking at her more and more oddly, almost as if she were a puzzle he was trying to figure out.

Resting a hip against her desk, he glanced at all the files laid out in front of her. "Please. I'm still convinced you get more work done here than is actually possible. Do you contract some of it out? How the hell do you keep the three of us all functioning at the same time with what we need?"

"Mwahaha," she said in the most evil laugh she could muster. "Like I'm going to give away my secrets to you. There's a price to pay if you want to know all of my talents."

Drew leaned over and got as near to her face as he ever had. It was downright intimate how, for that minute, they shared the same breaths of air. Up close, she could see almost silver-like flecks in his eyes. Maybe that's what gave them such a sparkle when he was happy. "Beautiful, I think I'm willing to pay any price you want."

While she sat there stunned speechless, Drew picked himself off the desk and sauntered over to his office door. *What the fuck was that about? And why can't I find something to say?* Turning back, he looked at her thoughtfully for a second, like he was figuring something out in his head. His grin made her think that whatever choice he just made, something was going to change, and she wasn't sure if she liked that.

"Since you did so much work on this bid too, how about meeting up for an early dinner after we're done with the presentation? It should last all morning and a good part of the early afternoon, but then you can leave work early. You deserve a little break. I can text you when we're done."

Whatever Val expected after that look on his face, she didn't really think this was it. Which meant something else was brewing, but for now, she'd just put it out of her mind.

Smiling back at him, Val replied, "Sure. Any chance for one of you to spring for a meal sounds like a good deal to me. I'll be waiting."

"So will I." The whispered words drifted over to her as Drew's office door closed behind him.

LEANING BACK against the booth in his favorite Chinese restaurant, Drew waited for Val to arrive. They often came to this place since it opened in her neighborhood. After having given, in his opinion, a rather successful presentation, he texted her to leave work a little early and meet him at King Panda. Val had assumed his brothers would be there, but he'd decided not to tell her otherwise. Drew didn't really know where this meal would go. Or really even what he wanted to do. He just knew that after spending all of Sunday thinking about what his brothers had said, it was time to do something. Unfortunately, that something was still up in the air. *That something is you making a move on her, you jackass. How much longer do you have to sit at home, tugging on your own cock to thoughts of Val, before you at least make an attempt? At this rate, there will be another Evan in the picture, and then you're fucked again.*

The movement of the front door opening caught his attention. He turned and Valerie stepped through. She had a slight flush to her skin from walking from her house since it was relatively close and she usually dropped her car there. He took in her white skirt with scattered, big, red flowers. *Poppies*, he thought, recognizing them from his mom's garden. The red blouse hugging her breasts made his breath hitch slightly. When she finally noticed him, he caught the minute hesitation in her step when she saw him sitting alone in the booth. Drew stood as she approached the table.

"I thought I would be joining you and your brothers. Are they on their way?"

"Nope. Just us." He wasn't surprised by her comment. He had a feeling she had gotten that impression, and he wasn't about to correct her, but he knew. He never intended for that to be the case. This dinner was all about them, only about moving them to a different place. Making a gesture indicating the opposite side of the booth, Drew waited for Val to have a seat.

Placing her purse down on the cushion, Val tucked her skirt under her and slid into her place at the table. As Drew took his seat opposite her, he could tell that her mind was working. It was there in the slight glance of her eyes away from him. Every time she was trying to work something out, her gaze tended to dart around the room, like she was actively looking for clues. She had to be surprised at a couple of comments he'd made today, but that was okay. He wanted to keep her on her toes. God knew she'd kept him on his for years.

Seeming to regain her composure, Val looked at him. "So, tell me. How'd it go? Were they blown away by the proposal?"

Drew decided to answer her questions, even though there was no way he was going to let this become the working meal she thought it might be. If he didn't, her curiosity would get the better of her for the entire time, and focusing on work was not the way he wanted to spend the rest of the afternoon.

"In my humble opinion," he drawled, leaning his elbows on the table, "we were fucking brilliant."

Throwing her head back in laughter, a bright smile lit up Val's face. He was captivated. Drew certainly hoped she hadn't segued into speaking because there was no way he could concentrate on what she was saying. His entire being was drawn to her expression. Wanting to see that look all the time. Wanting to always be the one that could put it on her face.

"Never let it be said that you lack confidence, Drew." Still laughing, she leaned forward too. So close that it wouldn't take much at all to lean in to kiss her, but this wasn't the place for that. She would think he had completely lost his mind. And as much confidence as she thought he had, it flew out the window when it came to making a go out of a relationship with her. "Tell me all about it."

"Well, they were extremely impressed by the fact that we consulted with experts. Knowing we had never built a lab before was definitely a drawback for them, and we knew that going in. But we could tell that our research paid off, and as always, Matt had them eating out of the palm of his hand." For as surly as his brother could be at times, he had a way with clients.

Over the course of the next hour, that included a shared meal of General Tso's chicken and lo mein, they talked more about the presentation and what they hoped would be good news on the bid. Drew had never felt as at ease with any woman other than Valerie. He had felt it right away, beginning their friendship not soon after she started working at the company. It was something that seemed to fit both of them, and they fell into it easily.

And while the friendship was still easy, his feelings were now anything but. For the past year, they had been growing and changing. And for just as long, Drew had been trying to push them down. His only thoughts had been fear that their friendship would be destroyed if he acted upon them.

As work talk died down, Drew realized that this had turned out like any other meal they'd shared in the past. Work and friendship driven. The exact opposite of what his intentions had been. *Good job, jackass. I thought you were going to do something this time. Anything!* Listening to his inner voice had gotten him some pretty good things in the past. It had also led to some dumb shit, but now was not the time to think of that.

Seeing a couple of pieces of chicken left on the plate, he eyed Val. She had put her fork down and leaned back against the seat cushion, clearly not planning on picking up anymore.

"C'mon, we can't leave two pieces on the plate."

Val smiled. "You go ahead. I'm good."

Drew stuck a fork in one of the pieces and went to raise it to his mouth. At the last second, he changed direction and extended his arm toward her, placing the morsel against her mouth. A slight gasp caused her lips to part. Drew slid the fork between her lips, even as he stared into her eyes. Pulling the fork away, he placed it on the table without breaking their stare.

"You have some sauce right here." Drew ran his thumb just under her lower lip, where some of the sauce had clung. Even as caught up in the moment as he was, heat flooded his system when Val moved her head slightly and caught his thumb between her lips. His heart beat faster and his cock got rock hard as she sucked the sauce off his thumb.

Letting go of his finger with a soft *pop*, he gently ran his thumb over her lips. *So soft. Like the finest satin.* He could practically feel them moving over his skin as she kissed her way around his body. His dick pounding in his pants, he was afraid it wouldn't take much more for this to become very embarrassing.

He pulled his hand back to his side and made a move to get out of the booth. "C'mon, beautiful, I'll drive you home."

Extending his hand, he waited for her to take hold to help her out of the booth.

The look she gave him almost brought him to his knees. Val sat there in what looked like shocked wonder, probably trying to decipher what the hell had just happened. Seeing her gaze move over his crotch, there was no way for her to miss the fact that their stolen moment had affected him just as much. Her gaze shifted away, but the blush that appeared on her cheeks was probably the prettiest thing he ever saw.

Placing her hand in his, somewhat cautiously, she stood. "Drew," she whispered.

"We'll talk. For now, just go with this feeling," he replied. "I'll drive you home." And with that, he placed a hand on her back to lead her out. His first move was made, and now he just had to hope it wasn't something he would regret.

CHAPTER SIX

Sitting in the passenger seat of Drew's SUV for the short ride to her house, Val's mind was a whirlwind of thoughts and feelings. Worry and fear over what she may have unintentionally given away of her feelings. Excitement at the desire surging through her body. Pleasure at the look in Drew's eyes, even as it made her wary. This was where she kept telling herself she didn't want to go, didn't want their relationship to tread.

So what the hell had just happened?

She remembered planning to tease Drew with a nip on his finger, until she caught the look in his eyes. A look that gave every indication that he was holding on by a thread. Pure lust had stared back at her from across the table, in a look she had never seen directed at her from her best friend before. Truth be told, she probably had never seen that look from anyone before. Drew had appeared as if he was one breath away from vaulting the table and inhaling her.

So what made her act the way she had? She should have laughed it off just to diffuse the situation. Instead, she'd done the exact opposite: taking his thumb into her mouth and sucking on it like it was her favorite lollipop. *Or my favorite dick. 'Cause I wouldn't mind making Drew my special treat.*

Heat blossomed in her face as her wayward thoughts drifted to using her mouth on Drew. What would he feel like in her mouth? In her hands? She was perilously close to losing it as he turned the corner of the street leading to her home. She risked a quick glance to her left and the man steering the car. His rigid posture and whitened knuckles told the story. Sensing that he was strung as tight as she was, her plan was to escape as quickly as possible.

Her little one-floor "cottage," as she liked to call it, sat at the end of a dead-end street. She enjoyed having one side free of neighbors. Of course, it wasn't completely free since she did abut the fields of one of the local high schools. For the most part, it was quiet when she was home, except on game nights and weekends. But she could live with the sporadic sports schedule that created a lively environment next door.

As Drew pulled into her driveway behind her car, she thought about a way she could try to end the evening on a non-awkward note. Though she didn't see how, especially since her pulse was racing and she could already feel her panties dampening. Looked like she might have to do a little stress relief before bed tonight. Maybe pick out a passage from one of her favorite erotic romance books for some inspiration. *Or I could imagine Drew. Imagine him slipping his hand under my skirt and feeling how damp I am.*

ENOUGH!

She had to get herself, and her apparently shaky limbs, under control. If for no other reason than to not make a complete jackass out of herself by stumbling to her front door.

Before she could make her hasty exit, a door slammed shut and Drew was already out of the car and coming around to open her door. Bracing herself for awkwardness, she gathered her purse and stepped out once the door opened. Keeping her head down, she fumbled in her bag to get her keys. With any luck, she could actually avoid talking to Drew even as he accompanied her to her door.

A firm hand on her lower back caused her nerve endings to fire fiercely. It was like a brand on her skin, even with clothes in the way. Imagining Drew's hands on her naked flesh had her nipples hard in the confines of her bra. Fortunately, the one she grabbed today was slightly padded. Val thanked her lucky stars she paired that one with her sheer red silk shirt.

With her back to Drew, she placed her key in the lock of her front door. Just a few more seconds and she was in the clear. She'd give herself the night to regroup and try to figure out what the hell had just happened this evening.

Val froze as Drew glided his hand sensuously up her silk-covered back.

"Tonight was a revelation, wasn't it, Val?" Her breathing rate increased as Drew purred into her ear. His body was flush against her back as he slid his hand around her waist, his fingers tracing feather-light strokes on her hips. He was so close, completely surrounding her. Trying to catch her breath, she wasn't sure if she could actually find words to answer him.

He whispered, his breath fanning her ear. "This was just the beginning though, you can count on that." He drew back, but only to move to her other side. "Things are about to change for us. Now go inside. Sweet dreams." Those last words flittered along her skin. A butterfly-soft kiss just below her ear was accompanied by a quick flick of tongue.

It took everything in her power not to turn around and grab hold of Drew's head to drag him in for a bone-melting kiss. This was getting out of hand. She could barely control herself, and part of her, the part that had been thinking too often about Drew, didn't even want her to try. The part of her that had been hurt before wanted to run in the other direction, and that was the part that seemed to be in control. Whatever control was at this point.

Slipping through the door, she closed and locked it behind her. That physically kept Drew out for now, but the thoughts and images of him, of them, were firmly planted in her mind. And not by a long shot did she think she would keep him out for forever. She didn't even believe she really wanted to. Kicking off her heels, she padded into her living room and turned on the standing lamp.

But what did she really want? Apparently Drew had come to some sort of realization and decided things needed to be changed. Was that what she wanted? Lord knew that right then she wanted to come. That was about the only thing she was thinking about. As she moved through her house, lit only by the light in the living room, she was lost in thought.

As she stepped into her darkened bedroom, she let out a scream of pain and quickly fumbled for the lightswitch on the wall. "Son of a bitch," she cried. Looking down, her feet were squarely positioned in a pile of broken glass.

"Val! What the fuck happened?" Drew's panicked shout echoing from the front of the house startled her enough that she shifted her foot, letting out another hiss of pain as she must have managed to step on more glass. "Valerie, answer me!" She could hear him making his way from the front door. She knew that stupid key-in-the-fake-rock would come in handy, and to think he made fun of her for having it.

"I'm fine, Drew. Just stepped on some glass."

"Glass from where?" Appearing at the door to her bedroom, Drew had a slightly crazed look in his eyes. A look that bespoke of fear—fear that something had happened to her.

Val nodded down at her feet surrounded by glass and answered, "That's a good question. I know I didn't drop anything this morning, and it's not like I have a cat that could knock something over."

As she lifted her head, she noticed that shattered window to her right. "Well," she said, "I guess that answers the question." Following her stare, Drew honed in on the window also.

"What the hell? How did this happen?" A frown marred Drew's handsome face as he took in the broken pane of glass in the window and moved to the shards littering the floor beneath her feet.

"Most likely a stray ball came flying this way from the field. It's happened before, though usually they just hit the side of the house or bounce off the window. Haven't had any that actually broke the glass before." While the noise may not be that bad, reflecting on it, this was definitely a drawback. It never failed that, just as she had gotten cozy with a book under blankets or relaxed into a bubblebath, her house would get jarred by some flying object.

"I don't see any damn ball."

And before she could speak, she felt herself being swooped up by strong arms and carried over to the bed. A sudden feeling of contentment battled with surprise at the move. She lifted her arms around Drew's neck for balance and took a brief moment to accept that this felt good right before turning her thoughts back to his question.

Having deposited her on the bed, Drew knelt in front of her and lifted her foot. As if the never-before sexual tension between them wasn't already ramped up over their meal, seeing him gently tend to her foot just increased it even more.

"You've got a few good size pieces of glass embedded." Looking up at her with eyes a slightly darker shade of blue then normal, she was drawn into their depths. "We need to get them out and see if you need stitches."

Momentarily overcome with a desperate want, it took Val a minute to formulate a response.

"I can do that." Seeing Drew ready to refute her statement, she continued quickly, "I wouldn't mind your help covering that window with something. I can take care of my foot if you could do that for me."

Valerie could tell he wanted to refuse and most likely do both, but she really needed a minute or two by herself at this point. If only to get her head back on straight from what had been a confusing couple of hours.

"There should be some spare pieces of plywood in the garage that you can use. That way I can tend to my foot and maybe soak it for a bit while I put a call in to my insurance and search online for places that can fix the window." Plans. Plans were good. Plans got her alone for a bit. Plans let her think.

Drew sighed, but finally responded, "I can do that. But if it looks like we need to get to a doctor, make sure you tell me. You can't drive like that."

What she hoped was a cheeky grin spread across her face, and she gave Drew a mock salute. "Aye, aye, Captain."

Shaking his head on a laugh, Drew smiled. Some of the sexual tension dissipated and it felt like they were just friends again, laughing together. She needed to get this atmosphere back and ditch the other because she was *so* not ready to go there and wasn't sure if she ever would be. And truthfully, she figured Drew didn't really want to go there either. Why ruin a good friendship?

AFTER GETTING Val situated in her living room with her laptop and everything she should need to get the glass out of her feet, Drew made his way to the door off the kitchen leading to her garage. Hitting the lightswitch, he scanned the one-car garage for wood. *I'll tell you where there's some wood. In my pants, and dayum I need to do something about it.*

He was not about to go there right now. As much as he wanted to, he could tell that he'd startled Val at dinner tonight.

Startled her even more at her front door. The sexual attraction was there, that much he could see now. Guess he'd have to give Matt some credit because the heat in her eyes as she sucked on his thumb said that she wanted to eat more of him up, but her silence in the car and the shell-shocked expression on her face told him she was not ready to jump into a different kind of relationship with him. And before he screwed anything up, he needed to get control of himself and slow the fuck down. This was a race he intended to win, and if slow and steady was the way to go, then that's what he would do. He'd become the fucking tortoise to win Val.

He spent the time searching for the plywood to cool down his raging libido and cock and to formulate a game plan. He didn't go into a presentation with a prospective client without a set of plans, so why would he rush into building a relationship without them? He could see now that just going by instinct and spur-of-the-moment moves would clearly stress her out, and a stressed out Val was one who put up walls.

Walls were not an option. Not that he wouldn't plow right through them, but he preferred she not put them up at all. Now that he had set his mind to winning her, he couldn't believe he had tried to talk himself out of it. *I've said all along to make a move on her. But did I listen? That would be a big fat NO. Instead, I listened to that head of mine that just keeps putting up stupid roadblocks and assinine arguments. Enough of that crap.*

Tired of listening to his dick, or his heart, or his subconscious...whatever the fuck that was talking to him almost nonstop lately...he decided to shut down all thoughts of wooing Valerie for the rest of the night. Get the window fixed so she could go to bed and he could get the hell out of Dodge.

"Ah ha!" A piece of plywood he judged large enough to cover the window was propped against the wall. He grabbed it and picked up nails and a hammer from the makeshift tool bench on the way out. Drew made his way back through the living room, after making sure the garage door was closed and locked behind him. A quick check on Val found her soaking her foot in a tub of warm water, clearly entranced by something on her tablet, so he proceeded down the hall, back to her bedroom.

"Shit." He muttered under his breath some ten minutes later, cursing the damn piece of wood for what seemed like the hundredth time. It would have been a hell of a lot easier with two people to at least get this started, but he was not about to have Val up on her feet again. Once he managed to devise a way for the wood to stay in place until a few nails were secured, he made quick work of the rest of the project.

Now that it was in place, Drew retreated a step to view his handywork. He felt relatively comfortable that it would stay in place and that it should be secure until Val hired someone to replace the window. As he turned to leave, there was a loud crunch under his foot and glass shards surrounded his shoe.

He couldn't leave this for Val to pick up, and it definitely needed to be gone sooner rather than later, so he went to the kitchen in search of a dustpan and broom.

"I'm just going to clean up the mess in there. The window's covered so you should be good for now. Give me another few minutes, and I'll be out of your hair," he told Val as he passed through the living room.

"Sounds good, Drew. I've left a voicemail for the insurance and already have a few numbers to call for the window. If it's okay with you, I may come in a little late tomorrow depending on what's going on here. I should be there around nine."

Stepping back in the room carrying his supplies, he spotted her practically half-asleep on the couch. She had taken her feet out of the water that was likely cool now and had curled up under an afghan. A blanket of warmth settled over him as he envisioned taking care of her. That warmth turned quickly to heat as a mental image of spooning her beneath that afghan jumped to the forefront of his mind. "Val, um, I hate to break it to you, but nine is actually the time you're *supposed* to start. You just like to show me up by coming in early, don't you?"

Her eyelids drifted open and she grinned with a twinkle in her green eyes. She answered, "You know it. And just for that, smartass, I'm coming in at ten. That way I'll definitely be late. Hello to sleeping in tomorrow."

The conflict that had been written all over her face earlier that evening was long gone. Instead a relaxed and drowsy smile had taken its place. His heart felt lighter just seeing her like this. Walking past her, he let his hand brush her shoulder. As her eyes began drifting shut again, his fingers lingered on the soft skin over her collarbone, where her shirt had dipped revealing her flesh.

Back in her bedroom, he made quick work of the pile of glass littering the floor. He glanced around, all the while trying to avoid staring at the bed and thoughts it may conjure, and scanned the room for any stray pieces. Based on where most of it had landed, there was a good chance that some managed to get under the raised dresser. That's probably where the ball wound up too, since there was no sign of it anywhere else. At this point it was just as easy to move it and give a quick sweep for any leftover pieces, so he tried to nudge it out of the way.

Damn thing was heavy, and it seemed rooted to the floor. Maybe taking out a couple of the drawers would lighten it up enough to move. Feeling just a bit guilty for what was paramount to invading Val's privacy, he made quick work of taking the bottom drawer out and placing it on the bed. Still not light enough to move without damaging the wood floor or himself in the process, so he went to pull out the uppermost drawer.

And stopped dead in his tracks.

There, lying atop a piece of lavender, next-to-nothing, silk lingerie, was a pink vibrator. One of those ones with the little ears. He slammed the drawer shut, but it was too late.

Just like that, his cock came to full attention again. Lost in a fog of lust, he turned slowly toward the bed as images of Valerie assailed him.

She was sitting up in her bed, dressed in a lavender silk nightie, a glass of white wine on the night stand and her Kindle perched in her lap. As she reached over to pick up the glass, a fine tremor shook her hand. She took a sip and her tongue darted out to catch the stray droplet that was left on her lower lip.

Her finger clicked to turn the page and her breathing started to come faster. Whatever she was reading was clearly turning her on. As she continued to read, her left hand moved gently to her neck. She slid it up and down her soft skin and slowly lowered to her chest, bared by the negligee. She ran her hand over the tops of her breasts and her nipples peaked against the fabric. Her Kindle forgotten about, it slipped out of her hand.

Grabbing both breasts she let out a moan and her head dropped back against the pillows. As she tugged on her nipples through the silk, her legs began a restless movement. First they spread wide, almost as if to welcome a lover, and then they rubbed sensuously against one another in an attempt to relieve her ache. Her right hand glided down over her stomach and under the hem of her nightie.

Her back arched as her fingers came in contact with her wet folds, she was lost in the sensations of her fingers toying with her clit as she pinched her nipples. She let out a low moan as one long finger penetrated her pussy. Nowhere close to satisfied, another finger soon joined the first. She pumped those fingers in and out of her vagina as her panting increased.

Her eyes closed as her left hand journeyed from her breast to her clit. She used her fingers of that hand to tease the little jewel, even as she continued to plunge the fingers of her other inside. Body moving deliciously against the sheets, a flush rose up her chest. Eyes closed in pleasure, she struggled for that elusive moment. Yet the release she longed for seemed just out of reach. She alternated the movements of her hands, which brought her to the edge, slow languid touches followed by faster ones, but she never managed to go over.

Her eyes opened the slightest bit, and she turned her head to the nightstand. A moan of torture tore from her throat as she moved her hand away from her clit, but she fumbled to grab the vibrator lying next to her glass. One button and the vibrations came to life. She glided the toy over her erect nipples and groaned at the sensation. She slowly ran the toy down her body, until it finally came to rest on her mound. Pulling her fingers out of herself, she let loose another needy whimper. She placed the toy at her soaked entrance, and she gently eased it in. Ever so slowly she moved the toy in and out, groaning with each stroke. As the vibrations in the ears came in contact with her clit, she gave a little scream.

Faster now. Both the toy's ears and her fingers played with her clit. The toy pistoned in and out of her hot, wet pussy, pounding into her as hard as she could. With one final thrust of the shaft and flick of the ears, she screamed, "Drewwwww."

"Andrew Stephens! Answer me!"

Gasping for air, Drew clutched the top of the dresser. *Sweet Jesus.* Trying desperately to orient himself and calm down the frantic pounding of his heart, he tried to collect himself in order to respond. Pulling in oxygen, he slowed his rapid breaths.

"I'm fine. Just lost track of time. I'll be out in a minute."

Drew hurried through moving the dresser, not really caring if he scratched the floor or threw out his back. He sure as fuck wasn't opening the drawer again, and he just needed to get out of there.

Images from his vision continued to assault him. The thought and sight of Val, stretched out on her bed, pleasure taking over her features was almost more then he could take. Envisioning his fingers taking over for hers, playing her body like a fine instrument almost had him falling to his knees. His cock was pulsating in his pants and it took willpower that he didn't know he had to keep from coming like a teenager. He took a few more deep breaths, trying to get his rampant erection to calm down a bit.

Plans. He needed plans now. That vision had put his mind into warp drive, and he needed to get this relationship moving because there was no way he was not getting his hands on her in the very near future.

After sliding the bottom drawer back into the dresser and giving one last glance around the room to make sure everything was in its proper place and the glass was totally gone, he moved toward the living room. Just a quick goodbye and he could be out of there. *Orrrrr I could try to make that dream a reality.*

No! Absolutely not. He was not jumping without a safety net of a relationship.

As he stepped into the open living room, Val stood by the couch, her foot securely bandaged.

"You okay on your foot?" he asked.

"Yeah. It's tender, but I can manage. Just going to get into bed now and read for a bit."

Turning around so she didn't notice how his cock was tenting his pants, especially with renewed thoughts of Val in her bed reading, he headed for the door.

"Well then, on that note, I'll be out of your hair. Call if you need anything." He almost made it to the front door, when he decided to bring back a little of the tension from earlier. It was only fair, considering the state he was in. "Oh, and Val. We'll definitely be talking about what happened tonight, and I don't mean a broken window."

On that note, he shut the door and walked to his car. An ice cold shower was calling his name. Maybe he'd even work on a plan to pursue her, so hopefully, those types of showers would be a thing of the past soon.

CHAPTER SEVEN

*V*al woke to the aroma of freshly brewed coffee, grateful every day for the invention of the coffee pot timer. At least it was something she didn't have to think about because functioning without coffee was not really an option for her. One cup and usually she was somewhat human in the mornings.

She didn't know if that would be the case this morning. Last night's sleep was one filled with images of Drew. The heat in his eyes from across the dinner table over their shared meal. The look of worry as he responded to her startled cry. And those were only the start.

Her mind had created images of Drew in bed with her, skimming her body with his hands. Softly. Urgently. His touches growing harder as *he* grew harder. His mouth following the path his hands had taken. Kisses. Flicks of tongue. Bites.

Those images had her tossing and turning all through the night. She tried to will her body and overactive imagination to calm down, but they were hearing none of that. Refusing to give in to the ache between her thighs made her even more irritable this morning. She had to create some boundaries in her mind, and masturbating to the thoughts of Drew would clearly not accomplish that.

Turning to grab her phone from the nightstand, she tapped the button to wake the screen. Eight a.m. She had finally fallen into a dream-filled slumber around four, so at least she got a somewhat decent period of sleep. Stretching to relieve the kinks from the night, she still had time to start to pull herself together before she needed to follow-up about the window. Val swung her legs over the side of the bed and gingerly brought herself to her feet.

Those first few steps on her injured foot brought a definite sting, but it lessened as she hobbled to the bathroom. Taking care of what she needed to do, Val then limped into the kitchen and her elixir of life. By the time she fixed her coffee and made her way back to the bedroom, her foot felt a lot better, but her normal heels were off the table for today. Luckily, she had lots of cute little flats she'd be able to choose from. Shoes weren't exactly sparse in her wardrobe, but she by no means apologized for that. Everyone had some vices; shoes were one of hers.

She stripped off the nightshirt and panties she had worn to bed and then made her way to the shower. Letting the water heat up as she sipped her coffee, Val made a mental list of all that she would need to do today for the window. Stepping into the shower, she let the hot water wash over her. She braced herself against the shower wall and peeled the now wet bandage off her foot to inspect the wounds.

She was lucky. None were too deep and it appeared as if they all had stopped bleeding. She gently cleaned them, washing away the dried blood. Val didn't think there was any reason to see a doctor, but she'd be sure to re-bandage and keep an eye on them just in case. After finishing up in the shower, she stepped out and wrapped her fluffy green towel around herself.

One day she'd have the spa-like bathroom of her dreams, but right now she'd have to settle for soothing colors and semiluxiorous towels. Padding into her bedroom, she rummaged through her closet, selecting her outfit for the day, including the perfect pair of shoes, and then went to dry her hair.

By the time she finished getting ready, it was just after nine a.m. and she could call the insurance company back. Even though she left a message, she really didn't want to wait for them to contact her. Luckily, her agent worked in a small firm, so getting through shouldn't be a problem.

Her call was answered on the second ring. "Hi. This is Valerie Milner. I left a message last night about a broken window."

"Hi, Valerie. We just got it. Tell me what happened."

Val described what she had come home to last night and what was likely the cause. She wasn't really surprised by what the agent had to tell her. Fixing the window definitely wouldn't meet whatever deductible she had.

"I will tell you what you could try. It doesn't hurt to bring the ball back over to the school and see if they're willing to pay for the repair."

Although she laughed at the prospect of that happening, she agreed to see what would happen.

"Let me know if they say yes. You'd be the first, if they did." And on that note, the agent said goodbye before disconnecting the call.

Pondering whether she would even make the attempt or not, she stopped short as she crossed the threshold to her bedroom.

Where was the ball? Val had just assumed that's what broke the window because of the numerous close calls before, but she also knew what happened when you assumed. *Ass. U. Me.* Giving a look around, she didn't see any type of ball lying around the floor. Thinking back, she hadn't seen one last night and Drew hadn't either. But maybe Drew had found it while sweeping up and forgotten to mention it, so she went to look at the bag he had deposited the broken glass into.

Nope, no ball there either. Not thinking of a reason he would have taken it, she decided she'd ask him anyway. Maybe he thought to play knight in shining armor and ride over to the school to complain for her. He'd done weirder things in the past, and at least it would be something not fraught with sexual tension to talk about.

Over a final cup of morning coffee, she made calls to a couple of places to see when they could come out for an estimate on fixing the window. Agreeing to be available that evening, she collected her purse and made her way to the garage door.

Staring at an empty garage, her brain tried to process why her car wasn't safely tucked in its nightly home. The realization dawned on her as she looked at the empty room. She had been running late to meet Drew last night and never took the time to pull the car all the way into the garage. Turning back into the house, she locked that door behind her and headed to the front door. Stepping out into the bright sunlight had her fumbling in her purse for her sunglasses.

Her car sat precisely where she left it last night, in her driveway. She walked the few steps to the driver's side door and stopped short as she took in the back left tire out of the corner of her eye. What used to be an inflated tire. "What the fuck!" Now it was decidedly not inflated. She stalked around the car to check the other side, her cursing only increased. "Motherfucker." The back right tire looked identical to its counterpart.

She really didn't have the time or energy to deal with this shit now. Obviously, the car wasn't going anywhere, so what was the difference? Val reached for her cell phone and pulled up the app that would get her a ride into work.

~

WALKING through the office door just before ten, Val was amazed she made it to work that early. It never failed; the one time she actually needed that damn ride sharing app, and there were no cars in her area. Hating being late to work, her nerves were frazzled when one finally appeared. At least the drive in was productive, with her second call to the insurance company that morning.

"Are you going to go for three calls in one day?" The agent had chuckled as they arranged for a rental car to be dropped off to her at work.

"Bite your tongue," Val had replied jokingly as she stepped out of the car. "I'm ignoring you people for a year after this."

Now that she was at work, she took a deep breath to calm down. It felt like a lot more than twenty-four hours ago when Drew leaned across her desk and, to her apparently lust-crazed mind, put a new twist in their relationship. So much had happened, not the least of which were her almost near constant thoughts of him. Val was able to avoid those thoughts for much of the morning, or rather she pushed them to the side to deal with everything else. Now, being here in the office, where images of him abounded, it was that much harder to do.

"Hey, Val." Pamela greeted her with a ready smile from her desk. "Drew said you'd be in late today. Something about damage at your house."

Walking across the reception area, Val leaned an elbow on the high desk. "Yeah, broken window. Spent this morning arranging for a couple of estimates."

"Well, that just sucks," the older woman replied.

Val's mouth dropped open at Pamela's blunt statement. She was like a mother to all of them in the office, but some of the things Pamela said still never failed to startle her. Still, she chuckled. "Yes. Yes, it does. Couldn't have said it better myself."

Coming out from around the desk, Pamela enveloped Val in a hug. That was one of the things she loved about working here.

From Pam, to the guys, to their parents, it was one big family. She'd always wanted to have that support since her actual family was practically non-existent. Her parents passed away years ago when she was in college, and her older brother spent his time flitting across the world doing God knew what. She loved him, but sometimes she could go months without speaking to him. And on those rare times, it was often like talking to a stranger. They knew so little about each other's day-to-day lives. Her parents wouldn't have wanted that.

But finding Stephens Construction when she had been looking for a job after quitting school and moving out to the East Coast was a godsend. Originally brought on in a temp position when Pamela was out for surgery, Mr. Stephens took pity on her when Pam came back. Not that he would agree with her assessment. He said he'd known a keen mind, and someone who would keep his sons in check as they took over, when he saw one. Either way, she was eternally grateful for that and the encouragement to go finish school. Now she was a proud degree holder and even considered going back for additional courses so she could be more of an asset to the company. There was no way she would ever jeopardize that.

And that's what getting involved with Drew would do, wouldn't it? If we started something, I would lose my family when it ended. But what if it didn't end? Wouldn't that be gaining so much more than I could ever lose?

Those thoughts swirled in her head as she headed back to her desk. She knew Drew, accepted that something seemed to have changed for him. Though she couldn't tell when, or why exactly, she felt that, sometime soon, things were going to come to a head. Val just hoped that, when they did, she didn't wind up all alone. Again. She didn't think she was able to go through that a second time.

Taking her seat and booting up her computer, she turned as Matthew's door opened. Always seeming to have a sixth sense of what was going on, it didn't surprise her that he came out of his office as soon as she settled in.

"Are you okay to be here, Valerie? Were you okay to drive?"

Probably the most formal of men she knew, hearing her full name always sounded weird to her. Everyone shortened it. Hell, most people shortened everything they possibly could nowadays. Not Matthew. He never once shortened anyone's name, not even his brothers'. Had he always been like that? It was an odd little quirk, but she guessed everyone had them. She didn't even want to ask what hers may be.

"I'm fine, Matthew. My foot hurts, but none of the cuts appear to need stitches, nothing that deep. I'll be fine." Turning to face him, she stuck out her foot and wiggled it around. "Look. I even wore flats today that are comfortable."

Laughing in response, the smile spreading across Matthew's handsome face made him even more attractive. She wished the rare glimpses she had of him happy could one day be more frequent. Though she didn't know if that would ever be possible for him. Being as close as she was to the family, she could see without anyone telling her that his was not a happy home life. Luckily, his biggest smiles were saved for his son, Aidan.

"Smart girl. Today was probably not the day for you to trot in here on a pair of those skyscraper heels you normally wear. But what about driving?"

Typing her password almost absently into the computer, she answered, "Oh, well, I didn't have to worry about that. Two flat tires. Couldn't drive anywhere."

Before Matthew even got a chance to respond, a bellowed, "What?" came from the opposite direction. Looking over, Drew marched from his office toward her desk, and she actually shrank back a little. She had never seen him so formidable and angry. He looked like he wanted to hurt someone, though none of that fury was directed at her. This wasn't his personality at all and Val didn't know how to handle it. And to be honest, it did something for her. Even with anger rolling off of him in waves, her body took notice of his intensity. Whatever change started in her mindset last night, was working overtime today.

"What the fuck do you mean you have two flat tires? How the hell did that happen?"

By this time, Jon had popped out of his office and was standing next to Matthew. Seemed like she and Drew would be the morning entertainment since neither one of them appeared to be moving from that spot. Though concern marred their faces, both still had sly grins. Most likely from their brother's overreaction to the situation. Drew could be a bit of a drama queen when he wanted.

"Well, two of those big rubber things on my car were no longer inflated with air. Hence they were flat." Rolling her eyes at Drew, she continued, "As to how it happened, I don't know. I don't normally watch my tires all day and night. Obviously something must have gotten stuck in them."

"Don't be a wise-ass, Valerie." It appeared her morning predicament had gotten under Drew's skin a lot more than it did hers. While it was a definite inconvenience for her, she wasn't that upset about it once she had a chance to calm down. "You didn't notice anything different yesterday driving home?"

"No, Drew, I didn't. I was running a little late to meet you for dinner, but I didn't feel anything different that would have predicted two flats this morning."

"So, you guys had dinner last night?" This from the peanut gallery in the corner, who appeared to be practically giddy over the news. That didn't make any sense. She and Drew wound up eating together quite a bit.

"Yeah. Drew suggested meeting after the big presentation yesterday. You guys were missed. Too bad you couldn't make it."

Jon leaned into Matthew's shoulder, giving him a slight nudge. Like they had a secret they were dying to tell. Matthew eyed her and Drew, then replied, "Maybe next time." In turn, Jon muttered something under his breath. Something that sounded a little like, "If we get invited." Why wouldn't Drew have mentioned dinner to them? And why would he have made it sound, to her, as if it was all of them?

"Hey!" Drew was getting just a touch impatient at the detour the conversation had taken. "Let's get back to the tires."

"What is there to get back to? I walked out of the house this morning, and as I went to get in the car, noticed the back tire was flat. Ditto for the other back tire." She really couldn't see what the big deal was. It's not like this was the end of the world. "You know there's a lot of construction going on by me. I probably just picked up a couple of nails or something on the way home."

Even his brothers were looking at Drew like he was crazy. He was getting way too worked up for something that wasn't that serious. Taking a breath, he shook his head.

"You're right." Looking like he was calming down, he continued, "But between the window and then the tires, I just got a little worried."

Even if Drew liked to stir things up from time to time, he still had the heart of a protector. She knew how worried he had been last night and should have predicted this news would not have gone over well. Truth be told, she was a little unsettled by the timing of both herself, but she was also more than a little superstitious. "You know things always happen in threes, so I'm expecting the other shoe to drop soon."

Appearing as if he wanted to stay on the topic of how this may have happened, Val could see him mentally pulling back the reins. "Let's hope not. You already have enough to worry about."

"Can we do anything to help?" Not surprisingly, Matthew was the most practical.

"Nope, I don't think so. Called the insurance and the garage. They are going to drop a loaner off today and get the keys to mine so they can pick it up." Really just wanting to get down to work and to what should be a normal day, she tried to wrap up the discussion. "Looks like I should be set. Matthew, do you have any e-mails you want me to focus on right away?"

All three brothers looked at each other. They were men—and in the way of all men, a little oblivious to a woman's signals—but in this case they understood. She tried to don her *stop making Valerie a spectacle* look and attitude. Thankfully, she could stop being the center of some unwanted overprotective brother-like attention, and it was brotherly affection she had to get them all back to. Fortunately, they seemed to take the hint.

"There's another 'emergency at the Lewis site' e-mail this morning. Let's talk after you've had a minute to settle in and go through your inbox." On that note, Matthew turned to walk back into his office.

Both Drew and Jon were crossing behind her desk as she said, "And I do appreciate all the brotherly concern. You know I do."

An uncomfortable silence descended over the area. Looking around she caught an unreadable expression on Drew's face. Why was he doing that? The looks he gave her lately were not something she was used to, and it made her doubt herself and what had been their relationship. Val just wanted things to go back to the easy way they had been. Before dreams of Drew kept her awake. Before he started saying and doing things that put her emotions and thoughts on a roller coaster.

"Yeah, brotherly," Matthew replied with a chuckle before shutting the door to his office. Jon gave a rather inelegant snort as he ducked back behind his closing door. That left Drew. He hadn't moved toward his office. Oh no, he seemed to stalk right up to her desk.

Leaning down, he placed his hand gently under her chin and tipped her face up, the care in his touch at odds with the almost predatory way he had approached her. As she caught herself staring into blue eyes twinkling with emotions she couldn't really discern, she didn't even realize he had moved his other hand to gently toy with her hair. Tucking strands behind her ear, he glided his fingers slowly to the nape of her neck. A not-so-gentle squeeze had her coming out of her fog, but still paying absolute attention to the man in front of her.

"I'm not your brother." A little yank on her neck dragged her out of her chair and close to him. "I'll never be your brother." Another pull and she was closer still. She could smell his earthy cologne and a scent that was uniquely Andrew. "But I will be your something very soon. Be prepared."

With that, he let her go and strode into his office. As her heart tried to beat out of her chest, she realized Drew was a man on a mission and she needed to prepare herself. She wasn't sure if there was a path for them to take back to the way they were, but more importantly, she wasn't sure if she wanted to anymore.

CHAPTER EIGHT

*A*s Val sat at her desk a few days later, she realized she had never asked Drew if he had found a ball. Things had been so crazy, what with getting her window and her tires fixed, that it completely slipped her mind. It was only after another conversation with her insurance agent that she remembered the missing ball. Planning on going over to the school to have a friendly conversation with the principal, she really wanted to at least have the object in question. She had already resigned herself that they wouldn't pay, but at least a heads-up would be nice in case a ball went sailing in her direction again. In the past, the times when she had been home anyway, someone usually came looking for whatever came toward the house and she received a token apology.

Hitting save on the document she was working on, she slipped into her heels and walked over to Drew's door. Better to get it done when she was thinking about it. Drew had been acting like an overprotective guard dog this week, but at least he wasn't staring at her like he could eat her alive. *That's not really true. He's been looking that way, all right. You've just decided to ignore it again. As usual. C'mon! You know you wouldn't mind him making a meal out of you.*

Muzzling her inner monologue was getting harder and harder by the day. Putting a lid on her feelings was also getting more difficult. Val was beginning to forget why she was hesitant to start a relationship with Drew. She had finally broken down and confessed to Chelsea what was going on.

"I don't see the problem," her best friend said. "Just fuck him."

Sighing at the fact she was just being obtuse, Val then bit out, "But then what? I fuck him and lose him?"

As she came around to her side of the table, Chelsea poured more wine in Val's glass. "Why are you so sure you're going to lose him?"

"How can you even ask me that question? You of all people should know why? You were there when my last friends-to-lovers went sideways." Val picked up the glass and continued. "And why are you so convinced I'm not? Am I just reading too much into things?" Taking a sip of her favorite Sauvignon blanc, she tried to relax. "Maybe he's not really feeling that way at all."

Chelsea shook her head like she couldn't really believe Val was that delusional. "Whatever you decide, I'm here if you need to talk. But in my opinion, you would be crazy to not go with what you're feeling. No matter what happened in the past."

Before Val could get a word out, Chelsea continued, "And that's the last I'm going to say on the matter. I'm not telling you what to do."

That had been last night, and Val still wasn't sure where she was headed. A part of her really just wanted to pretend that the looks, the touches, were all part of her imagination. That she and Drew would go back to the normal friendship that they'd had. *Yeah, well the other part of you wants more of those touches. Fuck friendship. Let's go get a lover.*

Taking a deep breath to try to dispel the voice in her head that was a lot louder than she would like, she gently rapped on Drew's door. Now was not the time to have thoughts of fucking in her head. Not when she was venturing to the proverbial lion's den, so to speak. Hearing a murmured, "Come in," from the office, she opened the door.

The sight greeting her did nothing to make not thinking about Drew any easier. His hair was messed up from what was doubtlessly numerous passes through it with his fingers, and his shirt sleeves had been rolled up to the elbows, putting muscular forearms on display. Though he was primarily in the office full time, he rarely turned down a chance to get out to a job site and get his hands dirty. All three brothers were the same, having done the construction end of the business long before they actually took over the operation of it. Their dad had made sure they could both do the work and lead the crews.

What that did for Drew's body was nothing short of impressive. No matter what she thought about getting involved with him, she wasn't blind or dumb. Drew was strong and just muscular enough that he cut a remarkably sexy image. Even more so when he was relaxed and natural, like now. Though, from the scowl on his face, Val wasn't sure how relaxed he actually was.

Lifting his sky blue eyes from the papers in front of him, a grin spread slowly across his face, like he was savoring every second. A grin that did strange, yet wonderful things to Val's insides. It was also a grin that caused her pussy to clench in need. This was so not good if she couldn't even be around him and not get aroused.

"Hey, beautiful. You're definitely a sight for sore eyes." Rubbing those eyes, he leaned back in his chair. "And I mean that literally. I've been pouring over more financials and projections for the lab bid. They had some questions, and now I have a headache."

"Let me know if you need me for anything." A salicious grin appeared on his lips, and she quickly rectified her statement, "To help you with anything." That was no better. "With the bid." *Oh, lord!* She was blubbering like a fool. This was ridiculous. He was her best friend. She had to focus on that and nothing else. *But the other parts are so much more fun. I'm sure I could focus on Drew's other parts.* Hoping that the heat she felt in her cheeks wasn't accompanied by a flush, she marched over to the chairs in front of his desk.

"Nah. I've got it covered. At least until I meet with Matt about it, then we may need a referee." Leaning back in his chair and crossing his arms behind his head, Drew nodded to the chair for her to sit. "Besides, by coming in here you've given me a reason to stop going cross-eyed for a minute. What's up?"

Taking a seat, she pretended not to notice Drew's gaze following her legs as she crossed them. Maybe she shouldn't have worn a skirt today. Not that it would have mattered. Chances were she would have caught Drew staring at some part of her body anyway. It was becoming a common occurrence. She was still trying to wrap her head around how that made her feel. On the one hand, it played into all of her fantasies. It fueled her dreams, that their passions were matched. On the other hand, the one that surfaced in the cold light of day made her terrified. She had gone down this road before, years ago, and it had wrecked her. Drove her all the way across the country looking for a new start.

She tried to tell herself she wasn't the same person she was years ago. Experience and time had changed her, made her see everything that happened with Timothy through a much clearer lens. They were too young to handle the change in their relationship and the pain that ripped through her life. Drew damn well wasn't the same as Tim had been, never in all the years she knew him did she think he was. Yet now she was hell bent on using the past to sabotage her future and it was making her nuts.

How did she even begin to reconcile the two in her mind? Or her heart?

Right now though, she needed to focus on what she came in here for.

"Just a quick question. Don't want to pull you away from that fascinating paperwork for too long." Letting a little grin play at her mouth, that laser beam gaze of his zeroed in on her lips. "Um. I, um. Where's my ball?"

It was only as Drew glanced down at his lap that she realized what she said. *Oh my God!* Lifting his head, a loopy grin plastered across his face, and she realized she was in for it.

"*Wellllll*, I have two if you're interested." The slowly spoken words sent shivers down her spine. The expression on Drew's face let her know his balls were hers for the taking, and all she needed to do was ask. Hell, she probably didn't even need to ask. She could probably just climb over the desk and straddle him. But she wasn't going there, she told herself for what seemed like the thousandth time. No, she wasn't, even if she really, really wanted to.

Shaking her head, she couldn't even hide the lifting of her lips in a smile. Maybe two could play at this game for a bit. Give herself the upper hand for a minute or two.

"I'll take that under advisement. Never know when I may take you up on that offer." Drew's throat moved in a swallow, giving her all the proof she needed that her words had affected him. What's good for the goose and all that stuff. She refused to be the only one twisted in knots if this was how he was going to play things. "But that's not what I meant, and you know it. I meant the ball that broke my window." A puzzled look crossed Drew's face as she went on. "I know we didn't see one right away, but I figured you found one when you cleaned up for me. But I checked the trash and didn't see one."

Drew shifted in his seat, his penetrating gaze of moments ago, drifting away from her. He actually looked uncomfortable. *That's weird.* It wasn't like she didn't know he cleaned up for her. He shouldn't be embarrassed by helping her out.

Clearing his throat a few times, Drew finally managed to speak. "Yeah, I cleaned up, but I never, um, found the ball." His brows furrowed as he seemed to catch up with conversation. "Wait, you didn't find one later that night?"

"No, duh. If I did, I wouldn't be asking you now. I wanted to return it to the school today and see if I could get them to pay for the window. Long shot, I know." This was bizarre. "I guess you didn't take it with you?" Though that didn't even make sense as she asked it.

"No. I never found anything in the first place." As he got up from his chair, she knew what was coming. "And why the hell would I take it?" Drew tended to do the nervous pacing thing when agitated. So Val prepared herself to speak to a moving target. "Have you looked again?"

"Of course I have. I checked under the dresser, the night-stands, and the bed. Even outside thinking it bounced off and some sly teenager took the ball back thinking I would believe my window mysteriously shattered. Nothing. But I figured you found it when cleaning, so I wasn't that concerned." Getting up from the chair and smoothing down her skirt, she turned around to head back to her desk. "I guess I'll just wing it with the school administrators. I'll let you get back to the bid now."

Before she made it to the door, Drew gently but firmly grasped her elbow. Val wasn't sure if she was more startled by the action or by the heat that raced through her body at the touch. Oh, this wasn't good at all. Something would have to give, and soon, because her mind was racing to places it had no business racing to.

She dragged her gaze from Drew's fingers, clasped on her elbow, and up into his eyes. Everything seemed to stop for a moment. It was just like the other night, when it felt like only the two of them in their own cocoon. He glided his thumb back and forth on her inner elbow. She couldn't hide the tremor that moved through her body at the touch. She had never considered that area an errogenous zone before, but under Drew's touch, her skin felt like it was on fire. Sensitive in a way she had never experienced before.

The seconds lingered on, with just the slow back and forth motion of Drew's thumb. The shortened breaths of two people feeling way too much. As Val stared into Drew's eyes, this would be a "moment" for them. Feeling herself leaning slightly into Drew's body, she sensed him lowering his head. Part of her screamed that the office was not the place to let this happen. The other, more feminine part of her screamed that it didn't matter. That this was what it wanted: to feel him. To taste him.

That moment in time was blasted apart by a strangled cough coming from the door way. *Oh God!* She had almost kissed him in full view of the office. Anyone could have wandered past. Well, apparently they did. Hanging her head she didn't even want to turn around. Jerking away from the hold Drew still had on her, she tried to rush out of the office before anyone could say anything.

Laughter replacing the cough, she heard Jon before she saw him. "Sorry to interrupt." A sharp growl erupted from behind her. She pivoted around to see Drew's brows furrowed again, like he wanted to argue with his brother's intentions. "No, really. I'm sorry. But the door was wide open. Probably closing it next time would be the wise move."

Next time? There wasn't going to be a next time. There was no way Val would let this happen again. *Well, not at work anyway. Maybe. Work would be okay, but not for the first time. Maybe after I work the sex angst out of my system the first few times.*

SHUT UP!

Val's inner voice was making her crazy. Not at work. Not anywhere. This was not going to happen. But oh, she so wanted it to happen. She hadn't felt that alive, that ready, with any of the men she had ever dated. Every part of her wanted that kiss, even her *can't make up its mind* brain.

Seemingly mollified, he gave Jon a wink and her a saucy grin. "Shut door. I'll remember that."

Val was sure this could be worse, but she was having a hard time figuring out how. Not that she didn't like to joke around during the day, because she did. But this wasn't joking around. This was more fooling around, and she never thought she would be the type to let that happen in the workplace.

"Well, now that you've cooled off, Matt and I are back if you want to quickly meet about the bid revision."

Seeing this as a perfect opportunity to make her escape, Val creeped toward the door. "I'll let you guys get to that then."

"Wait." Drew's voice had her turning around. He couldn't think to say more about what just happened could he? Not in front of his brother. "So if neither of us found a ball, what the fuck broke your window?"

"Huh?" Val's mind was still so caught up in that almost kiss that she wasn't even following what Drew was talking about. Taking a second to re-group, she thought about his question.

"Something broke the window, Valerie. If you and I didn't find anything that could have done it, what did it?" Pacing again, Drew ran his hand through his hair. "Did the repair shop say what happened to your tires?"

Biting her lip because this probably wouldn't help the situation, Val took a breath. "They, um, they said they looked slashed. There were no nails or anything embedded in them that would have caused the issue." That had honestly shocked her. For that first instant, when she had heard, she felt a shiver of fear run through her. But she convinced herself that no one was out to get her, so it must have been a fluke. She also managed to convince herself to not tell Drew. Precisely because of the reaction she was now witnessing.

He stopped on a dime and turned toward her, Drew's mouth falling open. "Excuse me?" He appeared really calm, only his hands flexing into fists at his side showed otherwise, and that's when things usually went to hell in a handbasket with him. Even Jon was staring at his brother like he expected an explosion.

"I'm sure it was nothing." Turning to Jon for support, the look he gave her told her he thought she was an idiot.

Damn. Could her first instinct have been right? Maybe she shouldn't have dismissed what had happened, taking it a little more seriously. But that brought along a whole other set of worries. And that was what she had been trying to avoid. Like a fool.

"Nothing? How the fuck could it be nothing? What, did a ghost just say, 'What the hell, let's slash some tires?' Or maybe it was some neighbor kid's imaginary friend out for a night's fun." His pacing picked up speed. "Your window was smashed in and your tires slashed. In the same night. And you aren't concerned?"

Val thought hard about how to answer this question. Honestly, she thought it was a couple of strange coincidences. But then again, she really did believe Drew had found a ball and didn't mention it to her. And it wasn't unusual to pick up a nail with all the construction areas in her neighborhood. It was only when the mechanic had mentioned what his assessment of the tires was that she'd started to worry. And putting two and two together, like Drew had automatically done, only slowly creeped up on her.

"Yeah, it does seem a little strange."

"A little?" Drew turned toward his brother. "Do you think it's strange? Me, I'm finding it more than 'strange.'"

Hoping Jon would back her up this time, she gazed his way again. Well, that was a longshot anyway. "Val, I have to agree with Drew. This is beyond *strange*. One of the two would be *strange*."

"Did you call the cops?" Drew's blood pressure was clearly

sky rocketing. He loosened his tie and looked like he was ready to have a stroke.

"No, I didn't call the cops. Why would I?" Before Drew could let loose a tirade, she hurried on. "I thought the window was an innocent accident. Sure the tires were a little weird, but it only gets really strange when combined with the window. And you need to calm down!"

Jon seemed to figure out that cooler heads had to prevail. "Why don't you stop at the police station and just see if there is anything you can fill out? Even if all it does is cool off Mr. Hot Head over there."

Val stopped and thought for a moment. There was probably wisdom in that plan. The old adage said, "better safe than sorry." What if it wasn't a fluke and a random set of coincidences? By going to the cops, at least there would be something on record. And Jon was definitely right about Drew.

"Okay. Yeah. I'll do that when I leave here. I'm sure they can't do anything. Especially a few days after it happened, but it can't hurt."

As she stepped out of the room, Drew called out, "Val. This isn't finished." Thinking he meant talking about the damage, she nodded. His voice took on a decidedly deeper timbre, as he continued, "Nothing that happened in here is finished." It was only then that she realized what he meant.

CHAPTER NINE

"Dammit." The growled curse, followed by the slamming of the phone, didn't surprise Val in the least. Matthew's door was open as he'd taken the call from his wife, and like so many of their conversations, it hadn't been a pleasant one. Val loved Matthew like a brother and definitely did not feel the same way toward Cassandra. A colder woman she had never met. As beautiful and elegant as she was on the outside, it hid a world of meanness. Even their adorable son, Aidan, didn't inspire Cassandra's warmth. How she wished Matthew would leave the woman and find happiness. But her own thoughts mirrored something she had once heard Drew and Jon mention—that Matthew seemed to be punishing himself for reasons only he understood.

Valerie turned to face Matthew as he stalked over to the doorway to his office. Trying to draw him out of what she could tell was a foul mood, she smiled. "What's up, boss?"

A forced smile appeared on Matthew's handsome face and made Val hate Cassandra more in that moment. She always believed the Stephens men had it in them to love deeply. After years spent with the family, seeing how their parents acted and how much all three idolized them, her soul told her this was the truth. To think, for whatever reason, Matthew wasn't allowing himself to love like that hurt her. It also made her think of Drew, and what being loved by him might be like. Luckily, Matthew's voice broke her dangerous train of thought.

"What are your plans for after work?"

"Nothing really. With all the craziness of this past week, I think I'm just going to go crash early and enjoy the weekend." A defeated look crossed his face and she asked. "Why?"

"It's nothing. I'll make it work." As he turned on his heels to go back in his office, Val spoke out to stop him.

"Matthew, stop playing the martyr. What do you need? You know I'll help in whatever way I can."

"Cassandra just told me, none too gently, that we are expected at a command performance at her parents' dinner party tonight. At five p.m. With the Lewises of all people." Val winced and cast a glance at the clock. It was already four o'clock, and knowing Cassandra's family, Matthew's current work outfit of khakis and a polo was not going to cut the expected attire. "I had planned on dropping off some new plans and materials, that got delivered here by mistake, at their damn site on the way home. Which, like everything else in this project, is a clusterfuck."

"Can't you drop them on Monday or over the weekend? Do you have a suit here you can change into?" Matthew definitely couldn't make it to the site and still be ready for the party on time. Travel on a Friday night in the northern Virginia area was a nightmare to begin with, but add in the fact that his house and the site were in opposite directions, and there was no way.

Looking down at his clothes, he shook his head. "No. I knew I'd be hitting some sites today and didn't bother wearing or bringing one."

Figures, one of the rare instances Matthew didn't have a suit on, or at least handy. Normally he was all buttoned up and professional, except for days he visited the sites. Val always thought of it as his suit of armor, and in many ways that may be accurate.

"As for the site, I would, but we actually have a crew coming in tomorrow to deal with some of the specs on the new plans. I really don't want to fall behind any more on this project. I just want it done and over." Val could completely understand. It had been a nightmare since practically day one. Materials had gone missing. Random vandalism. An owner who changed his mind as often as he changed socks. Matthew was definitely not the only one who would be happy when the project was done. Val always had to convince herself that she wouldn't just slam the receiver down the next time Lewis called to bitch and moan about something.

Focusing back in, Matthew was still talking, "Andrew and Jonathan are already out at different sites, and making them come back here to turn around is ludicrous this time of day. Would you mind?"

"Of course not." The site was in the same relative direction as her house. "Just give me the stuff, and I'll head over."

"Are you sure? The site isn't in the greatest area." Truer words and all that. The building was going up in an area that was aiming for re-vitalization. It hadn't exactly hit that yet though, so there was some trepidation.

"Yeah, I know. But it's still light out, and it's not like I'm going to be spending the night. All I have to do is drop the stuff. Someone will be there, right?"

"Yeah, Dennis is going to stick around. Especially if I let him know you're coming instead." The flirty grin that passed over his face was so much better than the look he first came out of his office wearing. "You know he has a crush on you."

Rolling her eyes at her boss, Val picked up a paperclip and threw it at him. "He does not!" The older man was one of her favorite employees, and by all accounts, a great foreman. "He treats me like a daughter." She gave a little shrug. "Though if he wasn't married, who knows."

Matthew gave in to a full-fledged laugh. "Don't let Andrew hear that."

That made Val sit up a bit. Both Matthew and Jon had been dropping hints and acting weird about her and Drew for a few days now. "What do you mean by that?" She wouldn't let on the way her thoughts were scrambled. Maybe he was just reaching.

Giving her a look that said she wasn't fooling anyone, Matthew came closer to her desk. "You know exactly what I mean. I'll tell you what I told Andrew: give it a chance. Who knows what may happen."

Staring up into blue eyes, similar yet much more brilliant then Drew's, she saw a world of wisdom and knowledge. What she read there was he wanted to make sure that his brother and friend didn't pass something up. That they didn't lose something. Not like he had.

"Matthew," she whispered, reaching for his hand, heart hurting for him. Shaking his head, Matthew took a step back.

"Just think about what I said." Sensing the moment was lost, she let him go. "I'll get you the stuff now, and then I have to leave. Don't want Cassandra waiting."

CHAPTER TEN

A black non-descript sedan sat quietly on the street. Blending in with its surroundings.

Normally he would never be caught dead in a car like this: something old and bland. But desperate times called for desperate measures.

Inside, he waited. Patiently impatient. Dreaming about all that would eventually come to him once he succeeded.

So far things were going according to plan, but he wasn't one to rest on his laurels. And no plan was ever perfect, though he figured this was about as close as he was going to get.

The problems at the construction site in front of him were just stepping stones. Things that were annoying but nothing more. Now it was time to up the ante, and he sat poised to do it.

The Stephenses had been sitting there, rolling through life like they hadn't a care in the world. Like one of them hadn't ruined everything. But he had, and he damned well would realize what he had done if it was the last thing he did.

No one would get away with it. Let alone a bastard who didn't even appreciate what he had.

Luckily, one fortuitous moment earlier played into his plans even more. How lucky was he that he overheard the foreman talking to *someone at Stephens Construction. Two birds for the price of one were in his sight tonight.*

And this one was such a pretty bird.

Of course, it wasn't the bird he really wanted, but he'd be patient. And he wanted that bird to know exactly who he was. Wanted him to know why he had done everything he had.

But for now, there was no need to rush into anything. He would do what he needed to tonight, and the rest would come when he was ready for it.

As he waited, he stared out the window at the site's office trailer, sitting off to the side of the half-constructed building. He originally thought the building would be a better target. More symbolic of the company. But the trailer... Ahh, the trailer made it more personal, because that belonged to the Stephenses. Especially knowing that the metal and wood structure was going to hold something even more precious in a short time.

Even with the few businesses nearby the site and the last of their employees still milling around, no one would take great notice of him. Just another guy walking down the street. Minding his own business. He'd wait until the perfect moment and then slip out of the car. Make his way to the trailer.

The job site was shutting down for the weekend, so the crew would be gone. He wanted the damage to be just drastic enough to make a point and hand out a little suffering of his own to the Stephenses. In his master plan, he didn't have anyone getting hurt at this point. But what would happen would happen, and he wouldn't be sorry for it.

He would adjust accordingly. But his plan would be seen through. Of that he was eminently confident.

Settling in, he checked his phone for the time; he still had some time to kill.

Kill.

How appropriate. Maybe tonight would be his first. If not, there was still time.

Putting the phone to his ear he pretended to talk. All someone would see was some guy, parked, talking on his phone. What a good citizen, pulling over to have a conversation.

And a good citizen he was. He could ask anyone, friend or business associate, and they would agree. After tonight, he was convinced he'd be an even better one.

CHAPTER ELEVEN

"Well, that sucked balls." Pulling up to the trailer, Val once again cursed the wretched rush hour traffic. "How the fuck could a ride that should have taken thirty minutes take almost two hours? How is that possible?"

Not that she expected an answer since she was talking to herself. Even if she wasn't, there was really no way to get a logical answer. All she knew was that her dashboard clock read a lot closer to seven then five, and it was not exactly hopping with people around the site like she had hoped for. Yeah, there were a few people wandering around, but this was definitely not a booming area yet, and in her skirt and heels she looked out of place. Luckily, it was still relatively light out, the days getting longer as May started to bleed into June. But it definitely wasn't as light as it would have been two hours ago.

Scanning the site as she put her car in park, she didn't see any other cars. At this point she wasn't really expecting to. Val had called Dennis when she realized she was trapped in the traffic jam from hell. After a standoff because he didn't want to leave before she got there, he finally capitulated. Only after Val agreed to call him the minute she got to the site. As if the overprotective Stephens family wasn't enough, now she had Dennis too.

Grabbing her phone out of her purse, Val dialed the number Dennis had texted her. Waiting for the call to be picked up, she gathered up her purse, stepped out of the car and then opened the back door. As she waited for the call to be answered she dragged the box Matthew had passed off to her for delivery out of the back seat.

"Valerie? You at the site?" Dennis's voice came over the line as she struggled to keep the phone between her ear and shoulder as she shut the door and then started walking toward the trailer.

"Yup. Just got here. I've got everything, so I'm just going to run inside and drop it off. That okay?" Putting the box down on the trailer steps, she pulled the key out of her skirt pocket. Thank goodness Matthew decided to give her the key just in case; otherwise, Dennis would have definitely had to have hung around.

"Do you mind dropping it in my office?" Hitting the light switch as she got through the door she turned to grab the box. "With all the trouble we've been having at the site, I'd rather lock the stuff up if we could."

Abandoning the box on the nearby counter and glancing around the room, she took in the open area workspace and four doors surrounding it. Most of their work office trailers were the same: an open space for reception and spare tables. The doors hid an office, a bathroom and conference rooms.

"Well, I can if you tell me which door is your office. Does the key to the trailer work on your office too?"

"It's got a combo code lock on the door. No key needed. Oddly enough I'm better at remembering a code then I am at remembering where my keys are." Sharing a laugh with the older man, Val knew the feeling. Not even mid-thirties yet and her memory was a thing of the past. "And it's the door in the back left corner. Code is six-eight-nine-one."

Val juggled the phone again as she tried to pick the box back up. She only had two hands, there was no way she could manage the box, the code, and the phone. "All right. Let me get in and put this away, and I'll call you back as I leave. You okay with that?"

Hearing a sigh on the other end of the phone, Val already knew that hanging up was not Dennis's first choice.

"Really, Dennis, it's fine. I can't manuever the box and hang on to the phone at the same time. Give me a few minutes and I'll call you back."

A louder sigh accompanied a response this time. "Fine. But just make sure you do, or I'll call you back. I don't like you being there on your own."

"Yes, Dad." Val smiled into the phone, even though he couldn't see it. Although she sometimes groused about it, a part of her reveled in the concern. Her parents were much older when they had her, and both passed away when she was in college. Though she missed them, she had been on her own for years now, especially since her brother had taken off for parts unknown even before they died. Knowing she had people here, Chelsea and Rick, all the Stephenses, even Dennis and Pamela, made her smile and reflect. This was home for her now, and this was her family.

"Yeah, yeah, yeah. Smart-ass." She could sense Dennis smiling. "Now you definitely sound like one of my daughters."

"Let me get going. The quicker I do this, the quicker I call you back and get home myself." With one last goodbye, she pushed the *end* button and disconnected the call.

Dropping her phone back in her purse, she lifted the box once again and made her way to the back office. Propping the box on her hip, she entered the code and turned the doorknob and fumbled for the light. She had to admit, though it wasn't that dark outside yet, the trailer was in shadows. She probably should have turned on a few more lights to get rid of the eerie feeling.

Shifting the box, she pushed through the door into Dennis's office. Eyes opened wide, she looked around, stunned. Where the hell did he expect her to put this box? There was crap everywhere. *Good thing there are conference rooms because when the hell was the last time one of those chairs was used?* Papers and boxes were piled high on what appeared to be every available surface except some parts of the floor. Wasn't there a saying about a cluttered space and a clear mind? If there wasn't, there damn well needed to be as this was a hot mess, and Dennis was always the most organized of the foremen when he came to the office for meetings. *Well, can't judge a book and all that.*

As Val went about organizing piles so she had a flat surface for the box, a door slammed, rattling the trailer. The front door must have blown shut. Cursing herself for leaving it open in the first place, she went back to finding a home for the box. At this point, she just really wanted to get out of here.

She made her way out of Dennis's office after finally placing the box on a cleared-off section of floor. It was only as she stepped into the reception area that her senses alerted her to changes in her surroundings.

The main area was shrouded in darkness, and the lights she had turned on when she entered the trailer were no longer lit and illuminating the space. As she took a moment to take in the situation, she questioned how the door had shut. It wasn't windy out, and the door opened in. Even if there was wind, how could it have shut the door? And why were the lights out? Whatever closed the door wouldn't have also killed the lights.

She tried to laugh off the concern, but she couldn't surpress the shiver of worry that slid down her spine. Something just didn't feel right. Every ounce of sense she had was telling her to get out of the trailer and to her car as quickly as possible.

Making sure she had her purse, she reached in with one hand to palm her phone and keys. Turning on the flashlight app on her phone before shutting the door to Dennis's office, she made her way across the floor to the trailer door.

That was when she noticed the smell. Acrid. Burning. Smoke. Somewhere something was on fire and the tension she felt moments before amped up. Rushing to the front door, she grabbed hold of the knob and yanked. Nothing.

"What the fuck?" Val tugged again. Still nothing. She tried the switch to get more light. Up. Down. Nothing there either. Putting her phone between her teeth so she could still see, she grabbed the doorknob with both hands. Turning the knob and pulling as hard as she could. She fell on her ass as her hands slipped off the knob, her phone went skittering against the wall, and she was enveloped in darkness.

"What the hell is going on?" Talking to herself was doing anything but calming her now. "Okay. Just think for a minute." She tried to take a deep breath, but it was in that minute that she noticed the smell getting stronger. She fumbled on the floor, searching for her phone. "Where the fuck did it go?" A dim beam of light peeked out from under a desk. She inched her hand along the floor, feeling for the phone with her fingertips. "C'mon, you damn thing." This was not good. The smell was becoming overpowering. As the smoke began permeating the trailer, Val coughed. Even in the darkness, she could see it filling the small area.

Finally, her hand alighted on her phone. Hitting the button to pull up the screen, she hissed as she swiped her finger. Shattered. "That's okay. Just need to be able to call for help." Dealing with the stinging in her fingertip, she was startled as the phone rang. Seeing Dennis's number pop up was a welcome relief.

"Hope my office didn't scare you too much, Valerie. You find a place for the stuff?"

"Dennis."

Before she could get another word out, he must have been able to sense something in Val's voice that alerted him.

"What's wrong? What is it?"

"I'm stuck in the trailer. The lights are off and the door's locked. And it's filling with smoke." Beyond a little panicked now, Val trembled. "I think it's on fire."

"Fire?" The panic in Val's voice was echoed in Dennis's. "I'm hanging up and calling 911. You just keep trying to get out." With that, the connection went dead.

"How the hell do I get out?" Val looked around the office by the light of her phone. Sure there were windows, but there was a fire out there somewhere. And staring at the windows in the office, they were long and narrow, no way her body could squeeze through one. Pacing, Val felt like she was at a loss for what to do next. By no means did she just want to sit and wait, but what if she made matters worse?

This was a bad dream. It had to be. The pungent smell of smoke filling the room told her that this was no dream. It was real, and she was smack dab in the middle of it. Shock beginning to overtake her, she just sank to her knees, still in the middle of the floor clutching her phone.

Drew. She wanted Drew. She'd always heard that dangerous moments made things clearer for people, and it seemed to be the case for her. Sitting in this room, filling with smoke, not knowing what move to make made her worrywart feelings about Drew seem so stupid.

Jumping sky high as the phone rang in her hands for a second time, she hurriedly swiped at the glass and yelped in pain as her thumb was shredded by the broken screen.

"Val, are you okay? Fire department is on the way." Dennis again. At least she had a lifeline at the moment. Maybe he could calm her. Though, by the frantic breaths, she wasn't sure that would be possible.

"Yeah." Her voice sounded so tiny, even to her own ears. This was not her. She was stronger than this and would find a way out. Clearing her throat to try that again, another cough racked her lungs. Inhaling smoke with every attempted breath was causing her trouble. "I think I'm okay," she said on another hacking cough.

"Good. That's good. They'll be there soon, Val. Did you break a window?" Listening to Dennis take a breath to continue speaking made Val long for some fresh air. She groped around for something to break the glass with. "I'm in the car heading that way too. I couldn't reach Matt, but got ahold of Drew. He's on his way to you."

He would be too. It was her he was coming to, not the job site. She was done being stupid, so maybe it was time to go to him too.

She managed to grasp a thick piece of metal, maybe some type of tool, and approached the nearest window. With every ounce of strength she struck the glass until finally a hairline fracture appeared. Zeroing in on that small crack she whaled at it again and again. The crash of glass and influx of somewhat clean air made her feel slightly better. But she was still stuck.

As Dennis continued talking, trying to keep her mind occupied on something else, she could hear the faint sounds of sirens. As they kept getting closer, she couldn't help but feel they were getting here right in the nick of time.

The screeching stopped right outside of the trailer, the flashing lights illuminating the inside through the windows, as she dropped the phone in her purse. Poor Dennis was probably still talking, but right now she just wanted to be alert and ready for whatever came next.

CHAPTER TWELVE

*D*rew arrived at the site to a scene terrifying enough to rob him of breath. The pain was so intense that he clutched at his chest even as he slammed on the brakes. Taking in gulps of air, he barely remembered to throw the car into park before trying to get out. The last thing he needed was to take attention away from the situation at hand because he was a dumbass and got run over by his own car. He made it to the site in record time, even for his driving. Nothing else mattered in those moments except getting there once he'd heard Dennis's frantic call.

Valerie. That one word, coupled with what very little information Dennis was able to provide, had him bolting out of his apartment with just enough wherewithal to grab his keys. But not enough to take along his phone which was sitting on the sofa where he'd dropped it. He'd desperately wanted to call Valerie on his drive over. Talk to her. Calm her down. Hell, calm him down. Tell her that he was coming. Did she know he was on his way to her? Did she find a way out? Was she okay?

Now, as he stumbled out of the car, he stared at the site in complete shock. Flashing red and blue lights lit up the neighborhood. The screech of sirens still blaring on the trucks was enough to make his teeth rattle. Water arcing onto the trailer. Plumes of smoke rising from its destroyed shell. He took this all in, unable to move. It looked so violent. So decimated. With that thought, terrible visions flashed across his mind.

No! I will not think like that. Valerie is safe and is coming home with me tonight, and that's that.

It was one of the few times recently that he actually wanted to listen to his inner voice. He had spent so many days and nights fighting with it and himself, but he'd deal with decisions tomorrow. Right now, all he wanted to do was hold Val.

As he made his way from the car, he was enveloped in a mass of people. All of these busybodies who came to watch the excitement were getting in his way. Pushing through the throng, none too gently, he came out the other side—and smack up against a police officer trying to keep him and everyone else back.

"I'm sorry, sir, but you're going to have to move. I need everyone behind this line." He pointed to the yellow police tape strung between two parking sign poles.

"Officer, I need to get in there. That's my business." Drew didn't have time for this. In his head, he realized the young officer was just doing his job and trying to keep everything organized, but Drew needed to be in there with Valerie.

Looking back at him, the officer spoke, "What?" Whether he didn't understand or didn't hear over the blare of the sirens, Drew didn't really care. He'd give him whatever information he wanted as long as it allowed him to get on the other side of that tape.

"My name is Andrew Stephens. I'm one of the owners of the construction company. It was my company's trailer and employee—" God his breath hitched at that word."—that are involved." She was so much more than an employee, more than a friend even, and he finally was getting his head out of his ass and figuring that out. And nothing, no fire, no avoidance, no hesitation on her part, was going to make him stop now that he knew what he wanted.

Speaking into the walkie-talkie clipped to the shoulder of his uniform, Officer Thorton, by the name on his chest, relayed that information to someone on the other end. With a quick "affirmative" spoken, he gestured to Drew to slide under the tape. "Sorry for the delay. Just trying to keep things orderly."

Drew had no problem with the guy doing his job. Especially now that he was one step closer to Val. "I understand and I appreciate it." Drew wanted some answers about this whole mess, so order and organization were not something he would bitch and moan about too much. "Can you point me in the right direction of where I should go?"

Officer Thorton pivoted to his left and gestured toward an ambulance parked up the street. The doors to the back were open, but he couldn't see inside. That had to be a good sign, right? If the ambulance was still here, that meant it hadn't rushed Valerie to the hospital with serious injuries. With that thought in his mind and a nod of thanks to the officer, Drew darted across the street. He tried to prepare himself for whatever he would find, but a racing mind did terrible things to that option. He was one step away from the ambulance door when he heard words that had him sagging in relief.

Cough. "No, really." *Cough.* "I'm okay."

Val's voice had never sounded so good to him. Even roughened from smoke and choking on the words she tried to get out, it sounded like heaven.

He struggled to pull himself together. He didn't want to frighten her any more than she probably had already been. Once she recovered a bit, maybe he would let her see how much what had happened affected him. Until then, he would be the rock she could cling to if needed.

Stepping around the ambulance door, his hard won composure took another hit. Val's face was flushed, soot and dirt clinging to her hair, skin, and clothes. Tear tracks on her cheeks leant a vivid picture to how frightened she must have been. She still hadn't seen him yet since she was looking the other way. That was good. Gave him a chance, once again, to school his features.

Strong for her. He had to be strong for her.

"Val." Not wanting to startle her, but having to speak over the wail of the sirens, he was forced to call her name a little louder than he planned. The mad dash, and maybe one ran yellow-red light, was all worth it when her gaze finally rested on him.

He planted his feet and was ready when she bounded into his arms and wrapped herself around him. With her head buried in his neck, the smell of smoke wafted to his nose, but it didn't matter. Considering what he could see of the burned shell of the trailer, he'd take her smelling like smoke as long as it meant she was okay. Closing his eyes, Drew tightened his arms around her and just held on.

They had shared hugs before, but never under circumstances like this. And most definitely not with an awareness of their feelings. Drew knew deep down that she was as cognizant as he was of the feelings that were building between them. They both just had to admit it and see where it led them.

Gently smoothing one hand over her hair, his other rubbed circles on her lower back. Letting her know he was there for her. That he would hold and comfort her.

Leaning back in his arms, Val looked up at him. Her green eyes glowed a little dimmer than usual, flashing none of the typical humor that they usually did. Which was to be expected considering what she went through. Taking both hands, he pushed the hair back, his touch tender as he cradled her face in his palms. He released a breath he didn't know he was holding when she turned her face and laid a gentle, yet searing kiss to the skin of his right palm. Leaning down, he complemented her touch with a kiss of his own. A butterfly kiss to the center of her forehead.

"Ms. Milner?" A booming voice from behind him broke the spell of the moment. Knowing it was really just the first of many, he didn't object to the interference that much. With Val still in his arms—he wasn't willing to let go just yet—they both faced the newcomer.

A tall man in his early forties, wearing dress pants and a sports coat, stuck out his right hand in greeting while flashing a badge in the other. "I'm Detective Parteleone. There's some questions I'd like to ask you about what happened here tonight."

He knew this was important, but Drew wasn't going to drop the overprotective thing any time soon.

"Does it have to be now? And what about the hospital? Shouldn't Val go to the hospital?" Turning, he narrowed his gaze on her and went on. "Shouldn't you go to the hospital? Are you okay?"

Running her hand down his chest as if soothing a beast, Val gave a small smile. "I'm okay. The EMT checked me out and said that I wouldn't need to go." As if she could sense he wasn't going to allow that to stop him, she just went on, "Really. I'm more shaken up than injured. If I need to go after, I will. But I just want to talk to the detective now. I'd rather get this over with for tonight."

Nodding Val's way, Drew mentally conceded that she was right. And the quicker the police got information, the quicker they could hopefully do something to figure this mess out. "Will you at least sit down?"

"Aye, aye." Well, he was glad to see some of Val's spunk was definitely coming back. "That I can do," she murmured as she hopped up onto the floor of the ambulance.

"So, Ms. Milner, I want you to tell me what happened as well as you can remember it. Start with why you were headed over here."

With that, Val launched into the story of helping Matt out, hideous Friday traffic and getting to the site way later than she planned. "I didn't really notice anything weird until the door to the trailer shut."

Drew hissed. "You hadn't closed it when you entered?" He was going to strangle her. The area around the site was relatively deserted at night. Anyone looking for trouble could have come in and found her all alone.

Looking a little sheepish, Val responded, "No." Turning to look at him, she answered what would have been his response if she had given him another second. "I know, I know. It was probably stupid to leave it open, but I was carrying the box and just didn't think to close it behind me."

"And you didn't see how that happened?" No wondering in the detective's voice, just a simple question. "The door shutting, I mean."

"No. I was in the back office, Dennis's office, and I heard a slam. When I looked out I noticed that the lights in the main office were off and the trailer door was closed."

Chills were racing along Drew's spine as he listened to her recount what happened in the following minutes. From the smell and sight of smoke. To Dennis calling her back. To her breaking the window. To the arrival of the fire department. None of this was giving him a good feeling.

"I don't see why we had to race over here, Matthew. It's not like you or I were going to put out a fire." *Oh, sweet baby Jesus.* Just what he needed. *Not.* He heard Cassandra's voice long before he saw her, which considering that she was bellowing and the sirens had finally stopped wasn't hard to do. Glancing at Valerie, she cringed at the words of his sister-in-law too. Now was not really the time he wanted to deal with the bitch. And he used *bitch* in the most loving of ways of course.

Matt strode directly up to the ambulance and winced when he saw Val. Drew would say Cassandra winced also, but it was more of a derogatory staredown. Something along the lines of "Couldn't you have come out of a fire looking any better?" *Breathe. Just breathe. Now is not the time to let the family dysfunction out of the bag.*

Drew could tell immediately that the detective's attention was taken by the newcomers. Figuring politeness was the way to go, he made the introductions. "Matt, Cassandra. This is Detective Parteleone. He's been interviewing Valerie, and I assume he is the lead investigator." Receiving a nod in confirmation, he went on, "Detective, this is my brother and his wife."

"Investigation?" Cassandra asked. "Why would there be an investigation for a simple fire? Is this necessary? It's not like anything bad really happened." In that single moment Drew swore he needed to convince Matt to leave her. The look on Matt's face said it all. There was no love there, just a deep and growing animosity.

"Yeah, nothing bad at all. Don't take into account that I almost died or anything." Leave it to Valerie to say something. Matt wouldn't because that would start a scene. Drew's protective instincts had him wanting to haul her away from here and the family, but there was that whole scene-starting thing again. Val likely didn't care though, and considering she was the one who had been trapped in a burning trailer, Drew let her have a go.

Cassandra raked another up and down gaze over Val. "Well, you obviously didn't," she said in about the snidest voice Drew had ever heard.

Luckily, it appeared as if Detective Parteleone had pretty much had enough of the family drama by the way he jumped in to stop the bickering. "Well, since we don't know what happened, of course there will be an investigation. If we find out it wasn't an accident, we'll deal with it then. But we need to gather as much information and evidence as we can at the beginning."

That stopped Drew dead in his tracks. Before he was able to verbalize his thoughts, his brother beat him to it. "Are you saying there's a possibility this wasn't an accident, detective?"

"Well, it's too soon to know much of anything. I haven't spoken in length to anyone with the fire department, though I've briefly interviewed the guys who got Ms. Milner out. And I'll be meeting with the arson investigator after he's through processing the scene. So we'll have more information as soon as we can." Looking at all four of them, the detective went on. "What I can tell you is I'm a little concerned with the fact that the lights were cut off and the front door to the trailer was shut and then prevented from opening."

"Prevented?" Having heard Val's recap of not being able to open the door, he now questioned, "I thought the door had just locked somehow. Are you saying that isn't the case?"

"Again, I haven't had a full debriefing with the fire department about what they saw when they first got here, but from initial talks, there was something in place preventing someone inside from opening the door."

All at once foreboding washed over Drew. If this wasn't some random accident, what was it? Even an attempt at arson would have been something they could ultimately deal with, but if there was someone actively trying to hurt Val? What then? There was no way he would let that happen.

"I would like to get in touch with you tomorrow." The detective speaking brought Drew out of his thoughts. "In fact, I would like to get in touch with all of you. The investigation will be further along by then, and hopefully I can get some answers to questions."

After ensuring Detective Parteleone had all the proper contact information and Valerie was cleared to leave by the EMT, Drew led her over to his car. With her leaning against him as they walked, he felt like he held his whole world in his arms. He also felt he held a ridiculously tired woman who could barely walk upright.

Opening the passenger door and gently lowering Val to the seat, he belted her in, shut the door and strode around to the driver's side. With a wave to Matt, Drew got into his car. Valerie was already fast asleep, head thrown back and mouth open just the slightest. Soft little breathing sounds came from her. Knowing that this was the start of whatever was going to happen to them, Drew pulled away and headed toward his apartment. No way would she go home and be alone tonight.

"VAL."

A whispered voice flittered through the fog in her mind. She could sense a featherlight touch lying gently on her hair. Exhaustion had her so firmly in its grip that she refused to let the voice penetrate and wake her fully. Instead, she tried to curl into a more comfortable position, so she could go back to sleep and that wonderful dream she'd had about Drew, and came up trapped. Startled, Val opened her eyes and stared right into a brick wall.

Brain still fuzzy, she slowly realized that wall was outside a car and what had trapped her was the seatbelt. Those touches and that voice. Well, that came from the man in the driver's seat as she made her head turn that way.

"Hey." Another gentle sound. "Wake up, sleeping beauty. Time to get out of the car."

Val wasn't sure she actually wanted to leave this cocoon. It was quiet with just the two of them, and it seemed so much calmer. Just like that, the events of the evening came rushing back to her in a tidal wave. The fear that she had when she was frozen in that trailer. The determination as she attempted to locate something to break open the window with. The strength to finally break through that glass. The sense of relief that came when the fireman had broken through the door and got her out. The gulping breaths she took when she was finally in fresh air. But mostly the sense of rightness that had washed over her when Drew arrived and held her in his arms.

"Huh?" Apparently her ability of speech was still lagging a little behind. "Where are we?" There was definitely no brick wall near her house.

As he tucked a stray piece of hair behind her ear, Drew answered her questions. "The parking garage under my building. No way were you staying alone tonight. I can take care of you here."

Val's brain tried to process all Drew wasn't saying, and knowing him, there was a lot. This wasn't just taking her to his home because of what happened. Somehow, someway, this was him bringing her here to stay. Staking his claim. And what she thought of all that, she didn't know. When she had been trapped, she'd felt so confident in her acceptance of a relationship with him, and the feeling of rightness from being in his arms afterward soothed something inside of her. Now that the threat had passed, she was still terrified of her feelings. She had been down this road once before, and no matter how much her body and her heart longed for Drew, something still held her back.

Her brain was such a muddled mess after all that had happened tonight. She wasn't really sure this was the time to deal with this situation and her tangle of thoughts and feelings. But she had a sense that, whether she liked it or not, their relationship would now be top priority for Drew, so she better get to figuring out her feelings.

Opening her mouth to speak, Drew laid a solitary finger over her lips, as if sensing she was going to make a token fight to go home. "No." And she was, but only a token it would have been. There was something about spending this night at Drew's that felt right to her, regardless of how mixed up her feelings were. "You're not going to your place." His smile mirrored her knowing one. "And we're not having any deep conversations tonight. Now, out you go."

With that, he opened his door and stepped out as she unlatched her seatbelt and went to do the same. Taking a wobbly step, she was soon gathered into strong arms once again.

"Can you make it? Or should I carry you?" A little wink told her he was serious yet teasing her too.

"I think I can make it, big guy. I'm just exhausted. Being trapped in a burning building can take a lot out of a person." Taking a step toward the elevator, she hadn't realized Drew hadn't moved with her. Now, turning her head to look back at him, she caught a myriad of emotions crossing his face. So startled by the expressions, she had missed him moving until he was right in front of her, grabbing her upper arms.

"Never make a joke about that again." Breath coming in short gasps she could feel warming her face, she witnessed his eyes practically shoot sparks at her. "There was nothing funny about that. There was nothing funny when I got that call from Dennis and imagined you in there."

Knowing his emotions were consuming him, she raised her hand to his face and oh so gently smoothed it down his cheek. The stubble rasped against her hand, heightening the sensations running through her body. This wasn't the place or time for these feelings, yet she wanted him to know she understood his terror.

"I know. And I'm sorry." *Stroke.* Her hand kept up a steady motion that seemed to be calming him down. "I need to joke about it so I don't get scared again." That's just how she dealt with things that frightened her. It was usually like that for him too, but it seemed this time things were different. She raised her other hand to gently cup his face. "I promise, no more."

Even as she held his face in her hands, he nodded. As Val went to once again move toward the elevator she was stopped short by Drew's hand on her arm. As she looked to where they touched, his fingers slid lower until they finally intertwined with hers. The roughened skin that came from time on job sites rubbed against the smoother skin of her fingers. That skin gave a her a jolt of awareness that had her tightening her hold on his hand in return.

Hand in hand, they moved silently to the elevator. Waiting for the doors to open, her mind was lost in thought, and it stayed that way as they stepped inside and rode the elevator to Drew's floor in silence. Exiting, they walked down the gray-carpeted hallway. Drew's apartment was in one of the new condo buildings springing up constantly in the northern Virginia area. And while she preferred the quaintness of her own house, she couldn't deny the fact that his place was gorgeous.

"After you," Drew gestured for her to enter as he swung open the door.

He'd first showed her this place when he considered buying it, and she wasn't that impressed. It had left her cold. But he had done an amazing job taking that feeling and throwing it away. Sure, it was still a man's place. A bachelor's place at that. It was missing some feminine touches, some lightness, but it was definitely a home now.

Taking her hand again, he led her back to the spare bedroom. She joked about him needing two bedrooms plus an office when he was house hunting. How much room could one man need? She doubted most of his overnight guests were going to sleep anywhere other than his bed. At that thought, her stomach gave an uncomfortable flip. Funny how things that never bothered her before seemed to now when it appeared as if their relationship was going to take a much different track than the one it had started on.

Seeing the bed as she moved through the doorway, all at once her energy drained out of her. It was as if the few minutes it took to get from the car to the apartment had zapped whatever spare energy she had after waking up. Moving to the bed on legs that felt like wet noodles, all she wanted to do was crawl under the covers and sleep for a while.

"No, no, no, missy." Drew jerked her back before she could accomplish her mission. The bed was so close, and he was withholding all of its comfort from her.

"But I just want to sleep." Turning her crystal green eyes up at him, she gave him her best pleading puppy dog look. "Pleaaaase."

"You can sleep." Excellent. Making to move toward the bed, she was once again brought up just shy of her goal. "After you shower. You'll sleep so much better when you're clean and don't smell of smoke."

Drew had a point. She remembered coming home from bars when she was in college and never being able to sleep because of the smell that clung to her skin and hair. This was so much worse. Every breath she took had her smelling the smoke that had embedded itself in the fabric of her shirt. She honestly didn't think she had the strength in her to make it through a shower, but she'd give it a go.

Nodding at Drew, she made her way over to the bathroom across the hall from the guest room. Yawning as she went, she swore to herself that this would be the fastest shower she had ever taken. Then she could go lie down and lose herself in sleep. Barely hearing Drew mention something about bringing her something to wear, she shut the door and sat down to take her shoes off.

And that was where Drew found her in what was probably a few minutes later, fast asleep, sitting on the toilet, with her head lying on the vanity. Not really even registering what was going on, her eyelids fluttered shut as he picked her up again and strode out of the room. The next thing she realized he was gently depositing her on the vanity in his bathroom, holding her head upright.

"I know you're exhausted, beautiful. But you need to wash. You'll feel so much better if you do." Taking a towel from the back of the door, he handed it to her. Then stepped slightly away from her and turned his back. "You have two minutes to strip, wrap the towel around yourself and move to the tub."

It was only then that she realized the tub was already running. Filling up with hot water, if the steam rising from it was any indication.

"Drew, I can't take a bath. I can barely keep my eyes open. I'll drown." Either a shower or a bath at this point would likely kill her. She'd drown in the tub or fall over in the shower. "Can't I just sleep for a few hours and then shower." Maybe that would work. At some point she was going to wake up because of the hideous smoke smell. She'd shower then.

"Nope. You are taking your clothes off and getting in the tub. I'll be here with you the whole time to make sure you don't go under."

Whoa boy! Even half-asleep, she realized that this had to be the mother of all bad ideas. Going under the water was the least of her concerns now. She was more worried about what else would go on under the water.

"Andrew. I don't, um, I don't think this is a good idea." Though she was considerably more mentally awake then she was a few minutes ago, her body still felt like it could sleep the sleep of the dead.

"Why? Do you think I'm going to cop a feel? Glide soap all over your body?" Shocked that Drew would put into words what had been a dance between them for a few weeks now, Val gave a hesitant nod. "Don't worry, I won't."

Oddly somewhat deflated, Val didn't respond right away. Swallowing and looking anywhere but at Drew, she said, "Oh. Okay."

"Oh, I want to. And I will. Just not now." Blue fire sparked from Drew's eyes. "When I finally get my hands on you for real, you're going to be wide awake, and you're going to revel in every second of my touch."

With that, Drew turned his back again. "Now strip."

CHAPTER THIRTEEN

*D*rew awoke to two realizations running through his head. One was that there was definitely no sunlight filtering through his blinds. A look out the window bore witness to the fact that it was definitely dark outside. Though not from the time of day it seemed. Rain fell in a steady pinging against the window and was all the explanation he needed to know they were in for a dreary day ahead.

The other thought was of far greater importance, and was definitely more interesting to think about. He turned his head from the wall of windows and witnessed the most mesmerizing sight. Val's head was tucked up against his shoulder, hand splayed across his chest, and she had one leg thrown over his as if she had burrowed in to get as close as she could. Smiling at the sight before him, he reached down to move her hair gently off her face so he could look his fill.

She was peaceful in sleep, her face relaxed and her skin no longer flushed from the heat of the fire, which made his heart warm after all she had been through last night.

Although he wasn't going to complain about the results, it

was definitely not his intention to wind up in this position. Especially after the exquisite torture of the bath.

He'd held true to his word of not letting anything more happen in the tub than a simple bath. Although it probably wasn't that simple at all, at least not for him. As Val had drowsily bathed herself, he took on the task of washing her hair. He hadn't thought it would be that bad. He was a dumbass.

Yes. Yes, you were a dumbass. How did you think that wouldn't be bad?

For all their years of friendship, there was something intimate about watching her bathe and taking care of her. Even without seeing her fully naked, he'd been left hard and wanting. Kind of like he was right now, with Val curled around him and images of last night filtering through his mind.

Closing his eyes, he remembered what had transpired the night before. Her wet tresses sliding through his fingers. The glimpse of wet skin as she'd lifted her legs out of the water one by one. The peek over her shoulder to catch the water sliding down the delicate skin of her collarbones and upper chest. Luckily, he'd had the forethought of adding bubbles to the water. At least that had kept her breasts covered. He wasn't sure how he would have gotten through the whole ordeal if he could see those firm mounds and the color of her nipples.

Shifting slightly to adjust his now raging erection, he was careful not to wake the sleeping beauty in his arms.

Last night, he had laid a sleeping Valerie on his bed with the intent of letting her sleep there while he bedded down in the guest room. He grabbed a quick, ice cold shower to relieve himself of the smoke that clung to him and the hard-on her bath had caused, then threw on a pair of pajama bottoms. A moment's rest on the edge of the bed to make sure all of his electronic gadgets were muted and wouldn't disturb her had turned in to him waking up two hours later with Val draped over him. At that point, he thought it best not to risk waking her.

At least that's what you told yourself. I'm sure it had nothing to do with how good she felt snuggled up against you, or how much you enjoyed having your arm around her. Well, he wasn't a complete idiot. Those were definite benefits he was forever grateful for.

He used to dream of finding the woman he could wake up with and feel utter contentment. Even with some of his longer relationships, the sense of rightness that washed over him as he gazed upon Val's slumbering face had never surfaced. When he sensed his feelings for her beginning to change, one of the arguments always pushing forward in his brain was that it could ruin not only their friendship but the sense of peace they felt with each other. Never had he imagined this soul deep joy that he felt having her curled in his arms and in his bed.

Because he had never had it before, he couldn't imagine the possibility. This must be what his dad had meant when he talked about his mom just "being right." Their relationship was something he always gained inspiration from and aspired to. But he had no idea what it would feel like. He recognized that relationships took work, but if this was what one platonic night with Val was like, he would sign up for it every night.

Looking down at Val again, he noted her breathing wasn't quite as even as it was a few seconds ago, and her eyes were blinking open.

As she turned her head, emerald green eyes still cloudy with sleep stared up at him. Val moved her hand lightly on his chest, but not to draw it away. Instead, her fingers toyed idly through his chest hair. Drew never realized how sensitive his chest was until it was Val making small circles on his skin. He felt like a live wire, ready to start shooting off sparks. She continued her stroking even as the sleep faded from her eyes. She had to realize the effect she was having on him. Hell, one look down his body would clearly show the effect he was having on the sheet. Drew was pretty sure he had never been this hard in his life, and considering the woman lying in his arms and in his bed, that made complete sense.

Without a word spoken between them, this was a moment in time that was going to change everything, and it seemed Val was just as on board with that as he was, if he was reading her right.

Slowly, giving her time to see his intent and change her mind if she wanted, he leaned in toward her. Moving his hand to the nape of her neck, he angled her head to his mouth. He never let his gaze leave hers, wanting her fully aware of who was in the bed with her. She glided her hand up his neck and buried it in his hair. Taking one last breath, he closed his mouth over hers and was lost.

He intended to go slow, but the heat that sizzled through his body prohibited that from happening. Tightening his grip on Val's hair, he ate at her mouth. Tongues entwined with each other, teeth nibbling at lips.

Drew turned so Val was under him with both of her arms encircling his neck. She had a death grip on his head, like she never wanted to let go. Drew's one hand was still anchoring her hair and head, but his other hand had a mind of its own. He caressed the side of her neck and over the T-shirt he had given her after her bath. He continued the trek down her body, molding his hand to the shape of her breast. The sharp intake of air coincided with the pebbling of Val's nipple beneath his palm. Moving gently in circles over that handful of flesh, her nipple got harder and harder.

Breaking the kiss, Drew took in Val's flushed face and closed eyes. He had never seen her looking more beautiful. The sensitive skin of her neck beckoned him like a beacon. Lowering his head, he let his lips skim across her skin. Her breathing became more erratic as her chest rapidly rose and fell. He continued his assault on her senses until he neared her ear.

Taking a quick bite of her lobe, he rasped, "Oh God. What are you doing to me?"

Her answer was to drag his lips back to hers for another scorching kiss. As they let the kiss grow in intensity, Val shifted on the bed, spreading her legs wide. Drew immediately found himself cradled between them and sanity completely left the building. Knowing she wore nothing underneath the way-too-big-for-her shirt, his hips sought the naked heat between her thighs.

As he rocked his erection against her, a groan was torn from both of their throats. She met him thrust for thrust. Like she couldn't imagine this not happening.

The somewhat rational part of Drew's mind was sounding alarm bells inside his head. He recognized that he should slow down. That they would be best served if they talked about this change in their relationship before jumping into anything more physical. That they were both still riding high on the adrenaline of the night before. But how was he supposed to listen to that when Val's hands were all over his body? When the inside of her thighs were rubbing along his legs. His mind was short-circuiting, with thoughts of how good, how right, this felt.

Val let her hand drift from his head, stroking up and down the skin of his back, her short nails dragging along as she matched his motions.

A whimper of despair escaped her lips as Drew moved his hand away from her breast. The sound was quickly replaced by a delicious moan of ecstasy as he found it again. This time without the barrier of the T-shirt.

Her skin was so soft, like the finest of silk. Drew trailed kisses down Val's neck, his focus as sure as a laser beam. With his hand beneath the shirt, he pushed her breast up to meet his mouth. As he closed his lips over the tight peak of her nipple, wetting the material of the shirt, she shook in his arms.

"Oh my God!" Val clasped onto his head again, holding him

in place. While her body rode the ridge of his erection. "Drew, please."

She was about ready to come apart in his arms, and all they had really done was kiss. Hell, he was about ready to come apart too. He could feel the pressure building in his balls as he continued to thrust against her. It wouldn't take much to send her soaring, so he started to drag his other hand down her body to her core. Just a few seconds and he could see her sated. What he wouldn't give to have her fly apart in his arms.

So close now. Val was rocking back and forth, whimpering and whispering unintelligible words. Just as he was ready to slide his hand into the slickness between her thighs, a noise blared through the condo.

He and Val jumped apart from each other, like two kids being caught making out by their parents. Except there were no parents here to yell at them, and they definitely weren't kids.

"What the fuck was that?" Valerie asked as she tried to tame her erratic breathing.

Drew's breathing was no better. He felt as if he had run for miles, but this sure as fuck beat any running he had ever done. This was the type of running he could get used to, and he had every intention of getting used to being between Valerie's sweet thighs.

Running a hand through his hair, he dragged air into his lungs. "It's the new doorbell system that the building put into place. They are still working out the bugs."

"Well, tell them to work out the noise, for Pete's sake. That will wake the dead." Breath still coming in jerking pants, she place a hand over her chest. As if she could simply calm her racing heart by applying pressure. Sadly for him, it wasn't only racing because of what they had been doing.

"Yeah, that's one of the bugs." Both of them jerked as the noise reverberated through the place again. "It looks like someone really wants my attention." Glancing back at Val as he rose from the bed, he winked. "Well, someone else."

It was so funny to see her blush, considering the way she had been rubbing herself against him not five minutes ago. But blush she did, even going so far as to lower her head so he couldn't see it. Well, that wasn't going to happen.

Leaning over the bed, he placed a finger under her chin and raised her head. "Let me take care of whoever is beating down my door. Then we'll talk." Her eyes wide, she nodded. "I hope you believe this. What happened this morning, just now, wasn't planned. It was damn sure enjoyed, but not planned. We'll talk before this happens again."

Seeing her open her mouth, he wasn't about to let her retreat behind whatever fears or doubts she had.

"And it *will* happen again. This and so much more. Now that I've had an appetizer, I want the whole damn meal. I'm a hungry man, Valerie, and I enjoy good food. I know you're going to be the best I've ever tasted." Grabbing a T-shirt from his bureau, he pulled it on as he made his way out of the bedroom. "I'll go see who's at the door. Come out when you're ready."

DREW HAD SLIPPED BACK into the bedroom to get dressed and let her know Detective Parteleone and the arson investigator were here to talk to her. Val decided to take some time to pull herself together after hearing that they were outside. With all of the emotions and feelings shuttling through her body, she was left with no other choice.

Grabbing sweatpants and a new T-shirt out of Drew's dresser, she made her way into the bathroom. Looking at the image in the mirror, she saw a very aroused and unfulfilled woman staring back at her. Lips red and swollen. A flush covering her face and neck. A wet spot on the material over her breast. She was damn sure that if she lifted the shirt's hem, she'd see glistening on her thighs giving proof to her desire. Grasping the counter as a life line, she sucked in a breath.

Sure, even in her denial she'd known where the dance they had been doing for only a couple of weeks was heading, but she never thought she would go up in flames like she had from some simple kissing and touching.

Simple? That was simple?

Okay, so maybe not so simple. She had tried to always see Drew in the friendship light, but that was blown out of the water today. She wasn't sure how she could go back now, and she needed to until she finally sorted out her feelings. Her body still vibrated with passion at the thought of how combustible they were together.

Mind reeling with the memory of Drew's hands stroking her body, she looked down to see her own hand moving toward her thigh. Stopping her hand just short of its target, she considered whether or not she should take the edge off while she had the chance. Going out to meet the detective when all she really wanted to do was crawl onto Drew's lap and ride him into oblivion was probably not the best idea. Of course, that wasn't a great idea for many reasons, namely her own confused feelings.

Though if she was really honest, Val would admit that seeing to her own pleasure alone didn't do much for her. She wanted Drew. Wanted him with a passion she didn't expect. That she had never really experienced before. One kiss from him sent her soaring, but her mind still raced with questions and worries. As high as Drew could make her body fly, she was worried he could make her plummet just as deep. Oh, not on purpose, that she knew, but she could still wind up hurt. Wind up alone again, like she had been all those years ago. Was this passion worth it? Her heart screamed that it was. Her brain was much more soft spoken, but sadly just as persuasive in its own argument, one that was years old and borne from previous heartache.

Deciding a quick, cool shower was the way to get over this fire running through her blood that Drew caused, she turned on the water. Tossing the T-shirt over her head and onto the counter, she then stepped into the tiled shower.

"Ahh!" Okay, so maybe the water was a little too cool. Adding some hot water to the mix, she stood under the spray and just decompressed. The past twenty-four hours had definitely been a whirlwind. From the terror of the fire to the absolute bliss she found in those few moments in Drew's arms.

Reaching for the soap, whatever arousal that had already lessened came roaring back to life. The woodsy scent she associated with Drew and usually took for granted brought a whole rush of feeling to her now. The warmth of the shower enhanced the aroma of deep pine. Her body was encapsulated in that familiar scent. So much so that if she didn't know better, she would have sworn Drew was there with her. Encircling her in his strong embrace. It was enough to send her temperature soaring and her blood rushing.

Reaching for the knob, she gave it a quick twist. "Time for more cold water." These thoughts running rampant through her imagination were not helping. Giving her hair another quick wash, she turned off the water and then jumped out of the shower.

After a quick towel dry, she slipped into the charcoal gray sweatpants—definitely too big on her given Drew's height. She rolled up the cuffs and hoped that they didn't slide down and trip her. A quick tug on the drawstring, followed by a secure knot, made sure they stayed up too. Looking at the black T-shirt she brought in with her, she gave a sideways glance at her bra. The pink lace teased her from its place on top of the clothes she had on yesterday. The thought of putting on something that reeked of the smoke from last night was not a pleasant one.

Throwing the shirt over her head and slipping her arms through, she gave herself a once-over in the mirror. Well, her breasts weren't that big and they were still relatively perky in her estimation. Hopefully, Detective Parteleone just thought it was cold in the apartment because Val really didn't think there was anything she could do to help the fact that her nipples were jutting out the fabric of the shirt. With one last longing look at the bra, she turned on her foot and went out to see if someone had deliberately trapped her in a burning building.

CHAPTER FOURTEEN

*A*fter a highly informative and slightly chilling meeting with Detective Parteleone and the arson investigator, Drew and Val headed over to her house so she could change into some real clothes. Not that he didn't love the fact that she was walking around in his clothes, but he damn sure didn't need anyone else seeing her braless. Drew wanted to wrap her up in layers of sweatshirts when she strolled out of his room, and he could so clearly see her nipples denting the shirt she wore.

Hell, it was bad enough he had sat there in jeans way too tight for the erection he was sporting while talking to the police. Looking at her and knowing that she was naked under *his* clothes almost made him come. *You need to save that, buddy. There will be plenty of time for coming later. Preferably when Valerie is naked and under you.* Yeah, that was definitely the intention.

Now, chaos was the name of the game as they all settled around the giant kitchen table at Drew's parents' house. He had Val next to him as they relayed the latest update on what happened last night. His parents, Paul and Linda, were fussing over Valerie, which wasn't really a surprise. Both of them had taken to her as soon as she started at the company and considered her one of the family. *Maybe she could officially be part of the family soon.*

Stunned at his thoughts, Drew sat back in the chair. Not that he hadn't realized how intense his feelings were, especially after this morning, but he hadn't yet gone to marriage in his head. Reflecting on it, he was still filled with a contentment he didn't think he'd ever feel. There was no nervousness or doubts like he had when past relationships seemed to be straying into a long-term commitment realm, but thinking of Valerie as his wife simply made him happy.

"Can we get on with this?" Cassandra spoke in a bored tone. "It's not like I don't have anything else to do on a Saturday. I have a spa appointment in an hour."

How the fuck did his brother put up with that attitude? On the best of days, Drew could barely stand to be around her, and he knew Jon felt the same. Their mom and dad had started out loving Cassandra. Okay, maybe that was a bit of an exaggeration, but they at least liked her. Or at least they wanted Matt to be happy and took his word when he said he was. Now he was pretty sure there was no one in the family that liked her, husband included. Yet he stayed for reasons only Matt knew and understood, though Drew had his suspicions.

"We wouldn't want to keep you from your botox, Cassandra." This from the woman on his right with a sugary sweet smile. "I'm sure that's important to you."

His woman could lay it on thick when she wanted.

Cassandra's mouth formed a perfect "O" of indignation. "I have never gotten botox!"

"Oops, my bad." Still with a smile on her face, Val lowered her voice. "Maybe you should consider it."

He should probably slip into the role of referee; otherwise, this was going to get ugly and nothing would get done. Before he had a chance to open his mouth, his mom jumped in to defuse the situation.

"I'm sure you'll make your appointment, Cassandra." Turning to her daughter-in-law, Linda smiled. "Why don't we find out what the detective told Drew and Val so you can make sure you can leave...on time?"

Wow. If that wasn't a backhanded statement, he wasn't sure what was. Drew couldn't ever remember a time when his mom wasn't unfailingly polite, but with that slight hesitation, she had come pretty close to bitchy. Looking around the table, even the rest of the family couldn't hide their looks of astonishment. And Val did a piss poor job of hiding the smile that crossed her face for a fleeting moment.

Matt finally chimed in, trying to move things along and no doubt wanting his wife to leave probably more than the rest of them did. "Mom's right. And considering it was the Lewis site, I would think you would be more concerned, Cassandra." The look Matt leveled at his wife dared her to say anything else at the moment. Looking back at the rest of them, he continued, "What did the detective have to say?"

Exchanging a look with Val, Drew could tell she preferred him to tell the story. She was still badly shaken by the events of the previous evening, and what they had heard this morning didn't help at all.

"Well, the fire was definitely deliberate." Seeing the paleness overtake Val's face made him want to wrap her in his arms. Though he wasn't sure if that would be appreciated in front of his family. They still hadn't talked about what was happening between them, and he didn't think his family's input was needed right now. But seeing his dad comfort his mom at the news made him realize how much he wanted with Valerie.

"They're positive?" This from Jon, sitting across the table with a frown marring his face. "No chance of a mistake on their part?"

Drew shook his head. "Not from what the detective told us.

I'm not great with the forensic or police lingo, but he said that there was plenty of indication that it was set on purpose."

Val nodded in agreement. "Yeah. He mentioned something about a trail of accelerant and cloth around the trailer."

"And that's not all. It seems as if something was definitely done to the door so it couldn't be opened from the inside. Which makes them convinced it wasn't an accident that the door slammed shut." Just saying the words sent a chill down Drew's back. Glancing at Valerie next to him, he could sense her shudder as he relayed the information.

"Goddammit." Matt slammed his hand down on the table. "Who the hell would want to do this?" Fuming, he stood and started pacing the room. "I'm so sorry, Valerie. This is all my fault. I shouldn't have sent you there last night."

"Well, you certainly couldn't have missed dinner." Six heads turned in stunned silence to stare at Cassandra. "It was bad enough you insisted we leave early to get over to the site." Drew was almost convinced she didn't realize how callous she sounded, until she glanced at her phone like the whole thing was just a bore and irrelevant.

Even as his mother prepared herself to speak, the silence was broken by another, much harsher voice.

"No. You know what was bad enough? Spending the evening with a bitch." Now the shocked faces turned in unison toward Matt. Never had they heard him speak like that to Cassandra though there were times they could tell he wanted to. Even Cassandra had taken on a look of shock as she raised her eyes to her husband. "Also bad enough was spending it with said bitch's family and friends."

Before Cassandra could even speak, Matt kept going, "Why don't you just leave now. Go get your fucking nails done or whatever it is you do, and leave this to family." Picking up her purse, Matt marched over to the door leading from the kitchen to the driveway and opened it. Noticing that Cassandra hadn't made any movement to go, he glared at her with eyes gone icy. When he finally spoke again, it was with a voice that was just as cold. "Go. Now."

A thick tension fell over the room as everyone waited for the fallout. But apparently Cassandra gathered some common sense and decided to leave before things got nastier. Though that didn't stop her from looking at Matt and seething. "We'll talk later, Matthew." With that, she grabbed her purse from him and slammed the door in her wake.

As Matt came back to the table, it seemed as if no one knew what to say. That was definitely the most public the animosity between the two had ever been. Drew wanted to comfort his brother but knew that he would be rebuffed if he tried. Matt was very private about all things, but his relationship with his wife most of all. Their mom looked like she was about to make a move to go to her eldest when a small voice broke into the room.

"Mommy make Daddy sad." Aidan, Matthew's three year old son, had wandered into the kitchen without anyone noticing, a little frown tugging at his mouth. Aidan was often quiet, Drew recognized, probably trying to keep out of his mother's way. While Matt doted on the child, Cassandra was little more than a figurehead of a mother, and Aidan could easily sense it.

Aidan came up to his father, laying his head on Matt's leg and gently patting him. A three-year old trying to give comfort to the most important person in his life. "Ove you, Daddy."

Drew felt the need to turn away and give Matt this moment in private. Looking at Valerie's face, the glassy sheen of tears in her eyes, told him she felt the same way. His mom was openly, yet silently, crying.

Matt gathered his son into his arms, laying a kiss on his head as he settled him on his lap. "I love you too, buddy. So much." As father and son shared a smile that lit up both of their faces, Val reached for his hand under the table. He gave her palm a squeeze in return but didn't let go. After everything that had happened in the last twenty-four hours, he needed this connection with her.

"You want to help Daddy and Uncle Andrew figure out why one of our trailers caught on fire?"

"Ire?" Blue eyes, the same shade as his father, lit up. Kids were so resilient. From sadness to excitement in the blink of an eye. "Ire truck?" Aidan loved the toy fire truck Valerie had gotten him for his birthday. Little did they know how prophetic that present would be.

Valerie leaned over the table, smoothing her hand over Aidan's head. "Yup, there was a fire truck. Lots of them." Eyes went round with wonder and delight. Val lowered her voice, like she was sharing a secret with the boy. "And an ambulance." The gasp of awe that came from Aidan was one of the sweetest sounds Drew had heard. Aidan scrambled off Matthew's lap and ran for the living room yelling, "ire truck," at the top of his lungs.

"You know he's coming back in here with that truck, right?" Jon had been silent since the incident with Cassandra, but finally chimed in now.

"Definitely." Matt sat, waiting for the inevitable return of his son. "At least he'll be mostly distracted as we talk." Putting his head down for a second, he raised it with a somber look in his eyes. "And I apologize for the scene before with my wife. She ..."

"Matthew. Stop." Looked like Mom had finally had enough. "There is no need to apologize for that woman. You and I will talk. Later. Right now, that incident is over and done with. Let's move on." And just like that, Mom had taken control, which wasn't unusual. Their dad may have been the head of a company, but Mom was definitely the head of the family.

"Yeah, let's move on to the fun stuff."

Drew glowered at Jon, showing his displeasure with his

words. "Is that your way of breaking the tension? You think that was fun?"

"What? Fire is a lot more fun than what just happened."

He was going to kill his brother. Val had been trapped inside a burning building only hours ago. There was damn well nothing fun about that.

"Jon's right." Val squeezed his hand, trying to calm the beast. "Well, at least about talking about what happened." Valerie gave her own glance toward Jon. "Though I'm not agreeing with you about the fun of a fire. You can get stuck in one next time. I'm good with my one-and-done experience."

The whirring of a siren broke through as Aidan came back in the kitchen carrying his toy like a precious gift. Climbing back on his father's lap, he moved the truck back and forth on the table, clearly lost in his play.

"Did you mention the previous incidents that happened at the Lewis site to the detective?" Matt managed to shut off the siren noise without much fuss from his son. At least they could hear each other now. "He left a message for me, but we've been playing phone tag for much of the day so far."

"I did." Drew had gone into a long list of what he could remember happening at the site. From the missing items, to the vandalism, to the annoying site owner, he'd given up everything he knew. "Detective Parteleone is definitely interested in seeing where that information may lead, but there's a snag."

"What snag?" Dad joined in the conversation. "Not that I like the idea of a client doing something like this, but it seems almost obvious as to what's going on."

"Yeah, that's what I would have thought too." Drew figured that the detective would have jumped all over this information.

"Until I mentioned what had happened to me recently," Valerie chimed in. "Once I told him about the broken window and flat tires, he became a little conflicted."

"So he doesn't know if it's someone after you or after the

company?" This from Matt, who was calmly bouncing Aidan on his knee.

"Or even you, Matt." Jon pushed the toy truck back in Aidan's direction with a smile. "You were supposed to be the one going to the site last night."

"True. It was only a last-minute change that caused Valerie to head out there." Matt ran a hand throught his dark hair. "But it wasn't a pre-scheduled visit, so who knew?"

Drew and Val nodded in unison. "Exactly. The fact that Val has had some things happen to her so recently makes what may have been a pretty obvious direction of investigation a little more muddied."

"So what do we do now?" Jon asked.

Drew turned his head and was greeted by Val's stare. "All we can do is just let them do their job and figure out what happened." He expected his next words may be met with some resistance, but that was okay. He was in too deep to back out, and he would do what needed to be done. Now he spoke directly to her, their gazes locked. "And Valerie will be staying at my place. I don't like the idea of her on her own with what's gone on."

Before Valerie could even open her mouth to voice her dissent, his mom jumped in. "That's a brilliant idea. You'll be safe there—with Drew protecting you." Drew caught the sparkle in his mom's eye and the look she shared with his dad. Looked like Mom was completely on board with his plans, even if she didn't know he was too.

CHAPTER FIFTEEN

*V*alerie leaned on the breakfast bar separating Drew's kitchen and living room, gazing out the windows at the far end of the room. The cloudy day hadn't dissipated any, but at least the rain had stopped. She thought back to the events of the morning and early afternoon and found herself wondering how she had been coerced into moving in with Drew. Though, if she was honest with herself, it didn't take much to twist her arm. After everything that had happened, she wasn't keen on staying alone right now. The neighborhood she loved wasn't the most active, and even before these incidents, sometimes she felt unsettled at the stillness around it.

She'd pleaded to stay with Chelsea and Rick, a half-hearted plea at best, and Drew had known it. She'd been so sure about her feelings while she was in the trailer, except then she wasn't. Maybe it was time to admit what she was really feeling. To herself and to Drew. Maybe he hadn't come right out and said the words, but his intentions were clear. To him, they were on the verge of being a couple. She just needed to get on board with it, if that was what she wanted. This is why she needed time alone, to think about everything.

Who was she trying to kid? It was definitely what she wanted in her heart. Her brain was asking her if it was what she should want? Val was not a woman who thought she lied to herself all that often. Yet thinking back on it, she lied to herself a lot about Drew. Yeah, they were friends. Though what she felt for him went so much deeper and that was always something she denied.

But those denials were stupid. She'd put Drew squarely in the friend category as soon as she met him. It helped that he was in a relationship when she'd started working for the company. Even though he had been taken, there was something about him that had made her heart stutter and— not to mention—her nipples sit up and take notice. She had never met anyone who managed to turn her on and wrap her in care all at the same time. It wasn't something she knew how to handle. So she didn't. And fortunately, at the time, she didn't have to. Drew became her friend, and she never consciously entertained the idea of him crossing over that divide. But, those thoughts always seemed to disappear when she'd dated other men. Maybe they never actually disappeared though. She was starting to think she simply told herself she wasn't interested in Drew, but maybe that wasn't the reality.

Now she was firmly stuck between a rock and a hard place. She could finally admit her feelings and see where things went with him, but that brought her right back to the whole "sleeping with your best friend" conundrum. Been there, done that, and have the scars to show for it. Or she could break it off in a way that wouldn't allow any coming back. It would probably destroy a lot more than her relationship with Drew, but that wasn't any reason not to do it. *Why am I even thinking about this? Stopping wherever this is going is not something that needs to even be contemplated. Go get some!*

Her inner voice was beginning to sound a little sex-starved. Not that she could blame it. After that taste this morning, it had taken everything she had to sit through the meetings with the detective and the rest of the Stephens clan and not manage to jump Drew. Her body definitely knew what it wanted. Her heart did too. Her brain, however, seemed to be the only holdout from full cooperation. *The brain is dumb; don't listen to it. Listen to the pussy!*

Val sputtered a little laugh just as Drew walked into the kitchen. "Something funny?"

Shaking her head, Val sure wasn't going to relay what had just crossed her mind. "Nope." She turned to face him, gifting him a brilliant smile.

Drew had managed to sneak up right behind her, so close she could oh so easily touch him. But she kept her hands to herself, even though she didn't want to. What Val wanted most in that instant was to reach out, grab hold of him and never let him go, but the doubts in her mind still held her back. The memories lingering from a time long ago were chains she was having a hard time figuring out how to break. Before, it had never dawned on her to want to break them, but now the pull was there to free herself. If only she knew how.

Instead, Drew made the first move, bringing a finger to the edge of her lips as they lifted in a smile. She glanced briefly at that finger, trying to come up with something to say. Raising her gaze to Drew's, all words were silenced in her throat. His stare held longing and passion and need. But tenderness and raw feelings blazed in those striking blue orbs as well. This wasn't something that was random for him. No. Instead, those eyes told a story of deep desires and emotions, something she knew well but never gave life to in her own.

Now was the moment of truth. Unlike what happened in bed this morning, they were both wide awake. There could be no doubt in their minds what this moment in time signified. Without saying a word, Drew was asking her a myriad of questions. Her answer could only be yes or no. No waffling. No regrets. No second thoughts later. If they started on this journey, they needed to see where it would wind up. She couldn't start and then let her fears stop her. She knew in her heart that if she did that, there would be no starting again.

Carefully, with full knowledge of what her actions were saying to the man in front of her, Valerie brought her hand up to his cheek. A whispered sigh escaped his lips as he leaned into her touch. Drew lowered his head and let the lightest of kisses brush over her lips.

Another pass of his mouth followed. Val searched for his elusive lips as he leaned his head slightly back. She followed his mouth and gently flicked her tongue against his closed lips. Drew responded, touching his own tongue to hers, before joining their mouths again.

As he ate at her lips, little nibbles and tugs at her mouth, she felt the moment that both of them let loose of the reins.

"You're mine, beautiful," Drew whispered in her ear with a passion-drenched rasp.

She gasped for breath as Drew held her face in his roughened hands and laid kisses at the corners of her mouth.

Val couldn't agree with him more. Never had she felt as consumed as she did with Drew, and they hadn't really even gotten past kissing. Her body was on fire, and all she knew was that she needed him. Needed him to bring out the passion within her.

"God, yes. Yours," she whispered as she moved her mouth in search of his. She needed his lips on hers. On her entire body. Reaching her arms up, she encircled Drew's neck, running her hands through his hair. Feeling the silkiness of it against her palms.

Val opened her mouth as Drew's came down on hers. His tongue darting inside, sweeping around for a taste of her. Chasing his tongue with her own, she gave as good as she got.

When they finally came up for air, she got her first inclination as to what her body was doing. She hadn't been aware of anything but her mouth on his, his invading tongue, but now she could sense what else was going on.

Drew had her completely trapped between the breakfast bar and his body. He ran his hands urgently over her, from her neck down to the edge of her skirt. She hadn't realized when she got dressed this morning what would happen, but she couldn't lie to herself and not think she had made a brilliant decision by opting for a skirt instead of jeans.

Drew grabbed her ass, yanking her lower body into even more intimate contact with his. She felt his erection through his jeans, pressing into her belly. Her panties moistened even more. Pretty soon she was sure they were going to be ruined. Never had she been this wet before, but she needed more.

"Feel that, beautiful." Another press of his jeans-clad erection against her body. "Feel how hard you've gotten me. That's all for you." Lowering his mouth to her ear, he whispered "Think how good it will feel inside you. Filling you. Making you come all over me."

Whimpering at Drew's words, Val's knees weakened and she felt faint. She hadn't been with anyone who really talked during sex before. She never imagined what hearing those words, and the images they garnered, would do for her.

Hands anchored to Drew's shoulders, she tilted her head to the side as Drew laid claim to her neck, sucking and biting on the sensitive skin there. Followed by long swipes of his tongue to soothe the ache.

Drew slid his hands to the backs of her thighs and under her skirt. The contact of his hands with her bare flesh sent chills through her body. He ran them up her thighs, slowly, finally encountering the fabric of her panties. Pushing his hands under the material, he gently massaged the flesh of her ass. "You like that? You like my hands on your ass?" She felt his fingers graze the crack of her ass, before grabbing each globe and squeezing.

Panting, she couldn't even bring herself to respond. "I think you do. I think you'll like my hand somewhere else even more."

With that, Drew moved his right hand to the front of her body, making a long sweep down her chest to where the skirt ended. With one hand still firmly gripping her ass cheek, he drew the skirt up her thighs. This was almost as torturous as when he moved up the back of her legs. She trembled with lust.

"*Ahhhhhhhhhh.*" A long groan tore out of her chest with the first touch of Drew's hands on the front of her panties. There was no way he could miss the moisture gathered there. As he moved his hands between her legs, he let her know.

"My, my. Someone is very wet." Playing with the material covering her pussy, she was consumed by the magic pull of his hands and words. "Do you like me playing with you? Touching you? Maybe you like me talking dirty to you?" She couldn't hide the rush of moisture that appeared with his words. "Oh, yeah. Your body tells me you do. If your panties are this wet, I can only imagine how slick your skin is. Is your little clit covered in juices? I bet I'll have no problem getting a finger inside. You'll be oh so tight, but I'm going to be able to slide right in."

Val's mind was barely functioning at this point. All she could do was feel, to revel in the sensations Drew's hands and words brought to her. She couldn't deny that her body was telling her she enjoyed Drew's version of dirty talk. It only added to the flames zinging through her body and made her want to melt into his embrace.

Running her hands over his shoulders, she ached for skin-to-skin contact. Val let her fingers find the skin at his neck and slid her hands under the material of his T-shirt. His body was hot, just like hers. It still wasn't enough for her. She wanted more. She *needed* more.

Starting to move her hands down the plane of his chest, her world dimmed as Drew's fingers came in contact with her aching clit.

"Oh, God." The words tore from her throat on a long moan. Her hands dropped off his body. One grabbed hold of the counter, trying to find purchase as she sensed herself slipping away. The other latched onto Drew's hand. Whether to keep it against her flesh or move it away to stop the torture, she wasn't sure. She just knew that her body was experiencing things that were brand new to her. Along with that, her mind raced in circles, trying to process every delicious touch and sensation Drew gave her. The very fact this was Drew caused her thoughts to whirl, a mass of confused feelings.

Drew circled the small nub of flesh with his fingers, making her more sensitive with each pass. Val's body was so ready, it wouldn't take much more for her to come, and it seemed as if Drew sensed that.

"You ready to come for me?" Whispering the naughty words in her ear while his fingers worked their magic was *so* doing it for her. "I can feel your body shivering and shaking. You know that this is only the start, right? If my fingers are making you feel this good now, imagine how my mouth will make you feel." Moving his fingers away from her clit, he slid them through the moisture of her pussy. The light touch on his return had her keening a cry of need. "I'm going to eat you so good. My tongue and lips are going to make a feast out of this sweet little pussy. I can barely wait."

Val needed more. She needed a firmer touch because now he was just playing with her. Taunting and teasing her. The need to come apart in his arms was overwhelming, stealing her breath. Panting, her body straining for more from Drew, she pleaded, "Please, Drew. Please, I need to come."

A wicked grin crossed his face before he spoke. "That can definitely be arranged."

He tightened the clutch on her ass. He rubbed the heel of his right palm roughly on her clit, while his fingers teased her opening, seemingly in all the right ways. As he latched his lips on to the sensitive skin at the side of her neck, she exploded. As the waves of pleasure rolled through her, she rocked into the hand still circling her clit. She could feel Drew's rigid erection at her hip, keeping time with her rocking rhythm. He changed his caresses to something more tender and softer as her body came down from its high.

Not even realizing she had shut her eyes, she opened them to find Drew staring at her face. Emotions she couldn't name flickering over his expression. *Or maybe you're too afraid to name them right now. Maybe you didn't think that word would come into play so quickly. No pun intended. Ha ha!* Her inner self had no business throwing around that idea or making fun of her for how quickly she just got off.

Still staring into Drew's blue eyes, gone icy with unsated lust, she was about to speak when she felt him pull his hands from her panties. The lack of his touch on her was almost painful. Her voice caught in her throat as he raised his fingers to his mouth.

Slowly, Drew licked her essence off of his fingers. Never once did he break eye contact, keeping her enthralled with his actions and on the verge of coming again. What about this was so sexy? Finally, he closed his eyes on a sigh and she could breathe again. "You taste delicious. See?" Val was unprepared for the ferociousness behind Drew's kiss as he leaned into her. Tangling his tongue with hers, she could taste herself on him. The flavor a unique mix of her and Drew.

As he continued to nibble at her lips and twirl his tongue inside her mouth, she felt herself growing hot all over again. A little aftershock rippled through her body just as he ended the kiss.

Raining fluttery kisses all over her face, Drew gently held her in his arms. She was pretty sure they needed to talk or something, but she could barely form a coherent thought at this point. Speech was definitely beyond her abilities right now. And she could feel herself growing just a bit embarrassed. Here they were, fully clothed in his kitchen, after what had essentially been her best orgasm in quite a while, if not forever, and she hadn't even reciprocated on him. She could still feel his erection. It hadn't subsided at all. If anything, it had grown harder as she was hurtled into her climax.

"Hey, there's no need for that." As if sensing her thoughts, Drew's hands gently lifted her face toward his. The scent of her arousal still clinging to his fingers made her face grow even redder than she was sure it already was. "Don't be embarrassed or ashamed. That was the hottest moment of my life."

Grinning a little, it made Val feel good to know that he was just as moved by the moment as she was. It still didn't do anything to hide her embarrassment of not giving back to him. Maybe she still could. Moving her hands down his chest, she let her fingers start to unbuckle the belt around his waist.

Masculine hands stilled her motion. "No. I'm okay." Seeing the question in her eyes, he went on. "Well, not really, but I will be."

"But ...".

A quick kiss stopped her words short.

"Not now. I have plans for us tonight, and I'm doing this right." Seeing the grimace on Drew's face, it almost seemed like he was a little embarrassed too. "I don't have to fall on you like a lust-starved man at every chance."

Val gave in to the slight laugh brewing in her throat. "The lust-starved man does have some things going for him." She stroked her hands up and down his chest and abs, hearing the strangled sound he made every time they moved lower. "I think I like that man."

"Well, you can like the gentleman too." Grabbing hold of both of her hands in his, he gently kissed her knuckles. "That's the one who's going to wine and dine you tonight. Provided the lust-starved one responds to the ice cold shower I'm going to take."

Val was pretty sure that, at this point, she was going to like any version of himself that he gave her. Whatever roadblocks and issues she kept throwing up in front of a relationship with him had been smashed. *"Hmmmmmmmm.* Are you sure that shower shouldn't be hot?" On a wink, she added, "And for two?"

"Stop it, you temptress!" They both laughed at Drew's exaggerated response. "I will not be lured into your sultry web."

Raising a hand to push a lock of hair behind her ear, Drew looked at her with all seriousness.

"Tonight we go out. We'll talk about this over a nice dinner. We've done almost everything but talk, and for this to work, I think it's time."

Valerie couldn't help but agree. They had gone from friends to almost lovers so quick her head was still spinning. After what happened in bed this morning and just now, they needed to see what they both were thinking about. This was either going to make or break their entire relationship.

"Okay. Talking and taking it slow it is."

Drew's eyes narrowed. "I said nothing about taking it slow, but we will talk before anything else happens."

With that, he wandered into the living room. Turning back, he called to her, "Wear something sexy. This is going to be a good night."

CHAPTER SIXTEEN

*D*rew's mind was still spinning as he waited for Val to finish getting ready for their date tonight. Oh, neither one of them had actually called it a date yet, but that's what it was. He had to make sure she knew sex wasn't the only thing on his mind. The only thing he wanted from her.

Though after what happened earlier this afternoon, he was worried that she only thought it was sex to him. He hadn't planned their kitchen encounter any more than he had planned what happened in bed.

But he sure as hell didn't regret either. The only thing he did regret was that they hadn't settled what was going on between them and where their relationship was headed before they got physical again. Although, he was pretty sure the sex gave him bonus points. Without that passion, she would find a way to talk herself right out of starting a relationship with him. After having experienced it, she wouldn't be able to convince herself not to try. At least that's what he hoped would happen.

Drew let himself relive those moments in the kitchen. He'd walked in and she was leaning over the bar, lost in thought. In that instant, a vision of her that way every morning had filled his mind. Of him walking into the kitchen to be greeted by the sight of Val having her morning coffee. The image had felt so real that it got added to the others showing them together in the future. Every time he saw her, the feelings deep in his heart just became more and more real. No, not real. They were already *real*. Maybe *pronounced* was a better description. It was like they took root in his heart and filled him.

He'd let all those corny, it's-never-been-this-good-with-anyone-else thoughts run through his head. While they may be clichéd, he admitted to himself that they were definitely true.

And then his cock had gotten in on the action. Seeing her rounded backside practically presented for him, skirt pulled tight across that firm ass, had been like a beacon in the night to the lust-filled part of himself that he was having a harder and harder time keeping in check. As soon as he'd neared her, was able to see the flush of her skin echoing her arousal, all bets were off.

And where the fuck had all that dirty talk come from? He couldn't remember ever talking like that to a lover before, but the words had flowed from his lips this afternoon. It seemed so natural; although, he was afraid he had startled her a little too much at first and had turned her off. Recalling her intakes of breath, speedy heartbeat, and heat pouring off her body, he realized she was most definitely *not* turned off. And he sure as hell planned on using that to his advantage in the near future.

He remembered talking to his dad once, right after Matt's wedding. Their dad hadn't seemed as excited about the recent marriage as he thought the father of the groom should, so Drew had asked him why. *"Because she's not the one, Drew. She's not the one for Matthew."* At the time he thought the whole thing about "the one" was a load of crap and he told his father so. He just laughed and slung an arm around Drew's shoulders. *"Laugh now. You won't when you finally figure it out."* Just then his mom had walked into the room and Drew saw the smile light up his father's face and thought that maybe, just maybe, his dad did know what he was talking about.

Now, as he sat in the living room waiting for Valerie, he reflected again on what his dad said and finally had to give him the credit he deserved. He had laughed at the time. But his father's wisdom proved to be prophetic because he wasn't laughing now. Valerie was the one. Of this he was sure.

Now he just had to find out what Valerie thought.

He wasn't under any illusion that she hadn't wanted to dive from friendship to lover with him. Part of the problem was that he didn't know why she was hesitant. But that ship had just about sailed, and there was no fucking way it was turning back around to dock. Tonight they would talk and go from there.

And he would take this slow, dammit. He was a gentleman, and there was no reason he couldn't act like it. Hearing a gentle cough, he looked up.

Well, fuck.

So much for controlling the inner caveman. His dick sprang to attention at his first sight of her. Dressed in a black wrap dress with a deep V that clung to her curves, she was stunning. A long silver necklace rested against her chest, falling gently between the mounds of her breasts. *You've barely had your hands on those beauties, buddy. And haven't gotten your mouth on her flesh at all. What the fuck is wrong with you?* His inner voice was going to make him batshit crazy at this point.

He was just about to speak when Val stepped in front of him and the words froze in his throat. Black strappy heals that made her legs look a mile long had his mouth watering. She was either oblivious to the effect she had on him, or she was torturing him.

Slowly lifting his gaze from her shoes, he let his sight linger in all the interesting places of her body. The skin of her knee just below the hemline. The juncture of her legs where the dress softly fell. The curves of her hips and waist. The swell of her breasts. Finally, his gaze landed on her face.

The fire brewing in her eyes spoke of the same passions and need he felt.

The small tug at the corner of her mouth told him she knew exactly what effect she had on him.

Standing was a bit tricky with his dick sporting the hard-on from hell. The custom made suit was tailored perfectly to his body, but he was pretty sure that didn't take an erection into account. Especially the likes of which he was currently sporting. He didn't even try to hide his actions from her as he sought to make himself more comfortable. A faint blush stained her cheeks even as a grin formed on her lips.

"So where are we headed?"

Slipping his hand into hers, he tugged her close. "To the bedroom?" He winked her way. "Ugh." The light slap of Val's purse into his chest, elicited a grunted response from him.

"After I got all dressed up? You just want to ruin me?" She indignantly huffed at him.

"In the worst fucking way." Pulling her up against his body, he let her feel what she had already seen. He didn't anticipate her rubbing against him to make his erection even harder. The woman was going to kill him.

"No. You promised me romance." Leaning her head forward and giving him a quick peck on the lips, she added, "And talking."

Val was right. They needed to talk, and talk over a nice romantic dinner they would. Didn't mean he couldn't do other things during said meal.

Releasing his hold on her, he bowed slightly.

"Come along, beautiful. Your romantic dinner awaits."

∿

DREW'S extended hand greeted Val as the car door opened. He was pulling out all of the gentlemanly stops tonight. And truth be told, she loved it. Sure, she was a "modern" woman, whatever that meant. But it didn't mean she couldn't enjoy the little gestures that showed more of an old, forgotten chivalry. Placing her hand in his, she let him steady her as she stepped from the passenger seat of his SUV.

Luckily the restaurant he was taking her to had valet parking. She hadn't relished the thought of navigating the cobblestone sidewalks of Old Town Alexandria and the puddles left over from today's rain in her heels. Val had actually considered changing shoes. Right up until the moment she'd caught Drew's expression when he saw her outfit. Shoes included. Val didn't consider herself at all vain, but she did nothing to hide the smile Drew's look gave her. Fortunately the thudding heart and moistening panties were slightly easier to hide. Because, yeah, she got those too. For a minute, she was afraid he was just going to drag her back to his bedroom, and she was pretty damn sure she wouldn't have protested a whole hell of a lot. She had trouble resisting whatever magic spell he seemed to weave around them lately. Not like she really wanted to. But she did want to talk.

Getting ready for tonight, Val had tried to remember and repeat the mantra she'd been telling herself for weeks: they were friends—best friends—no need to add something else. They would ruin their friendship. *Blah blah blah.* Her heart was no longer listening to her brain. All it was thinking about was how Drew had made her feel during their interlude in the kitchen. She finally gave in to the voice in her head that had been telling her to go for it. Or rather, she finally recognized that she had given in to that voice a while ago, and she just hadn't admitted it until the trailer. But had she really? Those lingering memories were still there. Still holding her back, no matter how much she wanted what Drew was so clearly offering her.

Thankful she had grabbed some nice, dressy clothes from her house, Val had taken her time getting ready for their "date." Not that either one of them called it a date, but Val was aware enough to call a spade a spade. *Did she know this was coming? Was that the reason she made sure to add the dress, not to mention some of her sexiest lingerie? Damn straight it was.* Apparently her inner voice was a step ahead of the rest of her. But whatever the reason, as she showered and slid into her lingerie and then the dress, she was glad that she listened to that part of herself. It seemed like forever since a man was taken with her efforts. Evan had paid lip service to her appearance when they went out, but there was never that spark in his eyes. Not like there was in Drew's when she had stepped into the living room. The fire she saw pouring off of him was worth every question her stubborn mind tried to ask when she was dressing. Every girl wanted to feel pretty and desired once in a while, and she was no exception. Fortunately for her, her date for the evening was broadcasting his desire loud and clear.

It also hadn't hurt that Drew looked like every fantasy come to life. The light gray suit he wore fit his strong body perfectly. It was his "good luck" suit at work, one he often wore for important meetings. Her body had always given a little stutter when he strolled in wearing it. She had passed it off as friendly appreciation. She wasn't blind and even though she didn't always play along with Chelsea's talk of the "hotties," she knew a good-looking man when she saw one. And Drew was definitely that. But maybe that stutter hadn't been random. Maybe it was her body telling her to pay more attention. Tonight he had it paired with a black shirt and tie. The stark color, making his eyes appear as a frosty blue. And every nerve ending in her body lit with energy when she had walked into his living room. It wasn't only the way he looked at her that set her aflame, it was also the way he looked.

"Val? Valerie." Drew's deep voice penetrated her contemplation. He was standing, holding the door to the restaurant open. "Are you okay?"

Realizing she had been lost in thought, she stepped forward and lifted a hand to his face. Smoothing the small worry lines from his forehead, she leaned in. "I'm fine. Just thinking about earlier."

That fire blazed anew in Drew's eyes, signaling that he was thinking about this afternoon too. Maybe Val hadn't been thinking about the same thing, but seeing his expression made those moments in the kitchen come roaring back to the forefront of her mind and senses. She could feel the heat from his touch all over again. Staring into those blue orbs, Drew and she were lost in a world all their own.

Maybe coming out to dinner wasn't the best idea.

"Good evening. May I help you?" Finally, the voice of the hostess broke their connection. At least the one keeping them trapped in the doorway. Valerie was pretty sure there wasn't much that would break their deeper connection.

Giving a slight cough, likely to regain his composure and cover any embarrassment for just standing there staring, Drew turned toward the hostess stand. "Yes, I have a reservation under Stephens."

Drew clasped her hand in his, fingers laced together, as they followed the hostess back to their table, a small circular booth, in a secluded portion of the restaurant. As she settled into her seat, she felt the heat from Drew's body as he found his place on the padded cushion. Right next to her. His nearness was not going to help the galloping of her heart.

"Soooo, this is cozy." Drew lifted the water glass the waiter had filled upon their being seated. His blue eyes pierced her as the glass rested against his lips. Drew slid his hand under hers as it rested on the space between them, entangling their fingers together. The rhythmic rubbing of his thumb over the sensitive skin between her thumb and index finger was completely distracting. Wasn't she supposed to look at a menu? Wine list? Something? She could barely do anything but feel.

Reluctantly, she pulled her hand away. They had to get the talking out of the way first; otherwise, they would be right back to where they were in the kitchen, with nothing discussed between them. "Drew, I thought we were taking it slow and going to talk?"

A sexy quirk of his brow preceded his words. "Why can't we do that as I touch you?"

Damn dangerous man. But she might as well start this off honestly. "Because when you touch me I can't think. And we both need to think."

The smile that spread across his face told her that he loved what he did to her. "Okay, beautiful. You have a deal. We'll talk over dinner." Grasping her hand again, he brought it to his lips in a gentle kiss. "But touching is absolutely on the menu for dessert."

Nodding her response, Val picked up her menu. She had a feeling this would be a very long meal.

After ordering—cedar-smoked salmon for her and a filet for Drew—they both leaned back into the comfort of the cushioned booth. Lifting her glass of wine to her lips, Val recognized the laser-like stare Drew had on her mouth. They had to start talking soon or they would be in the same boat as before.

Clearing his throat on a cough, Drew settled his glass of Scotch back on the table. Val felt pinned like a butterfly by those sparkling blue eyes of his. "So I said we'd talk. I don't think either of us can play like we don't know what we have to talk about."

Val gave a shake of her head. She wasn't going to pretend. The part of her that wanted to act like nothing was different between them had given up the battle after their encounter in the kitchen. Things had changed. Now, all parts of her were on board to see where this was headed. *Oh, some parts are more than on board. They are already at the wheel and ready to steer.* That still didn't mean she wasn't nervous about it though. Take that back. Not all parts of her. Unfortunately, her brain was the navigator and that part still had some reservations. Those pesky memories indicating that this would end badly.

"No, Drew, I definitely know. Wherever this attraction was hiding before, it's not letting us kid ourselves anymore." Wasn't she still kidding herself though? Thinking that her past wasn't having an effect on what was going on now. That it wasn't influencing every decision that she was thinking about making.

"I don't know if it was ever hiding, Val." Leaning forward, Drew rested his elbows on the table steepling his fingers together. Lying his cheek against his hands, he spoke solely to her, practically shutting off the rest of the activity in the restaurant. "I may not have acted on it, or hell, even acknowledged it. But I don't think there was a day that went by that I wasn't attracted to you. Even right from the beginning."

Those words made Val sit up and listen. She honestly thought Drew had never felt that spike of attraction or lust toward her until recently. "What?"

"Beautiful, you 'friend zoned' me pretty quick when we met." Val followed the movement of Drew's tongue as he took another sip of his drink. She wasn't a Scotch drinker, but she was dying for a taste of the amber liquid right now. Preferably from Drew's lips.

"You were my boss. And dating someone!" Val sputtered her response.

"Well, I've been single for a while now, and technically, I'm still your boss." Drew's gaze drilled into her. "What's your point?"

Val didn't exactly know where to go from here. The

thoughts running through her mind were tripping over themselves. Why did it seem that he was making this so difficult? And why was she such a mess?

Drew extended his hand forward, entwining his fingers with hers. "Valerie, listen to me. I'm not trying to make this hard on either one of us." Giving a glance at his lap, he lifted his gaze and gave a rueful laugh. "Well, hard on you. I think I've got the hard part covered on me."

It seemed he always knew how to put her at ease. Though maybe *ease* wasn't the right word for it. Because, now, she was thinking about his hard dick, and there wasn't really anything easy about that or what it did to her. Dammit!

"How about we both just lay it out on the table?"

Nodding in agreement, Val hoped he would take the lead and go first. She was clear in what her heart wanted. She was also crystal clear on what her body wanted. It was her mind that was the wild card in the equation. Her heart and body wanted to take the gamble, but her mind really wanted to make sure there was a net to catch her. Not like last time, when she broke apart. She just wasn't sure there was going to be a net around.

"I want you. I want you like I haven't wanted anyone else. I've wanted you since the second you walked into the office for the interview, but I pushed that aside for any one of a number of reasons." Drew stopped for a moment as the tuxedo-dressed waiter placed their dinner plates in front of them. Val wasn't sure exactly how she was supposed to eat with her heart lodged in her throat.

After ensuring that they had everything they needed, the waiter excused himself, and Drew turned all of his intense focus back on her. "I'm done with ignoring what I'm feeling. I'm done with watching you try to date other men who are all wrong for you. I'm done spending the nights alone, thinking and dreaming of you being in my arms and my bed."

Carefully palming her face in his hand like she was the most delicate thing he ever held, he caressed her cheek with feather light strokes. "I'm all in, Valerie. All in to bringing this relationship to life. Are you?"

"Relationship? What do you mean by that exactly?" Val finally let herself admit the reason she had been so hesitant. She worried Drew wouldn't want the same level of relationship she did. Oh, she didn't think he only wanted a one-night stand, but being brutally honest with herself, she worried he would be done long before she was over what they had. *Why are you letting the past fuck you up like that? Not everyone is just in it for what they can get in the short term, and not everyone is an immature boy.*

Fire, and a hint of anger, blazed in Drew's eyes. "Did you think I was just going to fuck you and run, beautiful?" Reaching his hand to the nape of her neck, she felt the pinch as he tightened the hold and focused her eyes on him. "There's no way in hell that's happening. We jump together, feet first, to see where this is going. I have no intention of putting a time limit on it. Because, honestly, I don't think there will ever be a limit."

Val's heart soared as she listened to Drew's words. Could she admit what just became clear in her mind? She realized that she was already halfway in love with the man sitting next to her. She didn't see herself as his sister, no matter what she had always tried to tell herself. Matt and Jon had fit into that brotherly role easily. But with Drew, it was always different, always something a little more personal and deeper. It was only her cowardice, and her past, that had prevented her from seeing what was right there all along.

"So what do you say, Valerie?" The tension radiated from Drew's body. From the lines radiating from his lips to the grip on her neck, she could tell he was holding on by a thread and honestly worried about her response.

She made sure her gaze captured his before responding, "I'm all in too, Andrew." The grin that broke across his lips warmed her insides. "Let's see where this is going to take us." Even as she took that leap, there was still some trepidation coursing through her brain. With or without that safety net, she was willing to make a go of this.

Dragging her forward, his lips met hers in a voracious kiss. Their tongues tangled together as she tried to pour all of her thoughts and feelings into him through the kiss. Leaning back, they rested their foreheads against one another and tried to catch their breath.

"Hold that thought, Valerie." Another little nip on her lips told her exactly which thought to hold. "Let's finish dinner and get out of here."

CHAPTER SEVENTEEN

*A*s they stepped out into the humid night air, a swirl of thoughts were running around Drew's brain. There was a sense of rightness and peace that came over him when Valerie had agreed to give their relationship a go. But any joy he felt was tempered by a wariness Drew still sensed within her. He wouldn't have believed she thought this could have been a hit-and-run relationship to him. That was never really his style, his college days notwithstanding, and even then there had only been a couple of one-night stands.

Accepting that she was scared of ruining their friendship still didn't take the sting out of seeing the shocked expression fill her eyes when he talked about having a real relationship. He'd die before admitting it to Val, but that look had been like a quick stab to the heart. But he had to get over it because the way her eyes had shined after that, after she fully understood what he wanted, more than made up for the original hesitation. At least he hoped it did, but he couldn't shake the feeling that all was not settled. There was something gnawing at him to be wary.

Clasping Val's hand while waiting for his car to be brought

around to them, he had to ask himself if she truly did understand how committed he was to her and this relationship. Sure, it was new, but Drew believed they should let themselves give things a go before running out and buying a ring. Though that was definitely a consideration, especially with the way Val was attracting looks tonight from male diners. She was his, whether she was fully ready to admit it or not.

A silhouette broke from the surrounding darkness and came toward them. "Valerie. It's good to see you." The slightest of pauses hovered before he was acknowleged. "Drew."

The words and accompanying smile of the man standing in front of them may have seemed friendly, but the tone he had spoken in hinted that he was not. And it made Drew want to demonstrate that Val was definitely his. Obviously, Valerie didn't get that same sense because she was just as welcoming as ever.

"Evan." Gifting him with a smile, she lightly touched his arm.

Anger flooded his system at the gentle interaction. His vision went a little hazy and then focused sharply on his perceived competition. A primitive feeling overtook him, to show Evan that Val was his and his alone. *Wow.* So that was the caveman, possessive vibe he'd heard about. Drew wasn't sure if he really liked it. Of course he didn't really like seeing Valerie touch her ex either.

Inching his arm around Val's waist, he gave a little tug to pull her in closer to his body. Noting that the move didn't escape Evan's attention by the flair of anger in the other man's eyes, Drew finally responded, "Evan. We were just leaving."

Drew could feel the glare coming from Val, without even seeing her face. He didn't really give a rat's ass that he was acting rude. There was no way he was getting into something out here, and by the look in Evan's eyes, that was a distinct possibility.

"So, what? You're together now?" Evan's words held nothing but bitterness and contempt.

"It's really none of your business." Drew hissed.

Val spoke at the same time, "No. Well, maybe. Yes."

Fuck it all! Drew wasn't sure if he was more pissed at Evan for the attitude and animosity he was showing or Valerie for hesitating about their relationship. Sure, he could have given a flat out "yes" when asked, but why the fuck did he have to answer to Evan? The next words spoken snapped Drew right out of his reflection.

"Fuck, that didn't take long." The muttered, "Bitch," under Evan's breath was enough to send rage boiling through Drew's bloodstream.

"What the fuck did you just say about her?" Letting go of Valerie, he took a step forward. His hands clenched into fists. No one spoke to her like that. He didn't really want to make a scene; that wasn't going to end well for anyone. But he was precariously close to throwing that concern out the window, just seeing the contempt on Evan's face.

Feeling a gentle tug on his arm, he glanced back at Val as she spoke, "The car's here. Let's just leave it." Nodding, he let Val lead him to the high road.

Unfortunately, it was blocked by a jackass who didn't know when to quit. "I called her a bitch."

Granted, Evan had an inch or two on him, but those inches were not backed up by any extra pounds. Drew was fairly sure he could take him, but talk about putting a damper on the evening. Somehow, he didn't think Val would be falling all over herself to thank him as the conquering hero. More than likely she'd voice, loudly, her unhappy opinion about him making a spectacle of them.

Or not.

"Bitch?" Green eyes lit bright with anger, Val whirled on Evan, raising a hand as if to take a swing. "I'll show you a bitch."

Whoa. Time to reign her in. "C'mon, Xena. Let's calm down." This was getting out of hand, and still, Evan stood there like he was welcome.

"You stuck the cops on me. So yeah, you're a bitch. I had nothing to do with any fire." Evan's breath was rapidly becoming more pant-like as he got agitated.

This had all the markings of things not ending well. He could see the valet manager step closer, probably trying to decide if he should get involved. Looking back at the man, Drew gave a slight shake of his head. Hopefully things wouldn't get that far where they needed outside intervention.

"Okay, let's all take a breath." How he went from wanting to clock Evan to being the mediator, he wasn't exactly sure. But taking a look at both Evan and Val, he didn't think that either of them would have any success at bringing things under control. Unless they wanted to end their night talking to the police, which was a big *no* in his opinion, someone needed to bring things down to a simmer.

"She didn't sic anyone on you. She simply answered questions." Trying to level out his breathing in the hopes that the other two would do the same thing, he slowly tried to let himself relax.

"Yeah. They asked about any recent breakups." Val must have been taking her cue from him because some of the tension had drained out of her shoulders. "I told them you could never do something like that."

And just like that, Evan changed on a dime. From snarling to almost in tears. *What the fuck? Pull it together, man.*

"I'm sorry. It was just so hard to believe you would do that. You know I would never, right?" Evan grabbed Val's hand before Drew could prevent it. Hell, before even Val realized what he was doing. "Maybe we could meet and talk sometime. We were friends before too."

Drew didn't really know what to make of the scene before

him. It was almost as if two different people were standing there with them.

Val gave him a look and a little shrug. Seemed like she was as confused as he was.

"Sure, Evan. Maybe we can."

Okay, Drew was not for that at all. But Val was her own woman, and he trusted her. Still, with this hot and cold attitude spilling from Evan, there was a fine thread of caution and concern that wove its way through him.

Evan moved from holding Val's hand to stroking it. "Excellent. And who knows what else could come from that. What we had was good."

This had gone on long enough. Well beyond long enough for Drew's liking. How did the evening take such a drastic turn from where it was going? This was sure as shit not what he planned to do after leaving dinner.

"What we had is over, Evan. But maybe we can still be friends." Drew breathed a semi-sigh of relief at Valerie's words. He most definitely didn't want her still being friends with this guy, but she couldn't have been any more blunt about their relationship being done.

Yanking his hand back, Evan turned roughly and marched down the street. No words, no gestures. But the angry set in his shoulders was a clear indication that Val's words were met with displeasure. A layer of discomfort settled over him. He had a very bad feeling about Evan and wasn't at all sure what to do about it.

Val settled her hands on his shoulders and started kneading. She leaned into his back, pressing close and whispered, "Let's get out of here. This has been too weird." Turning to face her, she ran her palms down his arms and grabbed his hands. Maybe they could salvage the rest of the evening.

Placing a gentle kiss on her nose, Drew responded, "Your wish is my command, beautiful."

CHAPTER EIGHTEEN

*S*hrouded in darkness, he watched the couple getting into a dark SUV.

It had seemed almost fortuitous that he had spotted them entering the restaurant as he was making his way up the street. They had been too wrapped up in each other to even notice him. And wasn't that just typical. Always ignoring those that were clearly superior.

But the sight of them, enthralled with each other, was not an unwelcome piece of knowledge to gather. He had needed to know more, so into the shadows he vanished.

And waited.

And remembered.

The night before had been almost an orgasmic experience. He thought he might've had some hesitation since the woman was involved, but that didn't come to fruition at all. Instead, a thrill had rocked his body as he closed and bolted the door of the trailer. Just the idea that she was completely alone and unaware of what was coming had given him a rush of excitement he hadn't experienced in years. Not since he'd lost what was rightfully his.

As he'd held the can of gasoline in his hand, he'd thought back on why he was doing this. What had been stolen from him and why he *needed to make the Stephenses pay. They had no idea what they had done. What HE had done. But know they would. And soon.*

He'd had to leave when the sound of sirens pierced the air, which had happened way too quickly for his liking. He hadn't been able to bask in the glow of the flames or his success.

His ruminations had been halted when he saw them exit.

Breathe.

He tried to get his head back in the game and think. Maybe he could work this new information into his plans.

He hadn't realized she was a Stephenses whore last night. His fists clenched in anger again. Dammit. His damage could have been so much greater.

Taking another deep breath, he calmed his worries.

He thought of the letter he had started earlier today. Just a little something to remind those bastards of what happened. But the thought of putting a more personal flavor on them made it so much sweeter.

There was still time. And now he knew what he was dealing with. And the fact that his revenge may be even sweeter in the end.

CHAPTER NINETEEN

"*F*uck me," Drew muttered as he searched in vain for a document on his desk. Plowing his hands through his hair, he felt himself growing more frustrated. And not just at the piece of paper that seemed to have run away and hid. *That's the problem: there's been no fucking.* Not after their dinner or in the days since then. *This is asinine. Go get some.*

It was a constant stream of inner monologue lately, and it was driving him crazy. Especially since it was right. Keeping Valerie at not-quite arm's length was killing him. *Can horniness be a cause of death? Sexual frustration? Incessant jacking off in the shower? For God's sake, isn't your hand tired yet?*

Crashing down into his chair, he leaned his head back and closed his eyes. Not that he was answering himself, but yes, his hand was tired. His morning session in the shower had only succeeded in making him run so late that he hadn't even had time to shave. It sure as hell hadn't relieved the ache that was his constant companion. There were only so many times a man could get himself off without it becoming just a bit worthless. This was even more true when the woman invading his thoughts was just across the hall from him. He imagined her lying in bed. In his mind, she was just as restless as he was when he crawled in between his cold and lonely covers.

Was she thinking of him too? Were those moans he heard? He convinced himself that they weren't, mainly so he didn't go storming into the room. But what if they were? What if she was just as tense and as frustrated as him? Though he wasn't really sure that was possible.

Val's stay at his apartment seemed to have taken on a life of its own. A week and a half had passed since the fire and their first date, with her becoming more entrenched in his place every day. She didn't seem inclined to leave, and he sure as shit didn't want her gone. He liked having her there with him. Liked sitting across from her and drinking coffee in the morning. Drew had come to realize very quickly that Val was not the most pleasant person in the morning before she had her coffee, and that was okay. He just made sure he had it ready for her. It was something little like that, seeing to her needs, that made him never want to let her go. The whole thing just felt natural.

Except for not having sex. That wasn't natural. That was decidedly unnatural and was slowly taking its toll on him.

"Earth to Drew."

Tipping his head forward, he opened his eyes as Jon strolled into his office.

"You were so zoned out you didn't even hear me calling your name." Taking a seat in front of Drew's desk, Jon leaned back and casually crossed his legs. "You look like hell brother. I don't really have to ask what's got you all tied up, do I?"

Seeing the knowing look in his brother's eyes, Drew wasn't going to be able to avoid this conversation, and maybe he didn't really want to. Or rather, maybe he shouldn't. Talking would help, or at the very least, it wouldn't hurt.

"I don't know how much more I can take, Jon." Frustration made evident as he plowed his hands through his hair. "She's practically moved into my guest room. Which is fine. If she doesn't feel safe at her place, I'm more than happy to be the person she turns to."

"But it's not fine, Drew." Tapping his fingers on the armrest, Jon looked him squarely in the eye. "You don't want her in the guest room, and that's the problem. Both of you are dancing around what you really want for no reason except that you are both chickenshits."

This was not exactly the attitude Drew was expecting from his brother. Usually Jon was the one who would agree with him and let him vent. The one he could go to when he tended to just want agreement with what he already thought. Jon rarely ever just told Drew he was wrong. That wasn't his style at all. Though, come to think of it, most of the times he vented to Jon, he changed his mind to something else along the way. *Dammit!* He had been played all these years. Without saying a word, his baby brother somehow got everyone to do exactly what they should have done in the first damn place.

"I'll be damned," Drew muttered.

"More than likely." This from the sneak sitting across the desk from him. "But that's neither here nor there. What is important is what you're going to do about Val."

Sighing, Drew was at a loss. He thought their talk over dinner had moved things forward in the right direction. That they were going to give "them" a shot. Everything had been set for them to move forward until they'd stepped out of the restaurant and encountered Evan. At the time, Drew didn't think that would alter anything, but the ride home was tense and the heavy weight of silence had filled most of it. Val had just stared out the window, not responding the few times he tried to engage her. She had gone right into the guest bedroom upon arriving back at his condo, definitely not the ending to the evening he had envisioned.

"I think seeing Evan has changed things." Drew had told Matt and Jon all about that little run-in. He still didn't like the way Evan had run hot and cold. And there was no fucking way he was as convinced as Val was that he wasn't responsible for at least one of the things that had happened to her. Maybe not all, but something was just not adding up. Add to that the fact Val seemed to back away from him a little after that. He still wasn't sure what that was all about, but it wasn't something he could deny. She had shut down a little afterward, and since then, he had tried to get her to open up. To let him know where her head was at, but with no luck.

He wasn't worried that she regretted breaking it off with Evan—that was clear by her reaction to the man—but that niggling fear was back. The fear that said she was afraid things were going to go south with him or that he wasn't fully committed to her. Did she think he was going to turn out like Evan? And with Val unwilling to really talk to him, there was no way to set her straight and gain back the ground that he had made that night.

He didn't like the feelings swirling inside of him. He was at a loss of how to get them back to starting the relationship he knew they both wanted. Every day was a new exquisite torture. The woman he loved, and he could easily admit that it was love, in his home morning and night. She was still far away from him emotionally, as if she was on a different continent.

"It's only changed things because you let it." Jon leaned forward. Slapping his hands on Drew's desk, he continued, "Why should that little prick keep you from what you want?"

Logically, Drew knew Jon was right. But that didn't make it easier to do something about it, or did it?

"Why the fuck not?" *Jesus.* Drew hadn't even realized he voiced the question aloud. He really was losing it.

"Drew, you need to go get your woman. You're overthinking the whole damn situation." Shaking his head, he got up and made his way to the door. "Val left early. Said something about some 'alone time.' Maybe you should go and make sure she's not too lonely."

With that, Jon shut the door. Drew couldn't discount his brother's sound advice. And what the hell was "alone time"? *I bet she's going home to get herself off. Maybe she knows I've been sneaking around her door at night waiting to listen to her fuck herself.* The images that assaulted him had his cock standing at attention.

"Fuck it." He needed to be where she was. He rose from behind his desk and grabbed his phone and car keys from the desktop.

A few steps and he was out of his office and into the wide open area Val normally occupied. His brothers' doors were open. "I'll be back tomorrow," he bellowed.

Not bothering to wait for a response, he left the office and headed home. To his woman. And she would most definitely be his woman after tonight.

STANDING under the steady stream of hot water, Val tipped her head back. Leaving work early today wasn't something she had planned. But dammit! How much was a woman supposed to be able to take? Over a week's worth of living and working with Drew had her shoulders scrunched up around her ears in tension. Sexual tension. And some damn serious sexual frustration. As Drew had walked past her on his way to a meeting, with barely a glance in her direction, she just snapped. When she had passed Jon getting off the elevator, Val hurriedly told him she wouldn't be back. Somehow, she thought they would all survive for the rest of the afternoon.

Ever since their "date" last week, things had gotten weird. She had finally convinced herself to give them a try. But did they? No. Drew acted like everything had changed since they ran into Evan. Now all he wanted to do was talk. There were no heated looks across the living room. No casual touches. And dammit, she didn't want to talk. Was it just because Val didn't tell Evan she didn't believe him? Because she didn't. And she sure as hell had no intention of giving them another chance. She was totally invested in moving forward with Drew now.

Totally invested? Am I sure? I think those doubts are creeping back into my mind.

Except he seemed to be putting on the brakes. Sure maybe she backed away a little that first night. She was still feeling a bit riled up and tense from seeing Evan and dealing with his personality flip-flops. But after that, things should have picked up from where they left off. Instead, it was like casual room-mates in his condo instead of two people who were interested in each other. Two people who had practically combusted in the kitchen.

Those memories and images ingrained in her head got her through the past few days. Under the covers at night, when the apartment was quiet, she closed her eyes and let herself relive those moments. Slipping her hand down her body, she'd tried to re-create Drew's caresses but nothing would match the feelings he brought to life in her.

Val opened her eyes and realized she had started cupping and massaging her breasts under the warmth of the water. Since she had the whole afternoon, and whole condo, to herself, maybe she'd make use of the solitude. At least she wouldn't have to be quiet this time. And if truth be told, she was dying for Drew to make her scream, even if it was only because of memories right now.

Turning off the water, she reached for a towel. Only to come up empty.

"Damn!"

She had walked straight into the bathroom after coming up

from the gym. The freshly laundered towels were all in a nice pile on top of her bed. Across the hall.

"Well, good thing I'm alone." It wasn't like she would run around Drew's condo nude. All she had to do was get from the bathroom to the bedroom. Since Drew wasn't home, that would be easy as pie. Brushing her still-dripping hair out of her eyes, she stepped out of the shower, opened the door and entered into the hallway.

That moment changed everything.

Hearing the harshly drawn breath from just feet away, Val looked up into a face tight with lust. The blue of Drew's eyes getting deeper and darker by the second. Sparks practically flaring within them. His entire body stiff. As her gaze moved down the length of his body, Val could see that everything was stiff. *Very, very stiff.*

Common sense fled her mind and she acted purely on instinct. The instinct she had been fighting for days—hell, probably for months if she actually thought about it.

Drew opened his mouth to speak, but before he got a sound out, Val was across the space. Lips fusing to his, she gave in to the passions that had been fanned to flames between them.

Pressed against Drew's hard body, she could tell the moment desire overcame the shock of finding her naked in his hallway. Drew took control of the kiss, deepening it as his tongue surged into her mouth. She met him, thrust for thrust, tangling her tongue around his. It was if they were trying to consume each other, making up for all the time they had wasted.

Strong arms crushed her to him as he moved forward, pinning her against the wall. Naked as she was, it took nothing to feel the caress of work-roughened hands over her skin. Trapped against Drew, the water clinging to her soaked through his clothes. The material molded to his chest, so she could feel the hardness of the muscles beneath. Water from her hair and face dripped in rivulets down her body. Those droplets could sizzle with the heat they were creating. Drew moved his palms up her arms and then down over her breasts. Kneading the globes as he moved the kiss from her lips, following thewater as it trickled down her neck. The sensation was mindblowing. His mouth took over from his hands, kissing and licking and sucking on the rise of her breasts. His fingers moved to her nipples, plucking and pulling them into hard peaks.

Breath caught in her throat as she looked at Drew's dark blond hair against the pale skin of her chest. The sight should have looked strange to her. Instead it looked nothing but right. All the doubts in her head melted away at Drew's touch. The pressure of his hands and lips lit fire along her skin as he learned her every curve. Goosebumps rose on her flesh in the wake of the roughened feel of his tongue. Her belly quivered where his erection nestled. *God.* She wanted it all. Everything that his body was promising. But it was more than that. She wanted what his words had been hinting at for weeks now. The physical feelings were amazing, but they were made even more so because of the emotional connection they had.

In a way this was part of what she had been struggling with. Her feelings for Drew went so much deeper than the physical. That was what could crush her. Almost like he could sense she was diving into her head, his teeth closed around a nipple, forcing her back to the here and now. Everything else she would worry about later. Now she would live in the moment, for the pleasure that they were sharing.

She tunneled her hands through that hair, to hold him closer, but he resisted, pulling away just enough for her to see his face. Gaze consumed with lust, he stared into her eyes. But only for a second. His head lowered, letting that penetrating gaze travel slowly, ever so slowly down her body until it rested on his hands cradling the heavy mounds of her breasts.

"I've seen these." Drew continued to caress and squeeze, pull and torment. "Seen them every night in my dreams." Leaning

161

forward, gaze coming back to connect with hers, he flicked his tongue out to graze her very erect nipple. Just a light touch that practically had her eyes rolling back in her head. "Imagined what it would feel like to finally get my hands on them. My mouth." She gasped as his cheek rubbed against her sensitive nub. That scruff she had found so sexy this morning was setting licks of fire along her skin as he dragged it against her flesh. "But nothing could come close to this." Lips closing fully around her pinkened areola, he tugged hard with his mouth. The groan that escaped from her lips was inevitable.

"What was that?" Closing his teeth over the tender tip, he gave a gentle nibble, followed by a flick of tongue. "You like my mouth on you?"

Nodding, she couldn't tell if he noticed through her now closed lids. "God, yes." The anchored hold she had on his hair tightened as the sensations cascaded through her body. This was crazy. He had only touched her breast and she was ready to go off like a rocket. "Please. Please, more."

Drew skimmed his hands down the rest of her body, grazing over her ass and coming to rest on her hips. His thumbs made little circles on the sensitive skin where her thighs met her body.

"There is going to be a fuck-ton more, but not in the hallway. I want you spread out on my bed like the delicious meal you are going to be. Where I can touch you and taste you and fuck you all damn day." Mouth going back to her nipple, he gave another tug, as if to show her exactly what she was in for.

On that note, he placed his hands under her ass and lifted her. It was automatic to wrap her legs around his waist as he took the first step toward his bedroom.

A first step that had them both groaning as his cock pressed against her. She was pretty sure that the water clinging to her body from the shower was not the only thing that would make his clothes wet. She could feel her pussy going all soft and moist as it brushed against the hardness contained behind Drew's pants.

Working her body over his, he stopped and gave a short tap to her ass, probably intending to dissuade her from doing it again. She was afraid her body didn't take the hint. Val rubbed up against him even more, tearing an anguished groan from his throat.

"Stop that." A harder smack this time had her freezing her movements. Her brain wasn't exactly sure if she liked that or not, though it seemed her body did. "I'll gladly fuck you standing up in the hallway later. Hell, I'll fuck you anywhere you want, but not now. Now is all about getting you underneath me."

Quickening his stride, he made short work of the remaining distance to his bed.

With her legs still wrapped around his lean hips, she felt Drew raise a knee to place it on the bed. Of course, that also brought his thigh in contact with her wet mound. Giving in to instinct again, Val moved her hips forward, riding the hard muscle of Drew's thigh. It tensed under her, adding to the sensations flooding her body.

"You trying to ride me, beautiful?" Moving his hands to her hips, Drew helped her motion. Rocking her on his leg, he never took his eyes off of her face. A face she could feel getting more flushed as her orgasm approached. The other day in the kitchen was the first time she could think of that she was this close to coming so soon. Of course, thinking wasn't easy to do at the moment.

Pretty much her only thought was how good Drew made her body feel, and how she could feel the pressure building.

"Hmmmmmm. I don't know if I should give in that easy." Whimpering at his words, her pussy clenched in need. Mindlessly she rubbed her breasts against his shirt-covered chest.

Another slap on her ass followed. "Stop trying to take it! I'm running this show, and you'll get it all. But only when I want."

Her mind didn't know what to make of her body's reaction to his control. She had never had a lover become so domineering in the bedroom. Or speak in the crass words that Drew did. But whether her mind jumped on board with it or not, her body had definitely climbed on for the ride. Every sexy phrase, every tap to her ass, every controlling move had her melting and more turned on than she had ever been.

Grabbing her hands from around his neck, he pushed her back on the bed, her naked body spread wide for his gaze. She could feel the heated flush that covered her chest. Hell, it felt like it covered her whole body. A live wire had nothing on her. Blood sizzling with the need to feel—to feel everything he could give her. Drew's hands as they skimmed her body. His skin as it brushed against hers. His mouth making a feast of her like his promise of the other day. His cock as he plunged within her drenched sex. She was envisioning it all, yet she knew that it would be nothing like the reality.

Even as his eyes darkened, they never wavered from her body. It was as if he could sense every thought racing through her brain. He could definitely see the slightest movement her body made.

"What was that thought?" Gaze fixed on her mound, he absently started unbuttoning his shirt. "I could see your pussy clench."

Embarrassment should have coursed through her at his words. But that was before she had listened to his whispered words in the kitchen. Instead, she just felt heat. And wetness. And a forwardness she had never experienced before.

"I clenched at the thought of your cock." Seeing his shocked expression at her speech, she continued, "Your cock thrusting into me." With that, she silently raised her hips in invitation. If Drew was experiencing anything like she was, he wasn't going to hold out much longer. Val's body was on fire, and the only thing that would quench the heat was him.

She pushed herself up to sitting, then moved her hands so they landed on Drew's belt and the treasure that lay beneath it. But apparently Drew was made of stronger stuff than she realized. And sure as fuck stronger stuff then her. Because, with a much less gentle shove, she was flat on her back again.

"What don't you understand about this being my show, Valerie?" Shirt fully unbuttoned now, he slipped his arms out of it and let it fall to the floor. Her gaze went automatically to the soft mat of hair covering his muscled chest. Tapering down to a trail splitting the ridges that defined his abdomen and disappearing into his pants. His still-closed pants. His covered erection pushed the limits of the material as it seemed to strain toward her. Her mouth watered at the sight and a soft sigh escaped her lips.

"Oh, I understand. I'm just hoping the curtain can rise on the first act already." Not really sure how she managed to put together complete sentences, as Val was reasonably sure her brain was mush.

A sexy grin tilted Drew's lips up on the right side. While it looked harmless and flirty, the steel in his eyes said otherwise. She had pretty much let the tiger out of the cage with that comment.

Kneeling down on the floor, Drew grabbed her hips and jerked her to the edge of the bed. "The curtain's going up, beautiful. And just to let you know, intermission isn't for a very long time."

With that, he pushed her knees wide open and leaned in with a long, slow lick of her pussy. Val heard a groan echo through the room, but wasn't sure if it came from her or Drew. And she really didn't care. A second stroke of his tongue followed the first, stopping just short of her aching clit. Val fisted the comforter as she tried to move her hips to entice him to make that connection. She gasped as the grip he had on her hips tightened. The dig of Drew's fingertips made the energy sizzling between them even stronger. He had full command of her and she gratefully gave it up.

Drew slowly moved his hands lower, coming to rest over the tops of her thighs. Fingers grazing the delicate skin resting between her legs and pussy. Back and forth, setting her nerve endings tingling. Valerie had never realized how sensitive that skin was. Of course, maybe that had something to do with the man who was currently touching it like the finest piece of art. Keening sounds emanated from her lips as just those fleeting touches and his breath on her bare mound seemed to concentrate her entire being to the area between her legs. Drew leaned his face against the soft skin of her inner thigh. The slight rub of the stubble on his cheek gently abraded her skin. Gasping at that sensation, he repeated the action on her left thigh. Alternating between legs, as his fingers continued to torment her with feather light touches.

Val was in heaven. She was in hell. Her body tight with sensation, limbs heavy with desire. Her fists opened and closed, seeming to want to reach for something, but not having the ability to truly move. Mind racing with feelings she couldn't put a name to. Hell, she could barely grasp them as they whirled around. She teetered on the precipice, yet her tormentor was seemingly unaware. Or maybe he was all too aware.

"I skipped lunch today." Hot breath came closer to her vaginal lips, and she could feel moisture flooding from her body. "Lucky for me, I have all I really want to eat right here."

With that, his tongue thrust into her in the most intimate of kisses. Fingers massaging her mound, he moved his tongue, mimicking the fucking she was dying to have. Her moans filled the room, nonsensical words, as she tightened her legs around his head, keeping him where she wanted him most. He began gently sucking on one lip. Then matching it on the other side.

Back and forth. The pressure in her body, and his tugging, built higher and higher.

Val opened her eyes and saw stars dancing above her on the ceiling. Her whole body was primed. She shifted her gaze down her body. Struck by the sight of Drew's dirty blond hair between her legs, Val gasped in a breath. Lips never leaving her body, his lids lifted and eyes rose to meet her in a stare that seared. She knew those eyes were reflecting her own emotions. The desire and lust, the frustration, the want. The love? With gazes still locked on each other, Drew's mouth moved. Hovering right over her clitoris, heated breath playing over the sensitive button, making her quiver.

She was there. Right there.

One more gentle exhalation of breath, and Drew's mouth enveloped her clitoris. Sucking gently, then not so gently, he had Val writhing on the bed. Gasps and pants tore from her. Head thrown back in surrender, hands moving to latch on to something more solid, they finally found his hands as they rested on her hips.

Drew gave one final suck to her clit, biting gently on the tender flesh. With their fingers entwined, Val flew apart.

CHAPTER TWENTY

*D*rew was barely keeping it together. His dick felt like steel in his pants. His every inhalation brought the scent of warm, wet woman to his nose. No, not woman. His woman. *Valerie.*

She was right where he wanted her, and nothing was going to stop him. When she didn't scurry back into the bathroom to hide as she stood there dripping wet in his hallway, she had accepted her fate. She sure as fuck was dripping wet now too. Pussy still sensitive from her recent orgasm, but that wouldn't stop him. The sweet nectar that had poured from her body as she screamed his name was too tempting to resist.

Lapping at her tender folds, he made sure that he got every drop. Hearing her pleas didn't faze him in the least. Settling in for another taste would torment her since her body was still on fire from the first climax.

"Drew, pleaaaase."

He was pretty sure Val didn't know if she was pleading for him to stop or continue on. Because if the way her body was trying to hump his face was any indication, it was definitely the latter.

"Oh, beautiful, I'm definitely pleased." Another suck to her delicate clit had her screeching in pleasure again. Barely calmed down from her first orgasm, it didn't take much to send her into orbit the second time. Good to know. Though, Drew would put money down on this not being normal for her. This was them. Together. Only with each other would they be that combustible.

Talk about combustible...I'm dying here. I need to be in her. Feeling that soft, sleek pussy grip me as I plunge into her.

Those thoughts had him moving up between her legs, settling his big body over hers. Legs still spread, he settled into the cradle of her thighs. They both shivered at the feel of Val's hard nipples rubbing against his chest hair. Looking down at Val's gorgeous face, he waited until her eyelids fluttered open. Bright green eyes clouded over from her orgasms, they finally rested on his face. Locked on to each other's gaze, he lowered his head and kissed her. The feelings that raced through him as he thought about her tasting herself on his lips and tongue had him pressing his hardened cock against her. Tongues tangling, he kissed her until breath was hard to come by. A soft nip, followed by a harder bite, he tasted his way around her mouth, all the while running his hands over her soft skin.

Which reminded him he was still partially dressed. The need to feel her without anything between them was a fire in his system. Caging her beneath him, he started to raise himself up. Only to be stopped short when Val tightened her grip on his head and brought his mouth back to hers. Her fingers drifted down his neck to his back, running over the sleek muscles there. Arching into her caress, he sucked on the sensitive skin of her throat, not caring if he left a mark.

Soft, yet firm, hands glided over his pants-covered ass.

"Off, Drew." She sighed the words as she broke their kiss. "I need you naked. I need to touch you. Feel you. Taste you."

Oh, hell yeah. He levered himself to his knees, and before he could reach for his belt, Val was already there. Staying her with one hand, he tangled the other in her hair and raised her face to meet his. "I thought we established I'm in charge here. No rushing the production." Drew moved her hands toward his chest. "Why don't you play here?"

She apparently welcomed the invitation, as she glided her palms across his chest, fingers combing through the light dusting of hair. When she reached his nipples, he gave a growl as she tugged. Still, with a firm grip on her hair, Drew guided her mouth to his body.

The feel of Val's warm, wet tongue moving over the muscles of his chest was mind bending. Her fingers followed, trailing her nails in a caress that made him ache. She made her way over to his nipple and circled the nub over and over with her tongue. Little circles that were going to drive him mad until she finally ended the torment with a bite. Nothing had ever felt this good before, and it was just going to get better.

As Val made her way down his abdomen, he wasn't sure how much longer he could let this go on. As much as he wanted to play, and would probably be willing to sell his soul to feel her mouth on him, he wasn't sure his willpower was that good right now.

Mind in a haze of sexual bliss, he hadn't realized his little temptress had taken control again until he heard the rasp of his zipper being lowered. Warm breath blew on his boxers-covered dick, but he was so sensitive he could still feel the heat of that burst of air. Val's arms encircled his waist, sliding her hands under his waistband and giving his ass a squeeze, all the while tonguing the fine hair on his lower abdomen leading to his dick.

Fisting her hair again, he took back some of the power she tried to yank away. He wasn't exactly sure where this domineering caveman act was coming from, but it sure was taking center stage. He figured it pretty much had to do with her. The nights, and days, of dreaming about her in his bed, wrapped around his body, were finally becoming a reality. And if the control made sure it happened, and made them both hot, who was he to wonder why he was doing it?

Tightening his grip, he pulled Val's head back enough to capture her gaze with his.

"You ready, beautiful?" The look in her eyes said she was, but he wanted the words. Needed to hear the words coming from her soft mouth. He needed to know that what they were sharing, what they were about to share, was more to her than simple sex.

"So ready." Licking her lips, she dragged his boxers lower. Levering himself off the bed to divest himself of the remainder of his clothes, he watched in rapt awe as Val lay back. Running her hands over her body, one tweaked a still hard nipple, while the other came to rest just over her clit. All the while, her eyes never left the sight of his hard-as-steel dick. Drew would swear it got harder and bigger just from her gaze alone.

Grabbing his cock, he stroked it from base to the mushroom shaped tip. Using some of the precum already gathered at the tip to ease his motions, Drew watched as Val licked her lips and strummed her clit in time with his movements. No porn had ever gotten him as hot as watching Valerie touch herself. Especially knowing she was turned on because of him.

Continuing his motions, he decided to increase the tension and let his dirty-talking caveman a little more off leash. "You want this hard cock inside you? Stroking in and out of that tight, wet pussy?" An answering groan was the only response he got. "It is wet, isn't it? Let me see how wet your pussy is." Val lifted her fingers, and they glistened in the sunlight streaming through the window. Her body moved restlessly as if it was in pain from having the touch removed.

"Why don't you show me how tight that pussy is? Show me how it's going to grip and suck my cock in." Lowering her hand to her mound again, Val slipped a long finger in her body. Now it was Drew's turn to groan. In minutes that would be his cock.

Just the thought alone was enough to make him come. Tightening the grip he had on his erection, he tried to get himself under control.

Val's sigh of pleasure had him testing that control. "Oh God, that feels good. So wet. I don't think I've ever been this wet. That big cock of yours is going to feel so good sliding in me. Driving into me." With that, Val began pumping her finger in and out of her greedy pussy.

Whatever control Drew was managing to cling to shattered in that instant. He fell on her, kissing her, like a starving man. And in a way he was. Starved for the taste of something he hadn't had before. While he may have thought he understood love, he was beginning to realize he hadn't truly known what the word love meant until Val. Until this second, when he felt more in tune with another person than ever before.

Tongues and limbs tangling, the hardness of his cock rocked against her lower lips, causing them both to groan. With each flex of his hips, the tip rubbed against her clit, causing her entire body to shudder. God, he had to get inside. Reaching down, he started to align himself with her center.

Condom. Condom. Sweet baby Jesus, this feels good, but how about waiting to go bareback for another time? Don't be stupid now.

A whimper of displeasure accompanied his slight withdrawl. "Drew, no. Please no. I need you." She tightened her frantic hands on his arms and pulled him back even as he reached into the nightstand drawer.

Coming back into position, he brushed the hair away from Val's flushed face. "I'm right here, beautiful. Not going anywhere. Just had to get something." Showing her the condom, he watched a wave of embarrassment cross her features.

"I...I didn't even remember that."

Leaning down, he kissed the chagrin away. The invade-and-retreat of his tongue was only a prelude of what was about to happen. Breaking the kiss, he tore open the packet and rolled the condom down his length. He grabbed the chance to get lost in the sight laid out before him. Her skin shone like cream in the rays of the sun through the window. The curves of her body beckoned him to touch and get lost in them. No amount of dreams could ever come close to what he had right now. It was all he never knew he wanted.

This was perfection.

Taking firm possession of Val's mouth, he positioned his dick and started to push in. *Dayum, she's tight. This is going to be fucking amazing.* For once, his inner voice was right on the money. A whimper from Val accompanied another thrust of his shaft.

"That pussy is going to take all of me." Thrusting, he gained another inch inside her. "I can already feel you clenching around me. Tightening like it doesn't want to let go."

"It doesn't." Turned on even more by her words, Drew rocked forward again. "You're cock is so hard and hot inside of me. Stretching me. It's making my nipples even harder than before." Val caressing her breasts had him slip the leash that had him controlled.

Caging her in with his hands, he withdrew to the very tip and slammed back into her, balls deep. Both of them groaned in unison even as hips moved to establish a rhythm.

"Keep playing with your tits." Bending his head to Val's neck, he bit down and sucked. She obviously liked that, considering the strangled hold her cunt had on his dick. He entwined his fingers with hers and together they gripped the hardened peak of her breast. Another shudder shot through her.

Raising up on his knees, Drew looked down to watch his cock shuttle in and out of her pussy. God, he was mesmerized. Not so much by the sight itself, but because this was Valerie. This was the start of something, and he was pretty sure they both knew it. Her entire body turned a faint pink as her passions rose to fever pitch. Val stroked one hand over her breast as she moved the other to glide down his chest as if she needed to feel the connection to him, in more than just a single place. Her eyes became a sparkling emerald green that he'd never seen before. In his heart, he knew those eyes had never glowed like that for anyone else before. Everything before him was something private and meant only for him now.

That one thought had him attacking her lips as he pounded into her. Even as his tongue tangled with hers and his cock sought the wetness of her pussy, he slid his hand up to strum on her clit. The minute he touched the tender bundle of nerves, a full body tremor passed through Val. Her breathing sped up as he ran his fingers in a circular motion around and around. Her body undulated in a dance, searching for that moment when the world went away.

Tongue pushing deeper into her mouth, he continued to play with the little button. Rolling it, rubbing it. Val broke away from his kiss, arching her neck back as she panted. Chest heaving, her breasts bouncing with the movements of her body and his thrusts.

"I'm going to make you come for me, Val. And then, when you're flying high, I'm going to take you like you've never been taken before." The words alone had her body shivering under his. Tightening the grip of her pussy as she struggled to find that one thing that would send her over the edge.

"*Dreeeeeeew.* Please. I need it. I'm...I'm so close." Her hands looked for purchase on the bed. Locked onto the sheet, she arched her back and continued to meet him thrust for thrust. "Make me come. I want you to make me come."

Drew didn't think he had ever heard sweeter words. "I always give a lady what she wants." Teeth locking onto the cord running from neck to shoulder, Drew gave another thrust and pinched her clit between his fingers.

"*Ahhhhhhhhhhhhhhhhh!*" The scream that pierced the air was music to his soul. Val shuddered with pleasure. Fingers still tormenting her clit, Drew aimed to prolong the sensations for her.

Her gasps continued to fill the room, even as he started to move his hips in a quickening motion. Looking at Valerie, still in the throes of her orgasm, was all the fuel he needed to go in search of his own. He could feel the pressure building, his balls drawing up tight. Slamming into her pussy, over and over again, rhythm lost, Drew felt the orgasm right there.

"Come in me."

Those words were all it took. A final thrust into her welcoming body and desire exploded from his cock. He threw his head back in relief, as a growl roared from his throat. He never stopped, still thrusting into the warm, wet heat of the woman he loved. Tremors coursing through his limbs, he fell forward, cocooning Valerie in his embrace.

CHAPTER TWENTY-ONE

*V*alerie floated in the blissful aftermath of sex, with Drew lying heavy atop her. Not an uncomfortable heavy, but rather a nice, safe, enveloping weight on her. With his head buried in her neck, all she could hear were the sounds of both of their breaths regaining their normal rhythm. Gently stroking her fingers through his blond hair, she reveled in the feelings he brought forth.

How could she not have imagined it would be this cataclysmic between them? Probably because she never pictured anything as powerful as this ever happening to her. Let alone with Drew. Maybe it was because it was the two of them that it was different. Even with deciding to give their relationship a chance, Val had pushed off really trying to figure out her feelings for Drew, but the time could be nearing where that wasn't a possibility anymore. She probably needed to start thinking of how deep they actually ran and what that fully meant. The funny thing was, though, she wasn't that scared of those feelings anymore, but she was still a bit fearful as to what those feelings may change or what could happen in the future.

Warm, wet kisses started covering her neck as Drew started a lazy thrust again.

As she glided her hands along his back and the nape of his neck, she whispered, "I can still feel you hard inside of me."

Rising up on strong, corded arms Drew kept moving. "I don't think I'll ever not be hard around you. And your pussy feels like heaven, so my dick has no problems staying up."

Val felt the rush of liquid at his words. She never liked dirty talk before, or it could be that she didn't remember other men doing it? But she sure as hell liked hearing it from Drew. It was almost like their own secret, because he wasn't generally crude around others. It seemed to be saved for her, and God help her, but she liked it.

Raising one leg, she stroked her foot along the back of Drew's calf. "Not to kill the moment..." A lazy movement that spread her legs farther out, allowing him to fit closer into the cradle of her thighs and briefly robbing her of breath. "But I think we need a new condom if we're going for round two."

Their separation resulted in mirroring sighs as Drew stood and hurried over to the bathroom, removing the condom as he went. Grabbing another on his return, he had it replaced and was back to her welcoming body before her skin chilled at the loss of his warmth. He resumed the steady thrusts that were igniting her passions all over again. Different this time, without the desperate ferocity of their first coupling, but no less intense.

Val felt the scrape of teeth across her breasts as he drew her hardened nipple into his mouth. Her entire body seemed to have a direct line to her pussy. She could feel herself growing wetter with every nip and suck on her aching breasts. Sliding her hands down Drew's back, she gripped the globes of his ass. She had always admired the way he looked from the rear, often letting her gaze wander as he strode away from her desk. Now she was literally grabbing the chance to get her hands on them.

Digging her nails into the firm flesh illicited a growl from her new lover, and a very firm thrust into her welcoming pussy. She was all for more of that, so she let her hands squeeze again.

"You want me to fuck you faster? Is that it?" At her slight nod, he increased the speed of his rhythm.

A low groan left Val's throat, relishing the feeling of Drew thrusting in and out of her pussy. She couldn't believe she was on the brink so soon after her previous orgasm. Sometimes she could barely manage more than one when she was flying solo, and rarely with someone. It seemed as if Drew had the secret key to making her body and mind soar. Though that probably wasn't all that surprising.

"Seems like someone needs to come again." Stilling his thrusts, he held himself tight to her body as she clenched around him. "I can feel your pussy fluttering around my cock." Left hand moving to her breast, he tweaked her nipple right before engulfing it in his warm, wet mouth.

The feeling of teeth closing around the distended tip sent Val reeling once again. Head thrown back and eyes closed, she clutched Drew in her arms and pussy, not wanting to let go with any part of her body. A long low moan tore from her throat, as she slipped into ecstasy.

CURLED UP ON THE COUCH, in panties and one of Drew's T-shirts, Val looked over at the man she had known for years but was now seeing in a totally new, and exciting, light. After what felt like her hundredth orgasm, she'd pushed Drew off of her. Though still hard, having not come a second time, he was slightly reluctant to leave her body.

She remembered a towel when she went for her second shower of the day. Drew tried to convince her that they needed to conserve water, but Val was pretty sure that her body wouldn't have been able to take any type of his "conservation."

Drew acquiesced, though he did his best to put on a sad, lost puppy look. That she totally wasn't falling for. Not much. Shoving him in the direction of the master bath, she'd grabbed her towel and ran for the guest bath only to hear his laughter following behind her. He stayed in her mind though. With every glance at the reddened abrasions from his beard, and every remembrance of his mouth and hands learning her body.

Now they both sat quietly. She knew that they needed to talk. Unfortunately, Val wanted to forego talking and begin nibbling her way down Drew's chest, which was conveniently naked. He really could have put on some more clothes instead of just workout shorts. How was she supposed to think clearly when all she wanted to do was feast on that skin.

Focus, Valerie! Talk then feast. There's a whole lotta Drew that your mouth hasn't explored yet, and it's starting to water for a taste.

"Ummmmm, so how come you came home early today?" She started with something innocent, mainly to draw her mind away from his body.

"For what we just did." Leaning back on the couch, Drew's expression could be considered nothing but smug.

"What?" That was not exactly what Val expected him to say, and definitely didn't help her thoughts.

Lowering the beer he was nursing, Drew smiled. "It's not like I expected to find you naked in my hallway, but the end result was the same."

Val was pretty sure he said something, but a droplet of condensation fell from the bottle and beaded on his chest, so she was a little distracted. This just wouldn't do. *Focus.*

"Hey, Val, my eyes are up here." Grinning like a fool, he wiped the drop away, though not without running his hand along his very fine pecs.

Guiltily caught in the act, she just played along. "Yes, I know that, but the view farther down is quite inviting." And she hadn't even gotten that much further just now. Raising her head to look into Drew's eyes, she noticed his gaze was riveted to the front of her T-shirt. A white, apparently very see-through T-shirt now that she looked down.

"You can say that again." Swallowing audibly, Drew took another swig of beer. Running the bottle along his forehead to cool off.

For all that her body was sated, for the time being, Val's mind was racing. What she had just experienced with Drew was like nothing she'd felt before. And it wasn't due to just the phenomenal sex and way he made her feel physically. Every second of their time in bed, there was a connection on a deeper level. Like she had finally come home to something that felt ever so right. But what felt right also felt scary because what happened if that rightness turned wrong at some point? *Why are you so convinced it's going to? Just go along for the ride right now and worry about that when, or if, it happens.*

She wished her brain could get on board with her heart and go with the flow. She had never been one to really take that leap before. Almost all of her other relationships had always moved in a predictable pattern, and Val liked predictable. Except for that one time. And that time was her sticking point. But this one, and she couldn't kid herself that it wasn't a relationship, didn't follow that. It was sexier and scarier then any of her others, but it had the potential to be the one she had always dreamed about because, in her heart, it just felt right. What might that dream cost her though?

Drew felt right, he always had. From the moment they met, there was something that called to her. She believed that to be a deep friendship, but maybe it had always been more. Could she have been deluding herself for years? Was that instant connection more than what she had always told herself?

Snap out of it! You are killing your post-great-sex buzz!

Grimacing inwardly, she had to admit that her inner voice was right. All of these self doubts and worrying over why she hadn't seen what was right in front of her was making her afterglow fade quick. Luckily, she knew exactly how to bring it back.

Stretching her leg along the couch, she stroked her bare foot against Drew's calf, the muscles bunching under her sole with each movement. "So you came home to ravish me, did you?"

"I came home to claim you."

Val lifted her gaze to peer at Drew. Intense wasn't the word for what she witnessed staring back at her. She was pummeled by the feelings that were clear as day in his gaze. Possession. Lust. Devotion. *Love*. Throat clenching, she continued to meet his stare.

"I'm done with pretending." Clasping her foot, Drew dragged it up to his lap. "I'm done with acting like our conversation at dinner didn't happen. I'm done with dancing around each other like we've done since that run-in with Evan." Gentle rubbing over the sole of her foot gave way to caresses up her ankle. "And I'm done not admitting how I truly feel. To you or to anyone." A firm tug on Val's ankle had her sprawling on the couch.

Before she was able to catch her breath at the sudden movement, a large, hungry male was leaning over her. Fire burned in his eyes and his touch as he ran his hands up the outside of her thighs. Val heard the tear of the material before her brain caught up to what he had done. Her torn panties dropped to the floor. Spreading her legs wider, he made a place for himself, resting against the heat of her pussy. Val could feel herself getting wetter as he wedged himself closer and closer to her core.

"Look at me, Valerie." Realizing her eyes had been traveling over the planes of his chest, she raised them to meet his and gasped. That same look was there. The same look from a moment ago. And the same look that had always greeted her. Sure, maybe the intensity, the lust, wasn't the same, but the base, the steel of that look was something that she knew only too well. How could she have been so stupid for so long?

"I love you."

She knew in her heart that he meant the forever type of love she had always wanted. Opening her mouth to speak, she was met with a finger stilling her words. But she had to say something, didn't she?

"You don't have to say anything." Lowering his head, he nuzzled the sensitive skin below her ear. "I've known for a long time, even if I took a while to admit it to myself." Dragging his mouth across her cheek, he neared her lips. "You're just coming around." A flurry of tender kisses peppered her jaw until they came to rest near left ear. "But I know anyway."

Plunging his fingers into her soaking wet pussy, he caught her cry of surprise with his mouth. His tongue dueled with hers as they tried to consume each other.

Val was emotionally lost as he withdrew his talented fingers. Her body completely agreed with her mind, since her womb clenched in an effort to draw him back inside.

"Missing something, beautiful?" His words, a sexy raspy whisper in her ear. He ran his supple fingers lightly up and down her slit, gently rubbing her tender clit, but never giving her enough pressure to ease the ache inside. Trying to increase the pressure, she grabbed at his hand but came up empty. The groan that was torn from her was one of painful denial.

Opening eyes that she didn't realize had closed, she saw Drew lean back. Reclining against the opposite arm of the couch, he draped his right arm over the back and looked like a sultan waiting for his favorite harem girl to come please him.

Who was she to deny him?

Sitting up on her knees, Val grabbed the hem of her T-shirt. Like the tease she wasn't used to playing, she slowly lifted the bottom until it came to rest just below her pussy. Hearing Drew's breath turn ragged gave her a confidence foreign to her. She'd enjoyed sex in the past, but this was different. She was having fun that went beyond sex. It spoke to the connection she had with the man who was now her lover and so much more.

"Like what you see?" Raising the hem a little more, she spread her legs as far as the couch would allow her. "Can you see how wet I am for you?" She was sure he could, considering she could feel the moisture from her body on the inside of her thighs.

Clenching the fist lying on top of his thigh, Drew swallowed audibly. "I can see you glisten." His tongue came out to run along his lips. As if he could practically taste her essence on his mouth. "Your pretty little pussy is flooded, isn't it?"

Another couple of inches the shirt rose, giving Drew an unimpeded view of her core. "Flooded thinking about you. About your cock."

"I like it when you think." Drew gave her a grin that would have had her stripping if she wasn't already in the process of doing so. "Why don't you come over here and think some more. Maybe think while you're sliding up and down on this cock I have for you."

Every word out of his mouth made her hypersensitive. Her skin was flushed and hot, her breathing shallow as she anticipated Drew's touch. The shirt lying against her skin was almost too much to handle. Easy way to fix that.

Baring her breasts, she lifted the shirt those final inches and pulled it over her head. Tossing it onto Drew's washboard flat stomach, she ran her hands up her stomach and finally cupped her breasts. Even though it was her own hands, her nipples responded to the touch. Gently kneading them, she witnessed Drew growing more flustered and more aroused, if the growing tent of his shorts was any indication.

"Oh yeah. Grab those tits." What was it about Drew's dirty talk that just set her on fire? "Pull those nipples. Make them hard for me." Following every direction he gave her increased her arousal exponentially. "Do you like playing with your tits for me? Did you touch them when you dreamed about me?"

"God, yes. All the time." Seeing the shit-eating grin that

crossed Drew's face, she realized she'd been duped. *Tricky, tricky man.* She was too far gone to care that she'd admitted dreaming about him—thinking about him as she thrust her vibrator in and out of her pussy. Maybe some turnabout was fair play. "Did you yank on that cock of yours thinking about me?"

Drew harbored none of the non-self-awareness she did. "Fuck yeah. I fucked my hand to visions of you more times than you can count." Rubbing the cock in question through his shorts, he gave a pained grimace. "But nothing beats the vision of you right now. This is what I want to see for the rest of my days."

His words caused Val to drop her head back in surrender. Still squeezing her breast with one hand, her other started the slow travel down her body until it reached the area that needed him most. One touch and she would likely go off, and she didn't want that. Didn't want to be alone in her pleasure. She wanted Drew along with her for the ride.

Coming down to all fours, she made the two-stride crawl to cross the couch and come to rest between his spread thighs. Raising her head and looking up through hooded lids, she could see Drew tense with anticipation. It was an anticipation that she would gladly fulfill. Sitting back on her ankles, she stretched forward. At least she was somewhat flexible thanks to Chelsea dragging her to those yoga classes.

Ass resting on her feet, she placed her hands on his hardened thighs, arched her back and dragged her breasts over the tented front of Drew's shorts. The hissed intake of breath, coupled with the automatic flex of his penis, told her all she needed to know about how her seduction was working. She continued her stretch up his body, using her hands to trace over his chiseled abs. Breasts now flush against his chest, she lowered her head and licked up the curve of Drew's neck. She could feel the abrasion his lightly stubbled jaw was already leaving against her neck as she leaned closer.

"You stopped me before," she whispered as she lowered her hand to the waistband of his shorts. Running the backs of her fingers against his skin, she started pushing them lower. "You're not going to stop me this time, right?"

A strangled, "No," escaped from her lover's mouth just as she grabbed the firm, hard flesh of his dick.

"It's my show now." A steady stroke from root to tip caused a tortured groan from both of their chests. Swiping her thumb over the tip, her finger came away moist with precum. "Looks like I'm not the only one who's a little excited." Moving back slightly, she used her free hand to move the shorts fully out of her way. "Of course, there's nothing little about it."

Dragging her body back down his chest, she peppered kisses along the way, all the time keeping a steady rhythm of her strokes until his hips were moving to match. Stopping as she made herself level with his engorged penis, she watched as her hand encircled and tugged on his length. Val marveled at the sight, the strength of him in her hands, the knowledge that all of that beauty was hers. She didn't think she really ever considered a penis beautiful before, but Drew's made her mouth water. Large and thickly veined, she reveled in the pleasure it had given her body.

Hand clasped tightly around the thick shaft, she briefly looked up to see Drew staring at the connection with the most intense look in his eyes. Without breaking that stare, Val leaned forward and licked the tip like it was her favorite lollipop.

Seeing Drew's eyes roll to the back of his head was the headiest feeling she'd ever had. Emboldened by his reaction, she matched her stroking hand to her licking tongue. Not wanting to end her teasing just yet, she licked and kissed every part of him not under her firm grip. She lowered her other hand to caress his balls drawn up tightly between powerful thighs.

So enraptured with her own sensations, she barely registered the pleas coming from him.

"What is it, baby? You want to feel my mouth wrapped around you?" Drew's dirty talk wasn't the only thing that could turn her on. "I can't wait to feel you pulse in my mouth." With every word she uttered her own moisture began coating her pussy and inner thighs. "Can't wait to taste you. Swallow you all up."

Dick jerking in her hands in response, she lowered her head and engulfed as much of him as she could. The cry that echoed above her spurred her on. Raising her head up his shaft, she let her tongue encircle as much as she could. Keeping one hand wrapped around him, she lowered back down. Hand, mouth and tongue all working together, she swirled her tongue around the head of his dick, tasting the pearly drop that gathered there.

Drew's hands fisted in her hair. Not directing her motions, but definitely not letting her go. It was the anchor she desperately needed as desire started to spin her out of control.

With each swipe of her tongue and kiss of her lips around his cock, she grew more and more aroused. Not thinking twice about it, she moved her hand away from his balls and stroked herself.

Her cry, muzzled by the rigid flesh in her mouth, didn't go unnoticed.

"Oh fuck, beautiful. Are you touching yourself?" The growled words just made her wetter.

Val thought she nodded, but between his stranglehold on her hair and her mouth wrapped around his dick, she wasn't sure. She just knew that her body was on fire.

"Yeah, I can see your hips moving. Play with your clit for me." Drew's own hips were moving too, forcing his cock deeper into her throat with each pass. "Put a finger up in that pussy." Doing everything Drew told her to do, the fire built in intensity. "That's not enough for you though, is it? You need my cock filling you."

The words, the touch, the taste. All were enough to make her come, but she didn't want to. Not this way. Not without him inside her.

Still she couldn't resist moving her finger in and out of her hungry body. With each movement, her need grew. She could feel Drew's need growing too, as evidenced by the swelling of his dick with each pass of her mouth.

On a rough groan and sudden movement, Drew grabbed her by the arms and positioned her so she was straddling his cock. With a whispered curse, Drew fumbled for the condom he must have stuffed in his pocket. He made quick work of putting the latex on, and without a second thought she lowered herself down, just as he surged upward, filling her in one primitive thrust. Raspy groans tore from both of their throats as their bodies met. His pleasure echoing hers.

"Fuck, that's a beautiful sight." Following Drew's gaze, she focused on where their bodies were locked together. The dark hair framing Drew's cock rested against the bare skin of her pussy, flushed with arousal. Keeping her eyes lowered, Val shuddered as she watched him slowly withdraw, only to lunge back into her waiting body.

The sight itself was almost enough to make her come, and knowing they were both on the razor's edge to begin with didn't help.

Drew tightened his grip on her hips, even as he reached his thumb to rub little circles around her clit. Her body squeezed his cock with each pass of his talented finger. Every stroke increasing her arousal to a fever pitch.

"Feed me your tit, Valerie. I want to suck on it as you come."

Her body gave out at his words, falling forward until her hands rested on either side of his head and her breasts dangled like ripe fruit in front of a starved man. Right before he made his move, a bit of wantoness had her sitting back up and cupping her breasts. Just as he asked she leaned back over and placed the hardened tip on his lips. Seeing the flare of blue fire in his eyes convinced her that following his command was worthwhile.

His lips surrouned her nipple and he lashed the furled bud with his tongue. All the while increasing the tempo of his plunging cock and talented fingers. Head thrown back, Val could feel the orgasm reaching that crescendo.

With a final bite of teeth to her nipple, her body clamped down on Drew's and she let out a primal scream of pleasure.

He released her tender breast and dropped his head back. With a grunt of his own, he bucked up into her one last time. His shout of completion echoed in the room as his cock continued to lazily move within her.

Body utterly relaxed in satisfaction, she curled up in Drew's arms, thinking back to those three little words he'd said to her. Her heart wanted to say them back, but she worried he would think it was just the magic of the moment and all they had experienced together that afternoon. Raising her head, she peered into the startling blue of his eyes to see if he could read her feelings. And he did. His eyes, his hands, his body, they all told her he knew exactly how she felt, even without the words. But he was going to get those words.

CHAPTER TWENTY-TWO

"*W*hat the hell do you mean you're moving back to your house?"

Drew stood at Valerie's desk, looking at her like she had grown a second head. He couldn't believe what had just come out her mouth. They had both called in sick on Thursday, and spent the previous day and nights tangled up in each other. This was the last thing he expected to hear when he stopped to see her after his lunch meeting.

Lifting her head from her computer screen, brilliant green eyes stared back at him. He could read those eyes a little better after spending most of the previous day inside her. What they said now was that she was reliving those moments on the couch, and the shower, and the bed, all of which there would be a lot less of if she moved the fuck out.

Cocking her head to the side, she gave him a slightly confused look. "You didn't think I was going to stay at your place forever, did you?"

Well, yeah. He sort of had thought that. Maybe not consciously, but they were together now. He had told her he loved her, so that changed things. And he wanted her with him. All the time.

Opening his mouth to respond, she beat him to it.

"I know you think that yesterday changes things, and it does." Tucking a wayward strand of hair behind her ear, she grinned. "But that doesn't mean we're running full speed ahead into living together."

Fighting to hold back his desire to have her lock, stock and barrel, he planted his hands on her desk and leaned in. The push to get into her personal space had her breath quickening and pupils dilating in response. He could see the rise and fall of her chest as she inhaled his scent.

"Just think of all the time we could spend on the couch if you moved in." Seeing the pulse in her neck kick up a notch, he continued the onslaught of words. It was the biggest revelation from their time together, how much she loved, and her body responded to, his words. If talking dirty to her would help his cause, he was firmly committed to every filthy word he could say. "You liked it these past days, didn't you? I know my dick liked it. And I'm sure that pretty pussy of yours enjoyed it too." Seeing the flush across Val's skin and the rapid beat of her pulse, Drew planned on moving in for the kill.

"Jesus! Not in the damn office, for fuck's sake."

The harsh words, laced with with a loving sarcasm, had Drew dropping his head. But not before he noticed that the aroused flush of Val's skin was now replaced with the red of embarrassment.

"Way to break up a moment, Matt." Drew was reasonably sure he could cheerfully kick his brother's ass.

"You want us to leave? I can call the fire department so they know to be on standby to put out the flames."

Dammit! Jon's distinct voice did little to hide the amusement in his tone. Nothing like getting caught by both of your brothers when you were trying to woo your girl. While he was aroused, yet not truly embarrassed, he couldn't say the same thing about Val who looked like she wanted to crawl under the desk.

Apparently there was a devil on his shoulder who decided to take over. Leaning just a bit farther, he planted a quick kiss on Val's lips before pulling away. Eyes still locked on hers, he offered up an explanation. "Don't worry, beautiful. They're just jealous."

Straigtening up, he turned to find his brothers making a vain attempt to cover their laughter and look away.

"Damn right, I am." Jon was the first to speak. Drew was startled to see a bit of jealousy in his eyes. Just a brief flare in the intensity of his blue gaze, followed by an almost wistful expression on his face. Drew had seen that look recently staring back at him in the mirror before Val finally fell into his arms. Could he have missed Jon's attraction to Val all this time? "I need to find a woman who looks at me like that." On a deep sigh of relief, Drew realized that it was the relationship Jon longed for. But even then, he could still see a wealth of happiness in his baby brother's face. "You sure you don't have a sister, Val? Friend? Someone?"

That coaxed a laugh out of the still-red woman behind the desk. He could tell though, that Val's embarrasment was waning. She was probably as much mortified by being caught by his brothers as she was by the words he'd used to build the slow burn within her.

"Nope. No sister." Smiling at the youngest of the brothers, he could tell his woman took the question seriously. She too could read the longing in Jon's face. A longing Drew had never really noticed before. "I'll see what I can do Jon and let you know."

While Jon and Valerie shared a conspiratorial laugh, Drew turned to his older brother. The look on Matt's face was much harder to interpret. It was also much harder to witness the pain that flashed briefly across it as he stared at the door to his office like he wanted to incinerate it. Drew had always looked up to Matt, wanted to emulate his older brother in everything he did, with the exception of one. There was no way Drew ever wanted to be in the hell that was Matt's marriage. As his brother turned back, that pain was replaced by the same sense of longing he had seen in Jon. And knowing the state of Matt's marriage, he wasn't surprised.

On second thought, he needed to make that two things. While the state of Matt's marriage may be hell, Drew didn't ever want to be in the place, or the mindset, that caused it. He may have been unwilling to admit his feelings for a while, but now that he had, there was nothing, and no one, who would stop him from claiming his woman. If his suspicions were right, Matt had let something stop him from doing the same.

The tumultous feelings now cleared from his expression, Matt tried to turn on the charm. "Valerie, I thought you had better taste." A lazy grin, with a raised brow was thrown her way.

A negligent shrug of her shoulder accompanied her words, "I thought I did too. Guess not."

Val joined his brothers in the laughter at his expense. Staring each of them down, he growled his reply, "You know what? I don't even care if you just made fun of me. I've got my woman, so nothing either of you Neanderthals can say is going to ruin my day."

Turning a pointed glance back to the woman in question that silenced her laugh, he continued, "You can however." Facing his brothers with an affronted expression, he explained, "She wants to move back into her house."

"You go, Val."

"Make him work for it."

"Traitors, the both of you." Flipping his brothers off, he gave Val a sizzling look. "I didn't have to work hard for it Wednesday, did I, baby? Or any other time yesterday?"

A chorus of groans accompanied Drew as he walked into his office.

~

KICKING off her shoes as she walked through her front door, Val let out a small sigh. It felt good to be back at her house. As much as she loved being with Drew, everything felt as if it was moving at warp speed. And in no way, shape, or form was that normal for her. Not that she was overly cautious, but she sure didn't jump in without some thinking. Of course, she definitely jumped in with Drew. Or maybe jumped *on* was a more accurate phrase.

A slight blush colored Val's cheeks as she remembered how quickly she had herself wrapped around Drew in his hallway. That blush gave way to shivers as she thought about the pleasure she found in Drew's embrace.

These past two days were some of the best days she had ever had with a lover. Not that there had been tons, but she was no timid virgin. Usually, though, sex was never the spontaneous combustion it was between her and Drew. She could try to convince herself it was because it was their first time together, but that was a lie. It had never happened with any of her other "first times." Especially since the combustion happened over and over again. No. This was solely because of Drew. Or the combination of Drew and her. Now that she thought about it, there was no question. It was definitely the best days with a lover she'd ever had. Possibly even the best days period.

Moving through her house, she started to flip through the pile of mail in her hand. An oddly addressed envelope caught her attention. On first glance, it looked like junk mail, but she'd have to take a closer look later. Placing the stack on the counter, Val went to the refrigerator and pulled out a bottle of wine. She was lucky she'd made her escape from the office while Drew was in a meeting with his brothers. Uncorking the bottle and pouring herself a glass, she thought about her chances of Drew not showing up here.

"Not good. Not good at all." Talking to herself was nothing new. "But I'm going to enjoy some me time until that happens." Raising her glass in a toast to herself, she took a sip of the crisp white wine.

Padding down the hallway to her bedroom, she hit the switch before stepping in. The window had been fixed while she was staying at Drew's. While the school listened to her when she went there, with no offending object, they did little more than pay lip service to her complaint. They certainly didn't offer to compensate her for it. And it took her a few hours of arguing with Drew when he tried to take control and cover the cost. It was her house, and she could afford a new window. Now looking at it, if someone didn't know what had happened, there was no indication that anything had been amiss.

But she did know what had occurred. She'd be lying to herself if she didn't admit she was a bit apprehensive to stay here alone. Telling that to Drew would have been like waving a red cape in front of a bull. With one sentence, he would have had her moved in to his place and a "For Sale" sign in front of hers.

Setting the wine down on the top of her dresser, she began to shed the trappings of the day. Jewelry off and into her case. All except the small, star pendant bracelet that never came off. A gift from her parents when she was just a child, she wore it all time. When they had given it to her, on her fifth birthday, they told her to always reach for the stars in whatever she wanted to do. Now she looked to the stars as a way of reaching out to her parents, knowing they were always there watching over her.

She smiled. She was pretty sure her parents would have liked Drew.

Stripping out of her dress, Val grabbed yoga pants and a T-shirt to throw on. It was Friday, and she was living it up. That was if a person's definition of living it up meant wine, TV, and maybe some pizza. She really just wanted to relax in her own house for the evening.

Pulling open the top drawer for a pair of socks she spied her trusty vibrator. Well, that would definitely be relaxing. And her fantasies about Drew, the ones she never consciously admitted to having, would definitely have more to work with. Before, she could only imagine his touch. His kiss. His cock. Now she had first-hand knowledge of all of them and would gleefully admit her imagination was crap in comparison to the real thing.

Hell, even her vibrator was woefully lacking in the size department now.

Val slid the drawer shut just as the doorbell rang. She should have known Drew wasn't going to simply give up.

Socks clutched in her hand, Val made her way back to the living room and her front door. That it wasn't her lover was obvious before she even cracked it open.

"Yo, my bitch, let your girlfriend in."

Letting out a cackle, she swung the door wide to Chelsea gracing her front porch. Takeout bag in hand, she pushed her way right past Val.

"Come on in. Val won't mind," Chelsea spoke over her shoulder as she made her way toward the kitchen.

Val turned to look at the other woman who had accompanied her best friend, an inkling of recognition trying to make its way forward. The newcomer was tall, with auburn, curly hair, maybe a few years older than herself and probably a little on the heavier side, but she had a warm friendly face that currently registering shock as she watched Chelsea just take over.

"Yeah, she has that effect on people." Val stretched her hand out in greeting. "We've met before, haven't we?"

"Briefly." Nodding, the other woman clasped Val's hand. "The day you helped Chelsea and Rick move in. I'm Angela."

Waving Angela into the house, she recalled their prior meeting. "That's right. Runaway dog."

"Sailor doesn't usually get away like that when I'm watching him, but at least I got to meet my new neighbors. I tend to work or stay home. Not go out much."

Val peered into the kitchen where Chelsea was moving around, setting out dinner like it was her own house. "Yeah, how's that working for you if you've become friends with Chels?" Lord knows Chelsea wasn't going to let someone languish away at home if she could do something about it. At least that's what she always told Val whenever the urge to become a hermit hit.

A shy smile accompanied a rueful laugh. "As you can imagine, not well. I was getting out of my car tonight when she essentially kidnapped me." Leaning in close to Val, Angela whispered, "I'm sort of afraid I'm her new mission. I think I'm too old to be anyone's mission." The look on her face was one of sheer terror, coupled with a little bit of anticipation. Seemed like Angela was slightly interested in letting herself become Chelsea's project. "I apologize for the intrusion."

"Well, any friend of Chelsea's is a friend of mine. Besides, take it from someone who knows, you'll need the support once she gets going. And there's no intrusion." Linking arms with Angela, they made their way into the kitchen. "Make yourself at home why don't you, Chels?"

"Thanks for offering." Brandishing her hand over the food spread out on the small center island like a game show girl, Chelsea smiled. "I figured I'd come to save you."

"Save me from what?"

"From that sexy man who wants to steal you away, back to his big penthouse in the sky." Turning to Angela, she elaborated on her explanation, "See, she finally hooked up with middle hottie. But now middle hottie wants her to stay with him so they can fuck like bunnies, even after the whole broken-window-slashed-tires-caught-in-a-burning-trailer thing has died down. For some unknown reason, dumbass over here would rather stay alone in her own house than burning up the sheets with middle hottie." Chelsea had to pause to take a breath, which didn't even last long enough for Val or Angela to get a word in. "So here I am, and you are, to protect her right to stay alone when middle hottie decides to go all caveman tonight and come over here to claim his woman."

The look on Angela's face was priceless. Val was pretty sure she thought Chelsea was certifiable. Hell, most of the time Val thought that too. Though honestly, to hear it all laid out like that, it seemed pretty silly she didn't want to stay with Drew. But this was her house, dammit! She wanted to stay here.

"Um, maybe Valerie prefers not moving too quickly with middle hottie." Angela, it seemed like, was going to try to be the voice of reason. Val appreciated Angela's interjection and felt like she had hit it on the head. She just wanted time to think and slow things down a little. "Or maybe the sex wasn't worth it."

"Ha! You haven't seen middle hottie. Or any of the hotties."

"Oh no, the sex was fucking fantastic," both Val and Chelsea answered at the same time.

A look of delight cross Chelsea's face and she knew she was in for it. They had only spoken briefly today, so there was no time to share any of the juicy details. Of which there were plenty, and Chelsea would want them all, right down to dick size. Val could also see the color spread up Angela's face. Looked like maybe she wasn't the most comfortable person with this topic. Which would make it hard to be friends with Chelsea, considering sex was pretty much her favorite topic.

"Before you scare the shit out of Angela, how about we sit down and start eating? I've got more wine in the fridge." Grabbing a plate off the top of the stack Chelsea had removed from the cabinet, she handed it to Angela.

"Yeah, I'm a step ahead of you. Like, I didn't find the open bottle while you two were gabbing at the front door."

Shaking her head, she gave her best friend a look that let her know she was insane. Sometimes she wondered if an unsarcastic word ever came out of Chelsea's mouth. And it looked like Angela wanted to make for the hills.

"If you two want some friend time, I can get an Uber and head home. Chelsea sort of grabbed me as I was walking into my place and said she wanted company to run an errand." Seeing Angela standing there, still gripping her plate, brought out all of the protective instincts Val had. She realized how in sync she and Chelsea were, and obviously Angela did too. Sometimes it was hard to be the new girl breaking into a group.

Opening her mouth to put Angela at ease, she was beaten to the punch.

"Absolutely not." Chelsea moved to throw her arm around Angela's shoulder. "We are formally inducting you into our little group. Well, it was a duo, not really a group, but fuck it. Whatever it was, you're in it now." Giving her a squeeze, Chelsea took a step away. "Besides, now I have someone new to corrupt."

Val couldn't help but laugh along with the wickedly gleeful Chelsea. All was right when Angela smiled and joined in. She thought for a moment Angela may have thought Chelsea was joking about corrupting her. Yeah, she was sure that was absolutely her bestie's plan.

Dinner passed uneventfully, with them getting to know Chelsea's new neighbor. Angela was a delight, but Val could tell that she was shy. Of course, most people would be considered shy when in the context of Chelsea, but she held her own. It was a pleasant surprise to find out Angela worked for the lab the guys were bidding on. Maybe they could see more of each other that way.

"You know what that means, right?" Leaning back against one of the plush chairs in the living room, Chelsea took a sip of wine. "She could spend time with the hotties. Lucky bitch."

A shy smile creeped across Angela's face. She was active in every conversation they had, until it came to men. Then she sort of sat back and observed. Val was sure the rest of the evening would be a struggle for her because they hadn't even gotten to gossiping about Drew yet, and not much could stop Chelsea from getting that information.

"Why do you call them the hotties?"

A salacious grin spread across Chelsea's face. "Because they are fucking ridiculous. Well, not as sexy and hot as my man, but they tie for a damn close collective second." Val could practically see the wheels turning in her head as she was planning to tell Angela all about the Stephens brothers.

"Stop drooling over my bosses." Yeah, that felt a little weird to say now that she had screwed Drew six ways to Sunday. "Well, Drew and my two bosses."

"Wait until you meet them, Angela. You'll want to lick them up like I do." Chelsea sent a conspiratorial wink in Angela's direction that appeared to terrify her. Like Chelsea was really going to introduce her to the guys and have her lick them. "First there's Matthew. All controlled and buttoned up, but underneath you know he's an animal. He's married though." The sad expression that accompanied Chelsea's description was classic. "But she is a grade-A bitch. That poor man probably hasn't gotten off in years. Unless he's jacking off in the shower 'cause she is a nasty piece of work."

Angela's eyes went wide, but Val couldn't tell if it was because of the depiction of Matthew masturbating in the shower or Chelsea's description of Cassandra. Truth be told though, that shower image would probably be something to make a woman's eyes pop out.

"It's true." Two heads swiveled toward her. "*No!* Not about the shower. How the fuck should I know that?" Chelsea just shrugged and waggled her eyebrows, while Angela turned a slight pink. She was beginning to think that was going to be Angela's default coloring around Chelsea. Val just laughed at the two of them. "I mean about Cassandra. She's a bitch, pure and simple. But they do have an adorable little boy."

"True that. Poor kid having her for a mom though." Refilling her glass, Chelsea topped off everyone's with the last of the bottle. "Jon's the baby of the group. And by baby I just mean the youngest in age, cause there is nothing baby-like about that stud. A little more relaxed than big brother, but just looking at him, you know that man could go for hours. Don't you just think there's another side of him waiting to come out, Val?"

"Um, I never really thought about Jon like that." Val blanched a bit. She had always considered him the sweet one, the gentleman of the three. And she had never, not a single time, pictured him in relation to sex at all.

"Yeah, yeah. He's all sweet and polite and the peacemaker of the trio. But he's just waiting for the right woman, I can tell. Then he's going to let his freak flag fly and get all kinky and shit."

Val contemplated if there was that side to Jon. She had never thought Drew would have the dirty talking, possessive side that he'd shown her. Maybe Jon was like that too. Suddenly, she recalled what he had said at work today, about having a friend. She peered over at Angela, sitting there silently taking all of this in. Jon was the gentle brother, the one who could probably tease Angela out of her shell. He put everyone at ease, from nervous clients to herself at times. Was there more that he could do though? Because Val caught the little hitch in Angela's breathing when Chelsea mentioned the word kinky. Something to think about and maybe, just maybe, she'd arrange for a little meeting.

"And now on to middle hottie. He's taken though, Angela." Nodding in Val's direction, Chelsea continued, "They may have just recently done the deed, but that man's been taken for a while."

Settling back against her seat like a queen holding court, Chelsea proceeded to pepper Val with every question imaginable. And some not so imaginable. Her cheeks heated, both from the questions and the images they elicited in her brain. A blush creeped up Angela's cheeks, as the questions became more and more personal.

This was going to be a long night.

It was well past midnight by the time Chelsea and Angela went home. Courtesy of Rick coming by to collect them since the three of them had done an exceptional job polishing off some wine. Well, maybe more than some, but less than alot. At least in her slightly tipsy—okay, more like drunken—state, that was what Val was telling herself.

Turning out the last of the lights in the living room, she went to make sure everything was away in the kitchen. Their wine glasses in the sink could definitely wait until tomorrow. Grabbing the mail, she cautiously walked back to her bedroom. She could admit to herself that she wasn't quite steady on her feet. Thank God tomorrow was Saturday and she didn't have to drag herself to work. Though she had a feeling Drew wouldn't stay away for long.

He had called when they were eating, ready to come over and plant himself by her side. It was only when Chelsea decided to accompany the conversation with groans that would do a pornstar proud that Drew backed down. Knowing she wasn't alone seemed to appease him a little. Which meant she wasn't going to explain that Chelsea and Angela hadn't crashed here all night. She had a feeling that would not go over well. Drew's protective streak wasn't exactly new. He had always been overly protective of his family, and in a way that had always encompassed her. But she wasn't used to the focus and intensity it seemed to entail now. Even more so after they had slept together.

Staring at the stack of mail on the dresser, she was trying to remember why she had brought it back in here with her. She wanted to look at something again, but the wine wasn't exactly making it easy to remember.

As she racked her brain, her phone did a little vibrating dance across her nightstand. She grabbed it before it bounced right off the nightstand and she was left with a brand new phone that was broken. Turning it screen side up, she then looked at the text from Drew.

"You alone?"

Somehow she didn't think he meant in the house, but on the bright side she wasn't lying when she answered him. *"Yup. All by my lonesome in my bedroom."*

Flinging herself back on her bed, she waited for his response. Maybe she was sober enough to partake in some late night sexting.

"Hmmmmmmmmm. What I wouldn't give to be there now."

Truth be told, Val wouldn't mind it either. She was trying to maintain some semblance of the status quo, instead of having any real issue with going back to Drew's or having him come over here. A part of her was still leery about moving too fast. She had been burned in the past, and she didn't want that to happen again. Though, in her heart, she knew Drew wouldn't hurt her like that. He couldn't guarantee anything, there was no way to know what would happen in the future, but there was no way Drew wouldn't do everything in his power to make sure she never got hurt.

The phone buzzed where she had dropped it on her stomach. *"Beautiful? You with me?"*

Realizing she zoned out, she fumbled to unlock the phone screen. *"Sorry. I may have had a little bit to drink."*

Apparently she spoke too soon about sobering up. 'Cause

right then, her eyelids felt like they weighed a ton, and she was pretty sure she nodded off for a second. Looked like no phone sex for her tonight. Val didn't think Drew would be up for a partner who kept falling asleep.

"Thought that might be the case. I'll let you all get some sleep."

Val was typing her response when a second message from Drew came in.

"I'll be over tomorrow. Enjoy your sleep in your bed while you can get it 'cause tomorrow there won't be any sleeping. But there will be a whole hell of a lot of time in bed. Preferably with me buried deep inside you as you scream out my name. Lord knows my hand is a poor subsitute on my dick now that it knows how it feels to be clenched tight in that pussy of yours. I know that little toy of yours won't measure up anymore. I guess if you needed a little relief it may do the trick. It won't fill you up like I will though. It won't whisper how good you feel around me, or suck on your tit, or bellow your name when I come. But in a pinch..."

Holy fuck! How the hell was she supposed to get to sleep now? Even drunk, she was horny as all get out. She eyed her drawer, thinking of her trusty vibrator. How had Drew known about that? Shit, at this point she didn't even care how he knew. The phone buzzed one more time in her hand.

"Sweet dreams, beautiful. I'll see you tomorrow. Xoxo"

Typing out a one word *goodnight*, she put her phone back on the nightstand. The thought still swirled to get her vibe and give herself some relief. The images Drew's words invoked played through her mind as her eyes closed and she fell into a deep sleep.

CHAPTER TWENTY-THREE

*D*rew checked his watch as he pulled up in front of Val's house. Eleven o'clock. He had wanted to come over earlier, but his dad showed up at his doorstep this morning. As much as he loved spending time with his father, he had been practically crawling out of his skin wanting to get over to Valerie while his dad was "just killing time" waiting on his mom to finish at the hair salon. He sort of thought his dad was jerking his chain and knew he was anxious to leave. Though showing up bright and early today, especially if Val was still feeling the effects of last night's imbibing, wasn't going to put him in good standing with her.

So here he was after what he could only label as a tough night. After only two nights of having Val in his bed, he was already lost without her curled up next to him. He tossed and turned, searching her out in his sleep, but never finding her. And when he did manage to fall into a semi-peaceful slumber, she starred in his dreams. Sitting astride him as she rode him to completion. Under him as he pounded into her. Whatever the vision that permeated his dream, the outcome was the same. He woke up hard and hurting, fist wrapped around his cock.

Striding to the door, he was confident he would be able to keep those base instincts at bay. Giving a firm knock, Drew pulled himself together and swore he wouldn't pounce as soon as Val opened the door.

Hoping he didn't look like a complete horndog, he grinned as the door swung open. And his best intentions fled in a flash.

Best laid plans and all that shit. How about just focus on the laid *part?*

For once, he was completely in agreement with that inner devil.

Pushing through the door, he slammed it behind him just as he pushed Val up against the wall and brought his lips down on hers. Driving his tongue between her lips, he savored the taste of her. Part minty fresh, but all Valerie. Nibbling on her lips, he continued to plunder her mouth. She fought him for control of the kiss, but he wasn't going to let that happen. He was in charge of this. That previously unknown dominant streak was charging to the forefront every time he came near her.

Drew pulled back slightly, feathering soft kisses on her lips. Flicking his tongue out to lick gently at her mouth. The soft little mewls coming from her throat were turning him on even more, though he wasn't sure how he could get any harder. Realizing that his kiss alone had Val on the cusp of pleasure was a heady thing.

"Don't think you're taking control of this, beautiful." Skimming his hands down her arms, he laced their fingers together and raised them above her head. "Keep them there." Drew dragged his fingers back down the tender underside of her arm. The little tank top she wore was no match for his desires. Lowering the scooped neckline, he nuzzled his mouth between the mounds of her breasts. "So very sweet." Licking his way toward her right nipple, he furled his tongue around it, engulfing it within the heat of his mouth. Val clutched his hair in her hand, the sensation making him bite down a little more roughly than he planned. *"No."* Tugging her hand back into position, he grabbed them both in one of his. "Don't make me hold you here."

Well, apparently that wasn't a deterrent judging by Val's quick intake of breath. This was proving to be a whole new side of them both, and damned if it didn't make him ready to blow. Dick pulsing in his pants, he would have a hard time focusing on Val's pleasure first.

"You going to keep them where I put them?" Returning to the tantalizing feel and taste of her breast, he sensed her whole body shake along with her head.

"Uh huh." Eyes darkening with desire, she clenched her hands together above her head. "I promise."

"Good."

Taking a knee in front of her, he glanced up at the vision before him. Flushed face, teeth coming out to nibble her bottom lip, breasts spilling out over the top of the tank. A masterpiece, if he ever saw one. No work of art hanging in any museum was more exquisite than his Valerie when she was losing herself to his touch.

Grasping the gray yoga pants she wore, he tugged them down to her hip bones. Low enough to tease her as he ran his tongue along the edge. He could smell her arousal. Equal parts sweet and spicy, but most importantly, all Valerie. Yanking a little more, they cleared one hip. Drew peppered kisses along that tender juncture of torso and thigh as Val undulated her hips. Seeking more. Wordlessly begging him to give her what she desired.

A tug to the other side had the loosened pants sliding down her legs and puddling at her feet. Drew grasped her left leg and hiked it up over his shoulder. Pushing her right leg farther out, he spread her open, ready to feast on what he was craving all night and morning.

"Looks like I'm in time for breakfast." Her arousal glistened off her pussy lips and thighs. Val was soaking wet. He leaned in, pressing a quick kiss to her mound. Even that light touch coated his mouth with her cream and illicited a tortured gasp from her. "I believe you even kept it warm for me."

Spanning his hands across her thighs, he gently ran his thumbs over the folds of her sex. So sensitive if her panting breath was any indication. Using his hands to pull back and expose her clit, he leaned forward and flicked it with his tongue.

"Andrew, please." His name as a sob on her lips was enough to have him abandoning his plans to move slow. Slow could be for later. Years later. If they ever exhausted this all-consuming passion and need he had for her.

Placing his lips over her clit, he sucked. The shaking of her body signaled that this wasn't going to take long, but he still had a little bit of deviousness left to torture her with.

Removing his mouth from around her clit, he spread her wide with his fingers and gave a long slow lick all along her pussy. He worked his fingers in the opposite direction as his mouth. As he tugged on her clit with his lips, he gently stroked over her opening. Moving his mouth back, he let his tongue surge into her as deep as he could. All the while, his fingers were circling and rubbing that small bundle of nerves.

Her rocking motion was becoming more and more frantic. As he latched onto her clit again, he looked up her body. Head thrown back, eyes closed, and her mouth open on soundless gasps. But, he was glad to see, her hands didn't stray from the position he put them in.

As if she could sense his stare, her eyes fluttered open and caught with his. The fire in them flared when he eased two fingers into her. Pumping them in and out of her hot channel, he kept his mouth latched onto her clit. Never once did they break their gazes from each other.

Everything he was centered onto this moment. Wordlessly, they spoke to each other, conveying everything they hadn't verbally said yet. But it was there, in his eyes he was sure, and in hers as she stared back at him.

With his love shining for her to see, he gently bit down on her clit and she flew apart. Even in that moment, she never closed her eyes. Never looked away. At that moment of ultimate surrender, she locked her gaze on him and showed him her heart.

SIGHING CONTENTEDLY, Val curled up next to Drew in the comfort of her bed. Their passion had taken them like a firestorm as soon as she'd opened the door. But now that the edge was off, they were reveling in each other's closeness. Even the other days and nights at Drew's, they hadn't just relaxed. Hadn't let themselves really experience all they were feeling and thinking. Everything had been such a hot, blazing need that they never took the time to relax into each other.

They'd moved from the wall to the couch, then finally to the bed. But they hadn't actually had sex in her bed. Drew had simply picked her up and carried her down the hallway. Nestled in his arms, she had felt a sense of peace and rightness wash over her. Right up until he threw her on the bed where she bounced. She had no time to voice her displeasure though, since Drew jumped right on up with her and tucked them both under the sheet. Seeing Drew nestled against her pillows, teal blue sheet pulled up to his waist, he could have rivaled any sexy model shot that Chelsea was always posting on Facebook. Nothing looked as good on a man as a sexy smile, and knowing that she was the reason for it gracing his face made it even better.

Now, feeling Drew's heartbeat under her ear, she realized any excuse she'd told herself had to be moved to the past. Drew wasn't Timothy, he wouldn't hurt her like that. Maybe Chelsea had been right when she questioned why Val had never shared that past with Drew. She shared so much of herself already with him, but this was one thing she had always held back. She didn't like to dwell on the whole sordid story. And she hated to think that Drew would have looked at her differently, with a sad sense of sympathy, because of what had happened. But could it be that it was because she knew their relationship was headed in this direction? For all of her denials and excuses and avoidance, maybe her heart was leading her here all along.

"I can practically hear you thinking." Drew ran his hands tenderly over her hair, making her feel cherished. Like he couldn't get enough of touching her. The thought solidified when he stroked along the arm she had curled over his chest. "Tell me, beautiful. You know I'll listen to whatever it is."

She could feel the slightest bit of tension fill his body. As if he was worried what she was going to say. She made him like this. Made him think that she wasn't as invested in this. All because she was scared of what had happened years ago, and because she was terrified her feelings were now a hundred times stronger than those old ones ever were.

Swirling her fingers through the light spattering of hair decorating his chest, she began, "When I was in high school, I had a few really good friends, but still a small circle. Two of those I considered my best friends: Chelsea and Timothy. Chelsea wasn't really all that different from the way she is now."

"Good lord. That must have terrified teachers." Drew laughingly took the punch she planted on his arm, but he soon sobered.

"Tim was my buddy from when we were even younger. We didn't go to the same high school, but we were always together.

Someone I could laugh with. Tease. Talk about boyfriends with. We hung out all the time and could practically finish each other's sentences. I told him damn near everything." Tension overtook Drew's body. It was there in the way his arms tightened and his breath paused for just a moment. She could tell what was going through his mind, without even asking. She knew he saw the similarities between her relationship with Tim and the one she had developed with him. "Hell, most people thought we were dating, and those who didn't kept asking us when we were going to start."

Drew never stilled his hands as they stroked her skin, never stopped offering her his comfort. She sensed that he wanted to ask questions, but was giving her the time she needed to tell her story.

"We stayed best friends even as we started college. Somewhere along the way, we decided that maybe we should be together." Looking back on it now, Val realized it probably wasn't a conscious decision on either of their parts. They'd simply fell into the role everyone had already put them in, but that didn't mean she had been any less invested in that relationship. And at the time, she believed Tim was as all in as she was. "We started dating. And really, the only change to the relationship was a physical one. He was already my best friend and then he was my lover. It seemed just a normal progression."

Leaning back, Val looked at Drew. Mouth pulled tight and eyes closed as if in pain, as he waited for the rest of her story. She wished she could fast forward and explain that she realized the difference now. That all she was worried about before was nonsense and how her stupidity had cost them time.

"He was my everything back then, and I thought I was the same for him." She could feel tears start to well in her eyes. Drew looked despondent, and she wished she could explain that they weren't tears for Tim, but for the loss of something more.

"Then my parents were killed in the accident. My world crumbled, and I leaned on Tim. I leaned on him for so much."

Brushing a tear off her cheek, Drew leaned forward. "Of course you did, baby. That's what you were supposed to do. You lean on the man you love for support."

Of course Drew would say that.

"Apparently it was too much for him." Grinning slightly at the growl and look of displeasure coming from the man lying in her bed, she continued, "I caught him, not that long after, in bed with another girl. Not someone I knew, so at least there was that."

Val grabbed Drew's arm as he made to get out of bed. Her heart soared at the thought that he wanted to right the wrongs against her, but she didn't need him to do that. She just needed him here.

"It was a long time ago, Drew. Lie back down." He reluctantly did as she asked, grabbing both of her hands and pressing kisses to them. "I was devastated. My parents were gone. My brother had flown off to wherever he was headed to next. And now my boyfriend was gone, taking my best friend along with him."

Raising her hand, she smoothed back Drew's hair. So soft to the touch. Running her fingers over his face, she lingered on the strength and gentleness of his lips. So much like Drew himself.

"Drew, you've been my best friend since I came here. Looking back now, I won't lie to myself anymore and say I wasn't attracted. But I had already crossed that line with a friend once before, and the fallout left me gutted." The tension returned to Drew's body. He was braced for the worst, even if she could sense the pleading in his eyes. "I did everything I could to keep you in that friend category. To keep myself protected from what happened before."

"Baby, don't you know I would never do what he did?

Never." Drew's crystal blue eyes were full of sadness as he stared at her from across the pillow.

"I never thought you would. That was never the problem."

"Then what was? I can't make sure it doesn't happen if I don't know what not to do." Drew was petting her relentlessly now. Almost as if he was scared that if he stopped touching her she would disappear. That was never going to happen. He'd pushed for her, so he was getting her and he would be stuck with her for a long damn time.

"The problem was me. And don't shake your head." Val returned to stroking his chest—the chest that housed his heart and all the love he had in it for those important to him. "I wasn't worried you would cheat, per se. I was worried that, if something happened, I would rely on you too much and I would lose my best friend again. I realized that with everything that happened with Tim, I hurt more because I had lost my best friend than my boyfriend. So I convinced myself that, if we started something, I would risk losing you as my friend, and I couldn't do that."

"But..."

"*Shhhh.*" Silencing him with a gentle kiss, she continued, "But I was judging the man you are by the child, the boy, Tim was, and that's not fair. It's not fair to the amazing man you are, and it's not fair to me because I know I would be losing out on so much more. I mourned the loss of Tim, but I mourned the loss of our friendship more than the romance. I convinced myself that if I let a relationship develop between us and it didn't work out, the mourning would be a hundred times greater. But not trying, not starting this with you, would forever haunt me."

Tears falling freely now, she clasped Drew's face in both hands.

"You are my best friend, my lover, and my love. Everything I want is wrapped up in you and what we could have together. I love you."

Drew's smile could have lit up the night sky. Moving his hands to mirror hers, he leaned in close. "You are my everything, Valerie. You have been probably since the first moment I saw you. I will never abuse the trust you've given me. I love you so much."

Claiming her mouth with his, they let their touches and their bodies speak their love.

CHAPTER TWENTY-FOUR

*V*alerie spent the next few weeks in a haze of satiated bliss and utter happiness. She had fallen in love with her best friend and knew this time wouldn't see the heartbreak of her past. Drew was his own man and one who was entirely different than the boy Timothy had been. She had changed over the years too, as everyone does. There was a strength to her now that hadn't been there before. Relying on herself and growing up does that to a girl.

All she knew was that, right now, she was happy.

She and Drew had fallen into a normal routine, including splitting time between their respective homes. Drew wasn't happy that she hadn't picked up and moved all of her stuff in with him, but he was dealing with it. Besides, they had to figure out where they were actually going with this relationship. Val knew what she wanted, and she was pretty damn sure she knew what Drew wanted too. He hadn't yet proposed, but she suspected that was only due to him thinking she still needed some time to adjust. She didn't. But there was just enough of a tease in her to make him stew a little while longer. Chelsea thoroughly agreed with her, telling her to hold out in order to make it tougher for him. Her BFF had a definite sadistic streak at times.

Sitting at her desk, she flipped through the mail that had been delivered. Since they were together nightly, driving into work together had become their new norm. It sucked not having a car at her disposal, but it's not like she usually went anywhere during the day. Drew had an early breakfast meeting today with a prospective client, so she was in the office before even Matthew showed up.

The quiet of the office usually settled her. No e-mails chiming in. The phone silent. The lack of hushed conversations. They were all things she relished. But this morning, that sense of calmness eluded her. This wasn't the first time she had been alone in the office since the fire, but for some reason it felt a little eerier to her today.

"Damn. I'm going to need some more coffee." She shook her head hoping it would mentally shake off that unfamiliar feeling and allow her to settle in. Unfortunately that crashed to a halt as she turned over the next envelope in the pile and stopped dead in her tracks. Dread filled her as she recognized the handwriting. She still remembered the first one she received, sent to her house. She had opened it right before Drew showed up on her doorstep the morning after her drunken girls' night. His passion had overtaken her, and she never thought about it again that day. Nor did she tell him. It wasn't until a few days later, when he accidentally saw it, that she told him. It hadn't been pretty. So she hadn't told him about any of the rest of them. This one matched the others she had gotten over the past month or so. The ones that chilled her with their ominous message of regret that she had survived the fire. Words that talked about what would happen to her the next time the person tried something.

Every letter made her re-live those moments when she felt surrounded by heat and flames. Yanking on the door and having it remain stubbornly closed. Thinking, just for a minute, that there wasn't any way out of the trailer. There had been a few nights since the letters started that the dreams of the fire took over. She'd wake with a startled gasp only to realize she was safe and snuggled tightly in Drew's arms.

At least she had done the smart thing and gone to the police with them. But why hadn't she told Drew about the others? And why had she asked Detective Parteleone to not mention anything to the brothers?

Because she was stupid, that's why. Because she was convinced Drew would pack her up and lock her in his apartment tower in the sky to protect her. But was that any reason to be that dumb about this? *No, no it was not. If I die, how am I going to be with Drew forever? Huh? Did you think about that? Until this nutcase is found, maybe it's better to be locked up. With any luck, Drew will lock himself away too, and then we can have sex all the time.*

Fumbling with the letter in her hand, she set it aside without opening it. This one would go to the police as is, unopened. She had given the others to the police, even if she had handled some of them. It's not like she hadn't watched a bunch of crime dramas on TV, no matter what Angela said about them being wrong. She at least knew enough to keep the evidence. Unfortunately she had opened most of them before catching on that she should have left them alone.

Val leaned over and grabbed her purse out of her desk drawer. Opening the top zipper, she reached in for her cell phone. She'd call the police right now, and then she'd call Drew. It was time to let him know the extent of what was going on, because it didn't appear to be stopping, and deal with the inevitable explosion when he found out she'd been hiding this from him. Punching in the code to unlock her phone, she searched for Detective Parteleone's phone number and waited as it rolled over to voicemail. Well, she guessed it was better than nothing as she left a message telling him about this latest letter. Afer hanging up, she was about to call up Drew's name when her text message notification chimed.

Sighing as she saw Evan's name at the top of the message, she briefly glanced away. This wasn't the first message he had sent recently. Far from it. Every day there were more and more. Some friendly, some pleading, some nasty. Ignoring them all had seemed like the best idea at the time. Looking down at the letter, had she been ignoring too much? Could the letters have come from Evan? It didn't look like his handwriting on the envelope. But did that mean it wasn't? Maybe he wrote it with his other hand and that's why it looked different. Her mind whirled with possibilities and out-there theories. As much as she didn't want to believe he would set that fire, a small part of her was doubting the faith she had placed in him. She had gone to the police with the letters but hadn't mentioned anything about Evan's attempts to contact her. The letters started arriving only shortly before his texts had become consistent. Maybe now would be the time to respond back and see what he had to say. At least then she would have something to relay to the cops when she told them about him.

After touching the message icon, she opened the text to read it.

"Val, please. I just want to talk. I'm sure you've seen these, and I'm sorry for some of the things I've said. You're with Drew now, I get it. But can't we just talk for a minute? Just one minute?"

Closing her eyes, Val pondered the wisdom of talking to him. He was all over the place in his texts. She seriously doubted that a minute would be all he wanted, but could it really hurt? *"Fine. You've got one minute."*

Figuring he'd call, she was startled when another text came through.

"I'm outside the door. Can you let me in? I promise it'll be quick. I'll be gone before anyone shows up."

Now she was really conflicted. Talking over the phone was

one thing, but in person? Okay, if it was only a minute she'd deal with it. She got up to move toward the door and paused. Her brain was trying to tell her something, but she couldn't bring it into focus. Crossing through the reception area, she made her way to the main door. Taking a deep breath she turned the lock, opening the door. Evan stood there, a look of pure menace on his face. In that single instant, the thoughts in her brain came into crystal clear focus. *How did he know I was here? Alone?*

She tried to push the door shut, but she wasn't quick enough. Evan's foot slammed into the door, crashing it against the wall. He stalked forward, into the office, forcing her backwards. Menace was splashed across his face as he grabbed her wrists and yanked her toward him.

"I followed you, bitch." Growling down at her, he twisted harder, fingers digging into her wrists. "I saw you practically fuck that piece of shit this morning up against his car as he dropped you off." Evan tugged both of her hands behind her back with one of his. She never realized how strong he was, but she couldn't even budge her hands.

"Evan, please." Hearing the tears in her voice, she begged, "You don't want to do this." Unsure of what he planned on doing, she tried to think that this wasn't the real Evan. How could she have been so wrong and blind when they were dating?

Face pressed up against hers, he snarled. "Oh, I want to do this." Gasping as he pulled her up against his body, she started to shiver. Her fear appeared to please him since he smiled as he spoke. "We're going to talk, but nowhere that fucker or his brothers can bother us. You're coming with me."

Val dug her heels in the plush carpet but found no traction as Evan dragged her away from the threshold of the office. He adjusted the hold he had on her and pulling the door shut behind him. He steered her toward the emergency stairs that let out along the back of the building to an alley that was generally free of people and prying eyes.

Val opened her mouth to let out a scream, only to have Evan's free hand come up and cover it. "Not a sound," he whispered in her ear, and she cringed away from the closeness of his face.

Hands clamped behind her back, mouth covered and tripping on her heels, she was dragged into the stairwell. The back steps were rarely used by tenants, and this early in the morning, they had an ominous feeling to them as the the overhead lights flickered. Val refused to go down without a fight and renewed her struggle. Even with her attempts at disloding his hold, Evan still managed to pull her down the ten flights of steps and out the back door. His truck was parked right in front of the door, leaving no doubt in Val's mind that he had carefully planned this entire thing. He pushed her against the extended cab, pressing her tightly against the metal with his body. Evan had released her hands, but with the weight of his body, they were still ineffective in helping her escape. With his free hand, Evan grabbed open the driver's door and pushed her into the front seat.

Scrambling to cross the seat to the opposite door, she felt a large, roughened hand grab her ankle in a blistering grip. Evan climbed into the driver's seat, never once relaxing his grip, and slammed the door behind him with his free hand. Val made one more lunge for the passenger door, but heard the telltale *click* locking her in.

The sheer terror of the moment immobilized her.She always envisioned herself fighting hard if she was ever grabbed. *I fought in the trailer.* Flashing back in time, she realized she had overcome her terror then and had found the fight to break the window. She could do the same now, and began to kick her feet blindly behind her. She heard the grunt when her heel connected with his thigh. She wasn't quick enough though, as Evan's weight landed on her once again. Pressed face first onto the seat, she did her best to kick and squirm away. But between his weight and the rope he was effectively wrapping around her wrists, her hopes of fleeing were taking a beating. Easing his weight up slightly, he shoved her onto the floorboard of the passenger seat. Stuffing a bandana in her mouth, Evan pushed her head down with an unyielding grip.

"Now we're going someplace to talk. You keep your bitch head down and don't make noise."

Firing up the truck, Evan sped down the alleyway. Away from safety and away from Drew. Val just had to hope Drew would find her before whatever Evan was capable of came about.

YELLING at whoever was behind the closing doors, Drew picked up the pace to make it in time. "Hey! Hold that elevator!"

"Do I have to?"

"Not on my account."

Fucking family. His smartass brothers were really going to let those doors close on him. "Son of a bitch!"

"Ohhhh, I'm telling Mom what he called her." Laughing hysterically, Jon stuck his hand through the doors with just enough time to prevent them from blocking him out. Apparently, Drew was just the source of his brothers' entertainment, as usual, since even taciturn Matt was grinning.

But he really didn't care. Nothing could sour his mood. He'd woken up with his arms full of his woman, enjoyed an early morning blow job and shower sex, and then a damn fine breakfast meeting. Today was shaping up to be a winner. Now, if he could just convince Val to get a little freaky in his office at lunch, he would call himself a lucky man. Well, a luckier man.

So far, she was reluctant to do that with his brothers and Pamela within hearing distance, but he held out hope.

"Mom would never believe I would say that." Slapping his brother on the back of his head, he leaned back against the wall of the elevator. Well, he was partially right. His mom would definitely believe he'd speak like that, but never about her. She knew the boys she raised, and hearing "bad" language was part and parcel of their personality. Growing up around construction sites tended to do that to a man.

They bickered back and forth about nonsense as the elevator made the slow climb up to their offices on the tenth floor. The stairs would have probably been quicker at this rate, but lately the lights had been flickering and the landlord had yet to heed the many complaints and actually resolve the issue. With the unreliable stairwell lighting, he preferred not risking a limb just getting to work on a daily basis. Though at times the elevator didn't seem like a better option.

The car came to a final, shuddering stop and the doors slowly peeled open. Drew would be so glad when their new place was finally completed and they moved in. Two floors and no "hope it actually makes its way up" elevator. *Bliss.*

As they walked leisurely down the hall, the topic of the lab proposal was the center of discussion. Looked like they had the inside track on that one, but there was one other fierce competitor. Supposedly, there would be a decision soon, but it wasn't stopping the three of them from doing everything they could to make their bid the most attractive. Drew was convinced that the work Jon had done to learn about a lab was going to push the decision in their favor. But even with all the promising comments coming their way, they just didn't know which way everything would come down.

"I'm sure there will be another e-mail about the bid in my inbox. Seems they come daily." Matt was scrolling through his e-mails on his phone as he spoke. "There it is. I'll take a look when I get to my desk." Stopping in his tracks, Matt sighed and a frown marred his face. "Oh, look. Something from Lewis again. When the fuck is that building done?"

Things hadn't gotten better at the Lewis site since the fire. Though they hadn't gotten that much worse. Instead, just a steady deluge of nonsense and frustration. And since Lewis and his son had the ear of Matt's in-laws, there was no end Matt got to hear about it constantly from Cassandra. At least Drew had a bright spot to give his brother.

"We have the inspectors coming on Friday for the final walkthrough. Damn, Matt, is that a smile I see?" Teasing his brother was something he did openly. Though sadly, Matt didn't always see the humor.

"Yes, it is, brother." Smiling some more, he grabbed the office door and pushed it open. "The sooner that building is theirs to deal with, the happier I will be."

"Pamela, darling. How are you this fine morning?" Jon went over and leaned his elbows on the high counter of the receptionist desk where Pamela sat. Drew tried not to appear antsy as all he really wanted to do was head back and lay a hello kiss on Val's sweet lips. But he was still a civilized man and knew enough to greet their longtime receptionist first.

"I'd be better if I didn't show up to an empty office with an unlocked door. Scared the crap out of me, I have to admit." Standing, she pointed toward the door they had just walked through. Even from there, Drew could see that there was something off. The door wasn't sitting right in the frame at all. "I think it's even broken, don't you?"

Drew started to walk toward the door when Pamela's words penetrated his brain. "Wait a minute. What do you mean empty office? Val should be here. And she wouldn't have left without locking the door."

Matt made his way to the door and peered at the frame. He shook his head and pulled the door open again. "The hinge looks bent." He leaned down to look closer. "And the frame molding is broken." Matt pulled a piece of the molding off in his hand as he spoke. "I didn't even notice that there was something wrong when we came in."

A spear of worry and fear shot through Drew. He could imagine Val taking off to feed her designer coffee habit, but the unlocked and damaged door didn't flow with that theory.

Pamela turned a worried glance his way. "Val's not here. I went back by her desk when I came in and saw the door, but she wasn't sitting there. I just figured she was running a few minutes late. It didn't dawn on me she would be coming in early before your meeting." Ringing her hands together in front of her, she continued, "I guess it should have since you've been coming in together lately. I should have called you when I got here."

Drew turned on his heel and hurried back to Val's desk. He could hear Matt trying to calm Pamela down, while Jon was breathing down his back as he came to a stop at her empty desk. Stepping around it, Drew stood behind her chair. Mail was sorted into piles, with one addressed to her set aside. The bottom desk drawer was pulled out with her open purse lying inside. The computer was on but it didn't look like she had logged in yet, or maybe it had just gone back to sleep. Her cell phone rested silently in the center of her desk.

A chill snaked down his spine as he took in the silent tableau. Val would have never left without her cell phone or purse. An ominous feeling was slowly settling in his stomach.

"Fuck."

Drew looked up to see worry marring Jon's face. He must have had the same troubling thoughts. But Val was Drew's to protect. She was his woman, and he couldn't shake the fear that she was in trouble. There had been too much going on lately, with her at the center of it. And he didn't like where everything seemed to be heading.

Matt walked back into the inner office area, with Detective Parteleone in tow.

"Andrew, I think you should sit down." The concern in Matt's voice did nothing to allay the terror that had taken root. He slunk down into Val's chair without even realizing it. Not that the muscles in his legs could keep him upright at this point.

"Mr. Stephens. Drew." Concern was etched on Detective Parteleone's face. "Ms. Milner left me a voicemail this morning and since I was nearby when I got it, I decided to come over and speak with her in person. Your brother tells me she's not here."

"What about?" Drew couldn't think of anything that was bothering Val. At least not about the investigation that involved the detective. Sure she was still struggling with thinking about moving in with him, but it wasn't like the police could do anything about that.

"She still hasn't mentioned anything to you about the letters, has she?"

"*Letters?*" The detective nodded at his question. "There was that one letter, but that's it."

The detective glanced at his brothers and received nothing but blank stares back. Seemed like his woman wasn't sharing everything with him, which was fine if it was girl stuff that was better shared with Chelsea. But when it was something that had prompted her to call the cops? *Oh, fuck no.* That shit was something he needed to know. He never wanted to spank a woman for punishment, but that was changing right about now. Guess that was part of that previously unknown dominant streak Valerie had dragged out of him.

Resting a hip against Val's desk, Detective Parteleone seemed to weigh his words. "I've been in contact with Ms. Milner a few weeks now about multiple letters she had been receiving recently about the fire. More specifically, they expressed regret that she survived, and hinted at what could still happen to her.

She left me a message this morning about receiving another one."

Bile worked its way up Drew's throat. He re-lived the terror he felt during the fire. "What do you mean multiple? She got one. She found it when she moved back into her place a few weeks ago." A sharp pain stabbed at his heart. Did she still not trust him to stick by her? Was this just another way she held herself back? He thought they had overcome all of that, but for her to keep something like this from him? Maybe he was wrong and kidding himself.

"Stop it!" Jon's expression revealed he knew where his mind had gone. "She absolutely trusts you. She's a stubborn woman though." Jon squeezed his shoulder in support. "She probably just didn't want to stress you out. You've already been the king of overprotectiveness since the fire, this would have compounded it."

The detective nodded and chuckled.

How the fuck could he chuckle at a time like this? Before Drew could call him on his callousness, the man spoke, "She had said as much when I suggested she tell you." Leaning forward, he pointed to the letter addressed to Valerie. "Her voicemail indicated that she was going to finally mention them to you. Guess she couldn't hide it if I showed up here." Pulling gloves out of a small kit he carried, along with a paper bag labeled "Evidence," he donned the gloves as he continued talking, "Apparently this one was the straw that broke the camel's back." Lifting the envelope gently by the corner, he took a look at the outside. "Anyone have a letter opener so I can keep the seal intact for the lab?"

Drew wasn't going to be of much use since he was sitting there stunned. The fire investigation wasn't bad enough, now he was dealing with threats that the love of his life had tried to handle on her own. Yes, he loved that she was a strong, independent woman. He didn't want that to change, but he was there to support her, to make her feel safer. He needed her to realize that she could come to him about anything and he wouldn't turn her away.

He watched as Matt rummaged through the pen holder on Val's desk and passed the opener to the cop. Slowly, he ran the edge under the corner of the flap and sliced the envelope open. He read it silently and then turned it. Drew realized both of his brothers had formed a wall behind him, Jon's hand still resting on his shoulder. He gasped as he read the letter, as Jon's hand tightened and Matt's growl let him know exactly what his brothers were thinking and feeling.

You're not safe, bitch. Don't think you are. You think I'd let a Stephens bitch survive? Whole fuckin' family needs to go. Next time, you'll burn for sure, or maybe that bastard you're fucking.

Drew froze at the hate that palpably leaped off the page. His heart clenched thinking about Val dealing with the other letters on her own. *Why, baby? Why didn't you trust me? As a lover or friend, you didn't trust me.* "She should have trusted me."

"I guess now would be a bad time to ask why you didn't trust your brothers enough to tell them about the first one." Matt's words dripped with sarcasm and just a little bit of hurt. "Because I'm thinking it's just about the same thing."

That caught his attention. Matt was right. He damn near lost his mind when Val had shown him that first letter, but to him it was all about her. Her safety. Why the hell hadn't he told his brothers? "Damn. Matt, I…".

"We don't need to go there now. One thing at a time."

Drew was having a hard time keeping it together, but his brother was right. He could deal with this later. He had to be strong. Right now, he needed to have one focus, one goal. Find Val before anything happened to her.

"So, where is Ms. Milner?" The detective's words brought Drew back to the present and the situation they were dealing with at the office.

"I don't know." Watching the letter get placed into the evidence bag along with the envelope, he lost his train of thought. A shake of his head later, he was refocused. "I left her here around seven a.m. as I headed off to a breakfast meeting. My brothers and I all arrived back at the office at the same time, and she was already gone. But her cell phone and purse are still here." As he repeated what happened with Pamela, the detective got up and moved toward the reception area.

Drew stood to follow. Matt grabbed him with an arm around the shoulders. "I'm not going to say don't worry, 'cause that's just stupid. Just know we'll find her and get this letter shit taken care of."

As Pamela showed the detective the damaged front door, Drew could sense that his concern was ratcheting up. Detective Parteleone was just about to make his way back across the room, when he stopped and stared down at the carpet. Drew tracked his gaze and noticed the glint off the light beige carpet blanketing the reception area floor. Squatting down, the detective put on a new glove before retrieving the item.

"Does this look familar to anyone?" Drew gazed down at the outstretched hand and open palm.

Laying in the detective's big hand was a fragile gold bracelet with a star charm hanging from it. Just this morning, he'd run his fingers over the delicate jewelry as Val's hand rested on his chest. Drew's wordless nod must have told the detective everything he needed to know.

"Could the letters have come from her ex?" Matt inquired. As far as Drew knew, they hadn't made any headway into the search for the arsonist.

Detective Parteleone was dropping the bracelet into another bag as he answered, "Mr. Kinner has been ruled out as a suspect, for the fire at least. His alibi is pretty much airtight. Apparently he was at some sci-fi convention that was being held in the District. Between the people he was there with and the social media pictures, there was no way he was anywhere in the area when the trailer was set on fire." Parteleone moved back toward the door, as if to exit. "That doesn't rule him out of what happened at her house. At this time, we can't connect the two incidents. But we can't separate them either."

"So what does that mean now? Where is she? Does someone have her?" Drew's mind was whirling a mile a minute.

"Well, it could be that she left for whatever reason. " Holding out a hand to stop Drew's words, he continued, "But from the little I know of her, that doesn't seem to be something she would do. Are there security cameras around the building that we can check?"

Matt spoke up first, "There is one by all of the exits." He was already pushing buttons on Pamela's phone when he spoke again. "I'm calling down to building security to see if we can take a look."

"Excellent. That may give us some answers." Parteleone swiped a finger across his cell phone to unlock it. "I hate to say that the letter could have something to do with her disappearance, but it's a possibility." He stopped scrolling and looked up. "I may specialize in arson investigations, but I'm still a cop. And this whole thing is beginning to sound a lot bigger than originally thought. I'm going to get some guys out looking for your girl."

Jon came forward from the back office, holding up Val's cell phone. "I think you need to see this." He moved next to the detective, and Drew came over on his other side.

"How the hell did you..." Drew began.

"Know her passcode?" Jon shrugged, "I'm brilliant." At Drew's scowl he shook his head, "Lucky guess. It's your birthdate."

Jon displayed the text messages from this morning, and Drew's stomach dropped.

CHAPTER TWENTY-FIVE

*S*ometimes it paid to follow the people that you weren't really interested in.

He had spent enough time recently watching his marks. All he got from that was endless hours of watching them on top of each other. Like they were fucking animals. He tried to think of his beauty every time he saw them pawing each other. But some days that made it worse.

He would never treat her like that. She deserved such gentleness, to match her tender soul. Not that savagery that he witnessed.

Enough about that now. He needed to focus.

They had arrived together at the office this morning. As they had been doing for weeks. It disgusted him that one of those bastards was happy when he was here, his beauty out of reach. At least for the time being.

Just as he was about to leave, that big jackass he had seen on the street that night by the restaurant showed up. Not that he hadn't been keeping tabs on him too. It was amazing to him that someone would just open up to him, a stranger, at the local coffee place. But even that had been an exercise in futility. This guy hadn't given him anything except a headache with all of his talk about that bitch.

Though he would agree with his new friend on that description.

Almost anyone connected with this damn family was a bitch.

He sat there, hidden in the shadows of the parking garage, watching him walk to the front entrance of the building. Stepping out of his car, he walked along his garage level, in the direction his new friend had come from.

There was a truck parked near the back entrance. Was it his?

He waited a little longer. Just as he was about to leave, the door came crashing open.

A smile bloomed on his face at what he witnessed. The bitch was getting dragged to the truck and shoved inside. Even from a distance he could see the terror in her eyes.

Everything settled in him at that instant.

Maybe it wasn't all in his hands, but he would take what he could get. The thought of that bastard losing what he thought was his. That set his soul free.

There was still more to do. His mission wasn't finished yet, not by a long shot. But at least he would see to their pain.

CHAPTER TWENTY-SIX

Stephens
CONSTRUCTION

*V*al sat huddled in the plush chair in Evan's living room. Her gaze followed Evan's every movement as he paced before her. The ride from the office to his house was one long diatribe about how she had ruined him and destroyed his love for her. This was a completely different person than the one she thought she had known. Sure, there were some weird moments when they were dating, but nothing that could have predicted this behavior.

Arms flailing wildly, Evan kept up a steady stream of dialogue with himself. He barely glanced her way, and she wasn't even sure if he remembered she was still there. Maybe, if she was careful enough, she could start to move away. It would be hard with her hands tied behind her, but her feet were free, so she had that to work with. Her balance would be thrown off, but it was better than just sitting there and waiting. As he turned away from her, Val started a slow slide to the front of the seat.

Having eyes in the back of his head apparently, Evan spun around and stalked toward her. Maybe he hadn't forgotten her presence. Grabbing her hair with one meaty fist, he snapped her head back and yanked the gag from her mouth. "Where the fuck do you think you're going?" Tightening his hold on the strands, he pulled again. "I told you we're going to talk."

Swallowing down the bile that had built up as he loomed over her, Val could only stare at him. She didn't dare try to move her head with the death grip he had on her hair. "Ummm, okay." She would go along with whatever he wanted right now in the hopes that it would make him calm. Moistening her lips with her tongue, she tried to speak again. "What about?"

Evan's free hand roared back and Val closed her eyes, waiting for the blow to strike her face. When seconds passed and it didn't come, she slowly blinked them open. Evan was clenching and unclenching his fist as it seemed it took every ounce of strength for him to not make the connection with her cheek. "Bitch." He spat at her. "Don't make me hurt you." As his fist opened, Val took a deep breath. For this second anyway, she was safe. Though she wasn't sure that would last. She just had to keep hoping for the best.

"Why did you cheat on me, you whore?" The hand in her hair grew tighter again, forcing all of her attention squarely to him. The pain slicing through her head from his grip was slowly becoming overwhelming.

"I didn't."

"I saw you! Saw you out with him." Using his grip to drag her closer to his face, she was barely sitting in the chair. As she took in Evan's bloodshot eyes and the veins pulsing in his neck, she could feel the anger and hatred pulsing off of him. "Saw you fuck him. Humping him like the cheating slut you are."

Tears clouding her eyes again, Val attempted to shake her head. "No, Evan. Never when we were together." Maybe, if she could just get him to accept that she hadn't cheated on him, he would calm slightly.

Dragging her fully to her feet, he reached his free hand behind her and pushed her body into his. She could feel his erection against her belly and his hot breath on her neck as he leaned in toward her. "We're still together. Nothing is going to take you away from me." Sliding his lips along her neck, Val tried her best to disguise the shiver of disgust that ran through her body. "You're mine, and that bastard isn't going to take you from me." The band of his arm tightened around her body, and she could barely move as he continued his assault on her neck. "I'll show you why we were meant to be together, baby. I'll show you, and you'll love it."

Val almost wished that violent Evan was back because this one nauseated her. She tried to struggle, tried to work her body away from his, but the hold he had was too strong. A deceptive strength, since she never expected him to have this type of power. But it was cutting off all avenues of her movement, and she struggled to find another way to free herself. Maybe she could get him to talk now and buy her some time, and some space. She needed some space.

"Please, Evan." Letting sweetness invade her speech, she tried to cajole him. "I thought you wanted to talk. Can't we talk?" Nothing would stop the tears, but her voice didn't relay her fears. At least in her mind it didn't.

Dragging his lips up to her ear, Evan whispered, "Nope. Time for talking has passed. I'm making you mine again and getting the stench of that Stephens bastard off of you." The hand at her back started to snake under her top. The feel of his hand along her skin felt like a million bugs crawling over her. Despite the pain in her head and the hold he had on her, she fought back.

"Evan, please!" she screamed. "Please, stop." Twisting with a jerk that violently wrenched her head, she brought her leg up and slammed her shoe heel onto his foot. A howl of pain pierced her ears as the hand in her hair dropped. Seeing her opportunity, Val made a lunge for the door only to feel herself be dragged back. Letting her body go limp, Val started to fall forward with Evan looming over her.

The thunder of a door being slammed open accompanied a roar that reverberated through the living room. Looking up, Drew pushed through the busted front door, barreling past a police officer with weapon drawn. Murder in his eyes as he saw Evan pinning her to the ground, he stalked toward them, ignoring every officer in his way.

Cops shouted all around them, telling everyone to stay where they were. That was easy for her, as Val felt helpless lying on the ground unable to move. That soon changed when that giant weight was lifted off of her with seemingly little effort. She rolled to her back, confident the danger was under control. What she saw was an avenging angel. Drew gripped Evan by the collar, flinging him away from her like he weighed little more than a bug.

The rage that was alight in Drew's eyes was only matched by Evan's. Brushing himself off, he stood and charged straight at Drew's chest. Wanting to scream out, but not wanting to distract him, Val forced herself to be quiet. She couldn't steal Drew's attention away from Evan.

Standing his ground, Evan's punch landed squarely on Drew's face. Grappling with him, Drew kicked a leg out behind Evan and took him to the ground. Drew grabbed the front of his shirt and hauled him up again, only to rear his fist back and connect squarely with the middle of his face. Evan let out a pained grunt and collapsed onto the floor, eyes closing as he fell.

Not bothering to wait another second, Val struggled to pull herself up into a sitting position and threw herself at Drew. Tears blurring her vision, she felt herself being taken up in loving arms and rocked gently.

"Oh, baby." Strong, gentle hands smoothed down her hair as he peppered kisses over her head. She felt another set of hands behind her and suddenly her arms were free. Flinging them around Drew, she held on. "I'm here, beautiful. You're okay. We're okay."

Sobs were wrenched from her as she finally let go, and all the fear she had tried to hold in came free. Drew's arms were safety, but they were also so much more. This was why he had always felt so right to her. She was home in his arms, somewhere where she could be vulnerable and safe. He was her somewhere that she could always come to and know that she was loved.

As her sobs abated and the power of her feelings took over, she voiced the words that were bubbling up within her, "I love you."

"I know." Wiping the tears from her eyes, Drew looked down at her with tears in his own. "I was so scared, beautiful. So scared." She could see the depth of his worry and despair as he spoke. She had caused that, not only by what happened with Evan, but by not talking to him. By taking so long to tell him what had been holding her back, she made him doubt her. As she stroked his hair, to convey her feelings, he continued, "I love you too. So very much."

They stayed huddled on the floor as the police went to work around them. EMTs came to check over a now groggy and very subdued Evan. Eventually, they moved to the couch as Detective Parteleone came in accompanied by a new investigator. As Valerie relayed the story, she could feel the anger and indignation pouring off of Drew next to her. A part of her was glad the police had already escorted Evan away because she was afraid of what Drew would have done if he was still in the same room, although a small part of her sort of wanted to see it.

The conversation didn't get any easier when Detective Parteleone brought up the letters. She chanced a look at Drew. *Oh, boy!* Her man was not happy about them. She was a little afraid she heard the word "spanking" mumbled under his breath. She had to have been wrong about that though. Turning her head, she peered at Drew. A gleam in his eyes shown back at her. *On second thought, maybe not.*

What felt like days later, but was only an hour, she was allowed to leave after securing a promise to be at the police station the following morning bright and early. They had tried to pressure her into going tonight, but Drew was like a dog with a bone and would not budge on taking her home. "Don't worry, she'll be there, but now I am taking her home."

As much as she wanted to get it over with, she was grateful. She just wanted to be home, even if it was Drew's home. Wherever he was, was her home now.

She took one step before she was swept up into strong arms. A smile spread across her mouth as she looked up into the face of the man she loved. Unfortunately, his mouth was drawn into a frown.

"We have some talking to do." Those damn letters were going to come back and haunt her. "Not here, not with everyone around. I need to know why you didn't tell me."

It looked like her day was definitely not over yet.

DREW GENTLY PACKED her into his car, doing everything in his power to hold on to his temper. It would have been ideal if he could have whaled on that jackass Evan some more, but the cops broke it up pretty quick. At least that way he would have been able to take out his agresssion on the true culprit. Now he was left with the woman he loved, who also managed to hide from him the fact she was being stalked.

He was not happy, to say the least.

They rode in silence to his condo. Drew was too much in his own thoughts to speak and he wasn't about to have the conversation when he was driving. No, he wanted them both free from distractions when they tackled this. And tackle it they would.

He thought they had gotten over the trust thing when they talked about her ex. Obviously they hadn't if this was what she did. He loved her and knew she loved him, but he couldn't have a relationship where she didn't trust him. Eventually that would kill everything they felt between them.

The silence continued even after they were in his apartment, a heavy pressure pushing down on him. If he didn't know better he would have thought he was having a heart attack. Was this what it felt like when your world came crashing down? *No.* He gritted his teeth. He wouldn't think like that. They could talk this out.

He took a seat, the same place he sat those weeks ago waiting for Val so they could go on their first date. It felt like he'd been waiting for her his whole life, and maybe he had. It's funny how you don't even know what you want one minute and the next everything you want is right in front of you.

Say something, you fool. What? His shoes seemed infinitely fascinating, so he'd just sit here and stare until something came to him. He didn't even know where to begin. Lucky for him, he didn't have to.

"I'm sorry."

Val's hand captured his and lifted it to her lips. The feather-like kiss she placed over his bruised knuckles kicked him in the gut.

"They're fine." Until she touched his hand, the bruising there hadn't even penetrated his brain. Now he could feel the sting, but still, it was the least aching part of his body at the moment. He only wished his heart ached as little as his hand.

"That's not what I'm sorry about."

She reached out a hand and cupped his face, turning his head toward her. God, she was beautiful. Even after everything she'd been through today, there was a glow about her. It shown brightest for him, but it was there in all her relationships. This was the woman he needed in his life. He just needed to know she trusted him, because right now if felt a hell of a lot like she didn't.

"Why?"

That was it. He just wanted to know why.

"There is no good reason. I was stupid." Her gaze caught his as she continued. "I was scared. Not of you and me, but of moving too quick. You wanted to drag me back to your place after the first letter. Are you going to sit here and tell me that wouldn't have definitely happened if you knew about the others?"

If he was asking for honesty from her, he had to give it in return. "No. I would have packed your stuff up myself."

She brushed her lips across his before she spoke again. "I know, and it wouldn't have really made me any safer. It wouldn't have stopped the letters. It just would have put us on such a fast track that I was worried what would happen." He reached out to brush her hair behind her ear and she leaned into him. "If I let myself, I would have leaned completely on you."

"I don't see the harm in that. It's what you're supposed to do."

"But I did it once before and it blew up in my face. Even though I told you all about what happened with Timothy, before I told you about the letter, my head still had a hard time believing that things wouldn't blow up again. Only this time it would have been so much more devastating to me, because you are so much more important to me."

Drew tried to wrap his head around everything she was saying. Maybe it was foreign to him because he hadn't gone through what she had. Who was he to doubt her fears and worries?

"You can't do that again." He took her face in both of his hands, gently stroking her cheeks. "You can't *not* trust me, not share with me." There was no way he'd survive that a second time.

She mirrored his hold and then tunneled her hands through his hair. "Never."

They gazed deep into each other's eyes for long moments. What he saw told him everything he needed to know. She was his. Sure there may be moments when her worries jump between them, but it wasn't going to be anything they couldn't tackle. They were in this together, they just needed to remember that.

He had almost lost her today. Now it was time to lose themselves in each other.

He reached for her hand and led her upstairs and straight back to his bedroom. They took their time, slowly undressing each other. So often their need for each other's bodies had taken over. This time, need for each other's heart, their soul, was leading the way. There was no rush, no race this time. Now was all about building their future and it started with long, slow love-making that connected more than their bodies. Deep, soulful kisses and sensation-provoking caresses carried them on a wave of passion. They lost themselves in each other, and yet they found themselves in each other.

Later, the room only lit by the soft bedside light, Drew disentangled himself from Val and leaned over the bed.

"Come back here."

"In a second." He fumbled for his pants, reaching into the pocket and pulling out what he sought. He curled back around her and placed his open palm in front her. Her gasp told him she saw what he was holding. He laid the bracelet that had fallen off in the struggle against her wrist and re-latched the slightly mangled clasp. Drawing her hand to his mouth, Drew kissed the star that lay nestled at her wrist.

"This star brought you back to me. It's always going to lead me to you."

Her hand stroked the star and tears spilled down her cheeks.

239

She twisted around, their bodies skin to skin, but more importantly, heart to heart.

"Always. You are my star, Drew. I love you."

Kissing her lips gently, he whispered, "I love you."

They fell back into each other's arms and kisses; Drew knew this was just the beginning. They would always be best friends, but now they both knew they could be so much more.

EPILOGUE
FIVE MONTHS LATER

*D*rew looked around at everyone gathered. Friends and family alike were crammed into Chelsea's townhouse, and no one seemed to care that maybe the space was a little small for the amount of people. There wasn't one person without a smile and joy in their eyes. Drew certainly didn't care. He had everything he wanted, and they were there to celebrate that fact.

"Don't you look smug?" Jon slapped him on the back as he sidled up next to him. "Thinking about all those gifts you got?"

"The only gift I need is the one I get to unwrap on a nightly basis." Gaze straying to find his beautiful fiancée among the crowd, he homed in on her. Winking her way, he could see the faint blush that stained her cheeks.

"Okay, stop being so disgustingly happy. It's depressing the rest of us." Jon laughed as he said it, though Drew could sense there was some truth to his statement. Jon seemed to be looking for more than a casual relationship, but he wasn't finding the person that called to him. It was only a matter of time though. It took him years to find his perfect fit, and she'd been right in front of him the whole time. Jon would find his too, and when he did, Drew would sit back and laugh at him as he fell. What's good for the goose and all that.

"I can't help it." And Drew wouldn't even want to try. His life was fucking wonderful, and he was happy beyond measure. Sure there was still the mess with Evan that had to go to court and put his beautiful Val through it all again, but he'd be there for her and they would get through it. The letters hadn't stopped though, and that made them all more alert. Some were directed at the company, even to him and his brothers. But it was the ones that still came to Val that had him the most concerned. He played off the ones that focused on him. But he would never brush off the threat to his woman. Though Val seemed to be more worried about him than herself. She was probably going to drive him crazy over the course of their lives, but he would relish every second of it. Everyone seemed to be at a loss as to why they were getting them and who was behind it. But that was all in the hands of the police now, and he had to hope they were doing their job. Right now, all he wanted to think about was the woman across the room and getting a ring on her hand to make it official.

Laughing, Jon slapped him on the back. "No, I guess you can't." Picking up a bruschetta from the tray in front of him, he popped it into his mouth.

A screech of rage came from the kitchen area. A loud, familiar screech. So maybe there was one person who wasn't smiling at being a part of the festivities. Jon turned to Drew with a look of *what could that possibly be* disgust on his face.

"Please, Matthew," Cassandra said on a huff. "It's not like there is any worthwhile reason for us to be here. We made an appearance, and now we need to go. Mother asked us over for dinner."

Drew watched his brother try to usher Cassandra into

someplace relatively free from prying eyes. Of course, that didn't stop the prying ears that could hear every high-pitched complaint.

"This is my brother's engagement party. I told you we weren't going to your mother's when she damn well fucking knew the party was tonight. I don't give a shit if she's pissed. If you're pissed. If anyone is pissed."

At this rate, his brother was going to have a coronary. Drew looked at Jon and they both moved toward them. For support, or possibly to toss that bitch out on her ear, either one.

"You can't make me stay here, Matthew. It's like I'm being asked to spend time with the riffraff in a place that isn't worth it."

Riff raff? Who the fuck did she think she was? Sure, she came from some money, but none of them were among the rich and famous. In Cassandra's mind and estimation though, she was far above the lowly lot of them.

"Well, fuck you, your highness." Chelsea stormed up to Cassandra with hands on hips. If nothing else, this would probably be entertaining. "Who the fuck invited you? I'm fairly certain I just invited oldest hottie and son. There was no 'nagging, ungrateful bitch' on the invitation." Turning around she caught her husband's eye. "You saw that I didn't invite this thing, right?"

The look of pure rage and indignation on Cassandra's face was a thing of beauty. Next to Drew, Jon tried, unsuccessfully, to cover a laugh. That earned him an elbow to the gut from their dad who had come up beside them. Whether to watch the show or support Matthew, Drew wasn't certain.

"How dare you!" Cassandra looked like she wanted to rip the hair out of Chelsea's head.

Leaning over, Drew whispered to his dad and brother, "My money is on Chelsea. That girl is crazy."

"Oh, I dare. If my house isn't good enough for your pompous ass, get out." With that, Chelsea stormed over and opened the door. "Now." The welcome had completely left her face and a chill had settled in. "You are not ruining this party for my friend, and you will if you don't leave because I will fuck you up."

Cassandra turned to Matthew as if expecting him to support her. With every fiber of Drew's being he hoped that Matt took a stand.

"Go home, Cassandra. Or go to your parents'." Pushing a hand through his hair, Matt sighed. "I really don't give a shit where you go."

Cassandra grabbed her purse and moved toward the door. The chance of her leaving without parting words were slim though. "You'll pay for this, Matthew." Slamming the door after her retreating form, Chelsea turned to the group of them.

"Well, how did you like the entertainment portion of the party? I thought at first some strippers, but said, 'Hey, why not a crazy bitch instead?'"

Walking up to Matthew, Chelsea surprised everyone when she wrapped him in a hug. "I make a joke because it's what I do. You deserve so much more than the misery that woman gives you. I see the joy on your brother's face and hope that, one day, you will have that too." Looking like she was close to tears, she kissed his cheek. "And your son is off playing with your mom. He didn't see anything."

Rick came up behind her, and she leaned into her husband's embrace. They quietly left the room, leaving the four Stephens men to look at each other.

"C'mon, son. We're going to have a drink and talk." Their dad wrapped a comforting arm around Matt's shoulders and led him away.

Drew just stared at Jon, almost not knowing where to begin

to get things back on track. At least Val was still out in the living room, hopefully unaware of the ridiculousness that had occurred. It did seem that most of the guests were blissfully preoccupied with talking, food, and drinks. Thank God for small favors. Somehow, he didn't think the gossip wouldn't spread though as the party progressed.

"So, I guess we're full speed ahead on the lab project."

Jon seemed to focus on the first thought that came to mind. They had won the bid last month and were still dealing with some red tape, but overall they were finally getting ready to move forward. Drew knew that Jon was looking forward to it. A definite challenge for him since this was a whole new design concept they had taken on. But if anyone was up for it, it would definitely be Jon. Drew turned back to him, ready to speak, when his brother's eyes went wide.

"Who is that?"

Following his line of sight led him back to Valerie...and the newcomer she was talking with. "That's Angela. She lives down the street here. Apparently, Chelsea and Valerie have brought her into the inner girlfriend circle." With fascination, he watched as Jon took in every detail of the woman across the room. His gaze ate her up like he had never seen a woman before. According to Val, Angela wasn't the most comfortable of women around men for whatever reason, and with the way Jon was staring at her, Drew was afraid that she'd be more uncomfortable than ever.

As if sensing his gaze, Angela angled her head slightly away from the conversation and froze. Val's faint flush of before was no match for the color rising along Angela's pale skin. With a quick word to Val, she pivoted on her heel and left, which caused Valerie to stare in their direction.

Jon stood there looking shell-shocked. "I have to meet her."

Seeing Jon's expression, Drew couldn't suppress a grin. It

looked like his baby brother was about to dive into the most challenging "project" of his life, and Drew couldn't wait to see what he designed.

The End

AFTERWORD

If you enjoyed In Case You Didn't Know,
please consider leaving a review on your favorite platform.

Join me for Angela and Jon's story in **Break On Me**,
coming August 4th, 2020.
Order Here
and read on for an excerpt

EXCERPT: BREAK ON ME

STEPHENS BROTHERS BOOK TWO

SHEA BRIGHTON

STEPHENS BROTHERS
BOOK 2

Break on Me

Angela Corcoran is perfectly content with her life. Okay, maybe perfectly is a stretch. Or content for that matter. Sure she has her career as a forensic scientist. She has her hobbies too, and they're awesome. Who needs love? Apparently, her new friends think she does. They're determined she live a little, and that includes a man. A gorgeous man. A much younger man. Like she has any idea what to do with one of those.

His entire life, Jonathan Stephens believed he would find "the one," just like his dad. He lets growing the family business consume him, but the hope is always there, nestled in the back of his mind, and it explodes to the forefront with one glance across a crowded room. She's it. Finally. He's found her. Too bad she hopes he'll get lost.

Angela finds herself the focus of a man who has attacked before, when one of her cases takes a weird and dangerous turn. As her world explodes around her, she finds solace in Jon, who's joined her in the crosshairs as the growing threat to Stephens Construction and Jon's family makes him a target too. With danger closing in, Angela falls back on her old habits and pulls back from Jon, determined to protect her heart. But Jon won't back down, even when violence comes for them. He's found his angel, and he's never letting her go.

CHAPTER ONE

"Seriously? What the hell is taking so long?"

Angela Corcoran fiddled with the strap of her purse as she waited for the elevator doors to open and sighed that the day still wasn't over. Today had been crazy from the word *go*. It had started off with over-sleeping and missing her normal bus to work, and then she wound up getting a call mid-morning that she would be needed to meet with detectives about a case this afternoon. Before it had hit nine o'clock, her day had been shot all to hell, which meant she wouldn't get as much done on the pile of cases on her desk as she thought. Two unanticipated meetings later, and she still had no case work done and barely enough time to race across town to meet with the cops.

God forbid she have any time to eat. *A skipped meal wouldn't kill me.* Feeling the slight pinch of the waistband of her skirt, she cringed. She wasn't unbearably uncomfortable, but the fit could definitely be better. She could do with losing a little—okay a lot—of weight, but skipping meals wasn't the way to do it. She was so damn hungry.

Grabbing her phone out of her purse, she checked the time.

Four forty-five. She was definitely a long way from the cup of coffee and banana at seven when she'd gotten in to work. What she wanted more than anything in the world was to go home and cocoon herself in silence. It wasn't that she was anti-social, but sometimes, when things didn't go the way she had planned or organized, she just wanted to crawl away from the world. Instead, she was on her way to a meeting with the construction company charged with building the new lab.

Apparently, she would be their "subject matter expert" for the DNA lab. Did anyone ask her if she wanted more to do? Of course not. But her boss was infinitely lazy and had likely decided he couldn't be bothered, so he passed it along to her. At the last minute. On a Friday afternoon. It wasn't like she had plans for the night, but it would have been nice to have some forewarning.

The one benefit of this task was that her new friend Valerie worked for the construction company. The new lab would be nice too, but that was still a far-distant thing. As one of her co-workers always said, when dealing with the government, take the time something was supposed to be completed by and double it. At the very least. They weren't moving into the lab for years at this rate.

The elevator doors finally slid open on a loud *ping*. Cautiously stepping into the car, Angela was a little afraid it wouldn't make it up to the tenth floor. Val mentioned Stephens Construction was building their own office building, which made her feel slightly better knowing they weren't responsible for this death trap taking her up.

Angela spent what felt like eternity on the slow climb, pulling her thoughts together. She crossed her fingers the meeting would be relatively brief. A quick introduction and then she could be on her way. Though figuring out how to get home from here wouldn't be easy. Sometimes she hated relying on public transportation instead of her own car. It left her navigating the entire city just to go home. Not to mention, Northern Virginia traffic on a Friday was a nightmare. Her day was never going to end.

The elevator jerked to a halt and its doors creeped open. She stepped out as soon as possible just to get out of the car and started down the hallway. Spying a ladies' room sign, she darted into it to check her reflection. She needed to make sure she looked at least somewhat presentable, even if the toll the day had taken probably showed on her face. She gave her curly hair a fluff with her fingers and assessed her makeup. Normally she didn't wear much, but she started the day looking pulled together. That wasn't the case now, but she couldn't do much about it. She dabbed on some lip gloss she found in her purse and glanced again in the mirror.

Angela was consumed by a feeling of inadequacy as she viewed her image. Red-brown hair that needed some new high-lights. Makeup the bare minimum. Blue-gray eyes that were nothing special, even if people told her all the time how pretty they were. At least she was somewhat dressed up today. Since she wasn't going into the lab, she had worn a pretty blue and white patterned skirt and a dark blue sweater, and of course, heels. She loved her heels. The minute she slipped them on, it was like pulling a cloak of confidence around her. Even though they made her even taller, she couldn't help but feel good in them. Grasping for that self-assurance now, she Ignored the pinching waistband and stepped back into the hall.

"Shake it off," she told herself as she stepped out of the room.

As she made her way down to the office, Angela thought about how much she enjoyed becoming friends with the woman who worked there. Not expecting to be fully taken under the wing of the younger Valerie and her best friend Chelsea, she was slightly stunned when they started inviting her out with them all the time. At first, she tried to beg off, not wanting to intrude on the friends. Chelsea, however, was a force of nature not to be reckoned with, so Angela gave up trying. She had deluded herself into thinking she didn't need to make good friends since she had moved to the area a few years ago. She had amazing online friends, yet so very few people she could actually spend time with. Sure, she felt like the fifth wheel at times since they were both in relationships and she was eternally single, but the girls, and their men, had been welcoming to her right from the very beginning.

I wonder if I'll get to meet the other hotties today? Good lord, she needed to stop channeling her inner Chelsea. These men had names, and they were not "the hotties." Besides, since she had only met Drew, she couldn't speak on the merits of the names for the remaining Stephens brothers.

A warmth flashed through her as she recalled the man she had seen at Val's engagement party. She had been talking to Valerie when, all of a sudden, she felt herself being watched—but not merely watched. Turning slightly, Angela had seen one of the most stunning men she ever laid eyes on. Well over six feet tall, with blond hair, a face that could stop traffic and what looked like a lean body under his suit jacket, and his gaze had been laser-focused on her. She couldn't understand it. Men practically didn't look at her at all, let alone like they wanted to memorize everything about her. As soon as she'd gotten over her shock, she fled the room, and the party, like a scared rabbit. Thinking she could put the interaction out of her mind, she'd never asked about him and didn't know who he was, but that didn't keep the images at bay.

Pushing the wooden door open, she entered a tastefully decorated waiting area. Light beige walls complemented the black and white photos of buildings hung around the room. Dark brown leather chairs looked both comfortable and professional and provided ample seating for visitors. A desk sporting a vase of tulips on the corner sat in the center of the room, in front of a hallway leading to what she presumed were offices.

"Hello," she called out since nobody was seated at the reception desk. "Is anyone here?" If she had come all this way for nothing, she was going to kill her boss.

Rooted to the spot in front of the desk for several minutes got her nowhere. There seemed to be no response forthcoming, so she needed to decide what to do. The door wouldn't be unlocked if there was no one here, and according to her boss's e-mail, there was a meeting scheduled for five o'clock. So, they must have been expecting her. Or at least someone from the lab.

Making sure the door was shut behind her, she moved down the hallway behind reception, hoping to find the person she was searching for.

"THE LAB GUY call to say he wasn't coming, or were we just supposed to guess?"

Speaking as he walked out of his office, Jonathan Stephens was greeted by a sight that was all too familiar lately. His brother, perched on their executive assistant's desk, trying to sweet talk her into a quickie. Luckily for the company, their EA was also said brother's fiancée or they would be looking at a lawsuit.

"For God's sake, can't you two take a break?" He grinned as he spoke his teasing words. Jon was genuinely thrilled Drew had found happiness, but there was still the sting whenever he considered his own love life. He had thought he had found the one, dating Susanna all through college and even when he pursued his advanced degree in architecture. Apparently, she hadn't felt the same and chose to not accompany him back to Virginia after graduation. He'd dated since then, but nothing serious. And he *was* looking for serious. He wasn't like Drew had been. Happy to date for a few months and then move on. What Drew now had was what he'd been wanting for years.

Someone to love and grow with. Someone to come home to so they could ease each other's burdens.

His mind scrolled back to brown curly hair and a curvy body. Maybe too curvy for some men, but the moment he'd seen Val's friend Angela, he was spellbound. There was something about her that had grabbed him from across the room the one and only time he'd seen her. The smile on her face when she had been talking to Val was genuine, but he could sense there was a part of her she held back. He wanted that smile trained on him, completely unfettered with whatever she was hiding. He had tried numerous times over the past months to see her again. This time to meet her. Talk to her. But every effort had been met with her absence. It made him all the more acutely sensitive to what Drew and Valerie had, and made for some long nights when the images of her filtered through his dreams.

Drew and Val's happiness, and his own hidden jealousy and longing, was dampened by their oldest brother and nephew's loss. The same night as Drew's engagement party, Matthew's wife Cassandra was killed in a car crash. Matt hadn't been the same since, and though it was terrible to say, his demeanor wasn't always sullen. Matt and Cassandra's marriage had been a horror to watch and consisted of pettiness from her and—more often than not—disinterest from Matt. He was pretty sure part of his brother wanted to relish the freedom, but Matt couldn't hide the flash of guilt in his eyes whenever Cassandra or her death was mentioned. Jon turned from the morbid thoughts and looked at Drew.

The sparkle of merriment was alight in Drew's eyes as he tried to drag Val away from her desk. "Nope." He didn't get far as Val made no move to get up. "Besides, it's quitting time brother. She's all mine now."

Rolling her pretty green eyes, she turned to Jon. "No phone call unless Pamela took a message."

Jon sighed. Why couldn't they get an easy client lately? "First

Lewis and now this jackass." They had been thrilled to get the lab job, designing and building a brand new forensics lab for the state. It was a huge undertaking and something they had never done before, but he was confident they were up for the task. All had been going smoothly except for one person. "Why are we having so many issues with this guy?"

Shaking her head, Val responded, "Matthew says he's like this on all of their planning meetings. Essentially any time he has to do work is apparently asking too much." She playfully swatted Drew's hand away from her neck. "Matthew said he wants nothing to do with helping, so who knows."

"I'm sure that's making Matt's day," Drew added with a rueful shake. "He could be the one who finally gets Matt to snap." They had all been waiting for the tether Matt always had on his temper to break loose. Jon had a sinking suspicion he knew what that last straw would be, and he didn't think this jackass was it.

"Fucking great. I know shit about building a DNA lab. Hence why I need an expert." Every section in the lab had assigned one person to work with Stephens so they could get everything right. Building a lab was a lot different than designing an office building. The other sections had been great. Their enthusiasm about getting a new lab, with their input, was infectious. But the one time Jon had met with David DeWhite, he'd felt like smacking him. The man was all pompousness and no excitement.

"Do you want me to call?" Val turned to the computer. "I can find the number in the file quick enough."

"Hello?" A quiet greeting from the hallway to the front reception area had all three of them turning in that direction, and Jon's heart stopping in his chest.

It was her. For six months, he had been trying to get in the same room with her again, and now, for some reason, she was standing in front of him. He took her all in, from the top of her hair to the pointy toes of her high heels. How could he have thought her hair was brown? It was brown and copper, auburn and blonde. He was sure it would glimmer out in the sun. And those eyes. A blue-gray that, right now, kept darting between the three of them. He needed to say something. And stop staring. He was pretty sure his staring would scare her away again, and that couldn't happen. He refused to let it happen.

Before he could pull himself together enough to utter anything coherent, Val chimed in.

"Angela? What are you doing here?" Val walked over to her friend and enveloped her in a warm hug. "Not that I'm not glad to see you."

Returning the hug, Angela answered, "I'm here to take Dr. DeWhite's meeting with your architect." She glanced over at Drew and smiled. "Hi Drew." Jon felt her gaze alight on him and just as quickly move away. Oh, that wouldn't do at all.

Stepping forward, he reached out a hand. "That would be me. I'm Jon, Drew's younger, far more handsome brother." A sizzle of electricity shot through his arm as she placed her hand in his. Angela abruptly removed it from his grasp, which he told himself was because she felt heat too. There was no way he was letting this angel slip away from him again.

"That meeting was for—" Before Val could complete her sentence, Jon spoke up.

"Now." Drew and Val both spun around to stare at him, but he ignored them. "This time was the only spot I had available today. The meeting shouldn't be more than an hour."

Angela looked like she didn't believe him. Of course, with Valerie and Drew standing there looking like he had grown a second head, he wasn't surprised. But this was the opportunity he'd been waiting for. A chance to meet the woman who had captured his attention from the first moment he saw her.

"Dr. DeWhite didn't mention it was going to be so long." Angela's shoulders slumped, and her gaze darted nervously between the three of them, looking for a way out. "He said it would be a quick meeting." Glancing at her feet, she spoke again, "I don't think I can do an hour."

"Do you have plans?" The mere thought of her on a date with someone else sent sparks of jealousy throughout his body. This was too much, too soon, and was sure to frighten her off. That was the last thing he wanted to do. Jon wanted to get her closer to him, not running in the opposite direction. "I had really hoped to get moving with your section of the lab." Maybe, if he sweet talked her with her new work environment, he could win her over.

He had no idea what Angela did for a living and never would he have imagined she'd be working for the same lab they were. He had been trying to get information out of Val about her for a while now, but subtly, yet his brother and Val had been remarkably tight-lipped on any details about the beauty standing in front of him. He hadn't wanted to make his interest too blatant, especially since every opportunity to meet Angela again had been denied as she never showed up to any of their group outings. He wasn't a man completely full of himself or overly confident in his charms, but he was beginning to suspect the way he looked at her at Drew and Val's party had frightened her, and that wouldn't do.

But now this serendipitous chance had fallen right in Jon's lap, and he'd be damned if he'd let it get away.

Angela's eyes lit up a little at the mention of the new lab, but still she had a weariness in them that didn't have her jumping at the opportunity. "I don't want to be responsible for anything delaying the project."

"Did you have a hot date tonight, Ang?" Val questioned. She clapped her hands together in a little show of excitement. "I'm sure Jon would be willing to re-schedule if you had plans."

No. No, Jon would not be willing to re-schedule. What the fuck did Valerie think she was doing? So maybe he hadn't made his interest in her friend blatantly obvious, but for God's sake, she should be able to read between the lines. He turned to glare at his brother, only to see him trying to smother a smile behind his hand.

Ahh, so Val was jerking his chain. I guess that was fair considering all the times he had made a smartass comment about her and Drew. He went still, waiting for Angela's answer.

"Yeah, right." Angela rolled those stormy-sky-colored eyes. "You know that's not going to happen. I don't get dates, hot or not." A wry laugh escaped her lips, but it didn't light up her eyes.

That concept seemed unfathomable. How was he standing here trying to figure out a way to fight men for her attention with her saying there were no others to fight? His first glance at her had taken his breath away. Other men who looked at her had to experience the same thing, right? But from the resigned look on her face, she really believed what she was saying. She had presented him with a puzzle he was intent on solving because something told him this was important.

He'd figure out her words and the meaning behind them later, but right now he wanted to get their night moving along—and away from pesky siblings who had managed to get a laugh out of the beauty while Jon was stewing in his own thoughts. Drew could definitely be a charmer, but he needed to charm his own woman tonight and leave Angela to him. Looked like it was time to make haste.

Shooting his brother a look he hope conveyed *shut up*, he turned toward Angela again. "What if I promise not to keep you too long?" This may actually work in his favor. "We can get a quick lay of the land and then schedule another meeting to go more in depth and work with your schedule." Any way he could get one on one time with his enigmatic beauty would work for him.

"That may work." She gifted him a shy smile and turned to Valerie. "I don't want to keep you guys any longer either."

Before he could open his mouth to speak, Drew jumped in. "Oh no, we're headed out. This is all in Jon's hands." He hoped Angela didn't see the smirk on Drew's face. Grabbing his fiancée's hand, he practically hauled her out the door. "Night."

And then he was left alone with a woman who was visibly shocked and nervous, the one woman who fascinated him beyond words.

Order Here

ACKNOWLEDGMENTS

If there's one thing I learned from when I started this writing journey, is that it takes a village. Especially when it's the first book someone ever tries to write.

Thank you to everyone who's helped, guided, answered endless questions, gave me a push, and overall just supported me. Thank you to Jacki, Maggie, Michelle, and Stephanie for the willingness to read and give awesome feedback. A huge thank you to Chloe, Hailey, Lexi, and Mari for sharing your knowledge with me, especially since sometimes my questions probably seem endless. Just know that it means a lot to me and I so valuable your opinions and expertise.

To my editor and cover artist, Victoria – thank you for being willing to take on my first book. I'm sure at some point you screamed into the void of your apartment about my missing descriptions, sentence fragments, and love of the word "that", but you've helped me immensely. Dawn, thank you so much helping again with the formatting – one day I'll learn it – and for answering so many of my questions.

Lastly, to my parents. I value your love, support, and help more than you'll ever probably know. Love you.

ABOUT SHEA BRIGHTON

Shea Brighton has immersed herself in the fictional worlds of her favorite authors for years, never thinking she'd join them in their story-telling journey. However, life leads you to places you weren't expecting. That's what happened to her a few years ago, and her writing pursuit began.

Shea makes her home in Virginia, having left her native New York years ago. You can usually find her watching some sporting event on TV (though baseball holds her heart), visiting a certain Mouse, winery hopping with her friends, or curled up with a book.

Find Shea online:

https://www.sheabrighton.com/

 facebook.com/SheaBrighton

ALSO BY SHEA BRIGHTON

Coming Soon from Shea Brighton
(click to pre-order)

Mine Would Be You

Also from Shea Brighton
(click to order)

One Man Band (Mystifying Music, Book 5)

In Case You Didn't Know (Stephens Brothers, Book 1)